The Queen Of New York

A Novel By: Visa Rollack

Published by: **Street Knowledge Publishing** Written by: Visa Rollack Edited by: Charlene McNiff Cover design by: Marion Designs/ **www.mariondesigns.com** Photos by: Marion Designs

For information contact:
Street Knowledge Publishing
P.O. Box 345
Wilmington,DE 19801
Email: jj@streetknowledgepublishing.com
Website: www.streetknowledgepublishing.com

ISBN: 0-9746199-7-3

Dedication

This book is dedicated to my nigga, Shayom Kelton; a.k.a. Shay-North. Gone, but definitely not forgotten. If it wasn't for you taking me to the spot to meet the real 'Johnny' I never would've had the vision to write The Queen of New York. Rest in peace, my nigga.

Acknowledgements

First and foremost, I need to give God his props. You definitely turned me into a believer.

Mike Smooth: if it wasn't for your editing skills, I'm not sure if things would've panned out the way that they did. Believe it or not, you taught me more about writing then you could imagine. You know what it is, bruh. If you need me for anything, you know how to get at me! And I look forward too seeing "Welcome Home Mikey Santana" in book stores. Continue to do what you do.

Linda Williams; a.k.a. Rhona Barret, a.k.a. Super Mom, a.k.a. Super Woman; you're quickly earning one hell of a resume for being a blessing to inspiring writers. It's not every day that I meet a person who isn't out to strictly make a dollar by any means necessary, and that doesn't turn their back on a person just because they're incarcerated. Your actions definitely speak louder than words. If we had more people in the world like yourself, this would truly be a better place. Thanks for everything you've done and are continuing to do for me, Super Woman!

Street Knowledge Publications; JoeJoe: I see now what you're trying to do with incarcerated authors, and I salute my hat to you for it. Believe me when I tell you, I'm going to show other publishing companies why dealing with incarcerated authors can be the best authors to deal with. Just give me a minute, and watch me get in it! JoeJoe and everybody behind the scene at Street Knowledge Publishing, it's time to turn people into believers!

Before The Queen of New York was sent to any publishing companies for review, many of my prison comrades read it with a fine tooth comb to thoroughly critique it. My homeboy Red Uptown, Add-A-Lesson, Sqeek-D-i-low, my big bruh Red Rum, Hass, my nigga Point Blank, and Mr. Murda. All of y'all know what it is! Final result, sit back and let Nina Nuñez show y'all how it's done. Next level, my niggas.

I gotta acknowledge my homegirl, Bethany. When I needed you to apply pressure on one of these silly-ass ho's of mine to get my script back, among other things, you came through for the kid. Trust me when I tell you, babygirl; when the tables flip, I will stick to the script!

It's a must that I acknowledge my mother and two sisters. No matter the pressure, the tons of cases over the years, the twenty year plead bargains, etc. I could always count on y'all to be right there by my side. I never would've been in the right state of mind to write anything if it wasn't for y'all. I guess you could say that it's more than love, and less than luck.

Last but definitely not least, Robert Frost, a.k.a. Bobby, along with all of the correctional officers and civilians who went out of their way to assist me with my writing; much respect!!

Words of encouragement for all inspiring authors behind bars:

WHAT I AM TODAY, I WASN'T YESTERDAY. Once upon a time, I made some comments that you've also probably made. Such as: Writing books just isn't my thing. I can't write a book. Or, I wish I could write a book. But then I began to learn just how promising and lucrative book writing can actually be. That's all it took for me to begin studying the craft of writing. **WHAT I AM TODAY, I WASN'T YESTERDAY**

Chapter One

Carol City is just one of the many sections of Miami unknown to a great majority of tourists, who come to visit the "Sunshine State." Unlike South Beach and other popular attractions Miami has to offer, Carol City was far from peaceful and hospitable. It was a large city, lined with hundreds of streets, which zig-zagged, criss-crossed, and ran parallel with one another to prove itself a quite healthy breeding ground for some of Florida's most violent criminals.

Jamil Stevens and Sadon Mitchell were two such individuals. Jamil was an on and off hustler who had taken more to life as a full-time stick-up kid than anything else. He was tall and slim-built, with a bald shaved head, quick eyes, and a heart that was every bit as dark and as black as his skin complexion. Sadon was just as tall as his best friend, but their similarity in height was all they physically had in common. Sadon had a dark, golden-brown complexion with thick, reddish-brown eyes that matched a head full of dreadlocks, which fell a good length past his shoulders. Every single tooth in his mouth was gold-plated and sparkled brightly whenever his lips parted.

Unlike Jamil, Sadon preferred the occupation of a drug dealer rather than that of an armed robber. Both were quick-tempered, cold-hearted and fearless by nature But, Sadon was more so the better thinker of the duo, and he was by far, the most patient when it came to handling his business. For Jamil, life was about sex, money, and murder, with little room for anything else in between; while Sadon better understood the mechanics of it all. Throughout the past month, he'd endured one set back after another. Yet, he still managed to save quite a decent piece of change for himself. Jamil, however, barely had a penny saved, but always kept at least a few thousand dollars in the pocket to spend.

Jamil and Sadon were like night and day. The love for the streets and the love they had for each other was all they truly had in common. And the trials and tribulations they had endured together throughout the years were proof enough of it being all they needed.

⸎⸎⸎⸎⸎⸎

48th Street was just one of the many streets that stopped short of 47th Avenue, one of Miami, Carol City's main strips. It was a spacious road with a row of homes on both sides; all of them protected one way or another from the criminal elements which roamed about the neighborhood. Doors, windows, sometimes entire porches, and even air conditions were guarded by the installation of steel bars. The combination of these prison cell-looking houses, combined with the trash-littered streets and sidewalks painted a rather grim and hopeless picture for this crime-ridden section of Carol City.

Jamil and Sadon stood near the corner of 48th Street and 47th Avenue, each of them sparring one of their many pit-bull terriers against one another as the bright, Miami sun began to fade away into the darkness of night. With the dimness of night came an invisible surge of apprehension. It was only on the corner, where the lights of 47th Avenue somewhat shone down from above. The streetlights on 48th Street, however, were either malfunctioned or deliberately broken. The scant sight of drug dealers and addicts roaming about further down the street, gave 48th Street a very menacing appearance. For Jamil and Sadon, two thugs who'd run these Third World-looking streets since childhood, this grim and threatening sight was home sweet home.

Sadon was standing on the struggling end, to keep hold of the leash while watching his dog play a fierce game of tug-of-war with Jamil's. It was an incredible competition; both dogs were huge and extremely muscular, huskily growling while fighting to loosen a flavored bone from the grasp of each other's monstrous canine fangs. The remainder of Sadon and Jamil's dogs was tied to the banister of an abandoned home, yelping excitedly as the tug-of-war carried on.

It was only when Jamil had finished speaking that Sadon even noticed that he was talking.

"Hold up, hold up, nigga," said Sadon. "Say that again?"

Jamil stifled his impatience. With the sudden death of Sadon's mother, his woman skipping town with a great deal of his savings, not to mention his constant beefs with nearly every drug dealer in Carol City, Sadon was undoubtedly having the worst year of his life. If there was ever a person to have patience with, Jamil silently agreed, it was with Sadon. The constant yelping of their dogs, to Jamil, seemed to play a great part of hindering what he was trying to say.

As if reading Jamil's mind, Sadon turned and began screaming at his dogs to be quiet.

"Man, chill the fuck out!" he exclaimed. "Shut the fuck up!"

Each of the dogs, including those currently engaged in their battle of strength, ceased their activity. They all fell quiet while resting themselves on their hind legs. Jamil's urge to smile was thwarted by his recollection of Sadon's decision to leave town. Leaving and settling down somewhere outside of Carol City, was an idea that Sadon had toyed with for months on end.

After hearing Sadon mention it one too many times, Jamil soon questioned him about how serious he actually was about relocating; thus the quarrel began. Sadon argued that he was sick and tired of the same drama, and he needed some type of change. His name was becoming known as a threat, which would inevitably lead him to either prison or death. Jamil on the other hand, argued that moving out of state to avoid trouble was purely a "bitch move," and that only a "true gangster" has the courage and will power to make something out of nothing while in the face of adversity.

It was a super-sensitive subject between the both of them, and after seeing how adamant Sadon truly was about leaving, Jamil never bothered to speak on it ever again. He could only hope that Sadon would reconsider. As the days passed by, Sadon seemed more and more absorbed in his thoughts while hustling, which told Jamil that his best friend had thoroughly made up his mind about leaving town. It was only a matter of when.

"What's up, dawg?" Sadon asked.

"Oh, yuh" said Jamil. "Listen, my nigga," he began. "I ain't wonna tell you this shit, but you my nigga, so you know I gotta keep you on point. You know that hoe, Tweet, that you was fuckin' wiff? Well, the bitch done sparked up some bullshit between you and this fuck-nigga, Rod, from Overtown."

The glint in Jamil's eyes was an exact reflection of what he was feeling inside. No matter what the situation, Sadon knew it would inevitably be solved with violence.

"Listen, dawg, that bitch tryin' to get some bullshit started," Jamil continued. "I can't call if she was drunk, but after poppin' so much shit, homeboy done went in her mouth; and you know what happened next; Yuh man, "I'm funna get Sadon to split yo' shit.

Tweet was nothing more than a whore who lived far across town. There weren't enough fingers and toes on the human body that could count the amount of men that had slept with her and that was only the number of those bold enough to admit it. Sadon had literally laughed in Tweet's face when she had found the nerve to strike up the possibility of them being a couple. They both knew that such a thing would never, ever happen. The very thought of Tweet stirring up this unnecessary beef was enough to inflame Sadon with anger. Beneath the light of the street lamp on the corner of 48th Street and 47th Avenue, his eyes twinkled with rage.

Having full knowledge of the hardship Sadon had endured over the past year, made Jamil a bit reluctant to tell him. His first instinct was to handle it all by himself without even bothering Sadon; but Sadon was a man who was always serious about his business and would've been offended by not having the chance to settle his own problems. It was one of the characteristics Jamil loved most about his best friend.

"That's only half of the bullshit, my nigga," Jamil continued. "That nigga started runnin' his fuckin mouth. The bitch nigga even said that you could suck his dick."

Sadon's eyes went wide with disbelief.

"What?"

"Hell yuh, dawg," Jamil confirmed. "That nigga got outta line."

Sadon's face went rigid, his eyes as blank and as calm as the stillest river. The understanding of what was to come next between Jamil and his best friend went far beyond verbal communication.

"Then you know what it is, my nigga," Sadon said calmly. "When you wanna ride on this nigga?"

Few things excited Jamil more than the thrill of committing a violent crime. The weight of the pistol in his hands, the powerful recoil of the weapon as he fired it, and the brilliant flash of light which escaped the muzzle when squeezing the gun trigger, all of this combined to give Jamil a feeling far greater than any orgasm ever could. Now, however, Jamil was thinking more about his friend. He wanted nothing more than to ease Sadon's mind, and what better way to do so than to treat him to a night of unadulterated lust?

"Nigga! I'm down to ride right now!" Jamil answered. "Matter fact, we gon' get at that nigga regardless, so we might's well just go on 'head and get our dick wet right quick, you heard me?"

A tight-lipped smile spread wide across Sadon's face. He knew that Jamil had his back regardless to whom or what.

<hr>

1:30 a.m.

It was a typical early summer morning in Miami. A scarce number of stars burned brightly against the jet-black sky. The absence of any type of wind, combined with the ninety degree temperature, to provide an oppressively humid climate. Sadon wholeheartedly appreciated the breeze he was enjoying, while riding shotgun in Jamil's red 1964 Oldsmobile convertible. He frowned as the car slowed and crept into the parking lot of a local strip club.

"You ready?" Asked Jamil while passing Sadon what was left of the blunt they were sharing.

Sadon took a few more tokes and finished it off.

"Yuh. Let's go play wiff some pussy, my nigga," he said while tossing it out of the car and onto the pavement.

After enduring a lengthy wait in line, only to be handled roughly by one of the seven foot, three hundred-plus pound, bouncers at the door, Jamil and Sadon finally entered inside. The club was air-conditioned, but did little to ease the warmth of the summer temperature. It was just cool enough inside the bar to keep from sweating.

With exception to the team of strobe lights, which were fixed from different angles in the club, and a brightly illuminated stage where featured dances performed, the place was relatively dark. Teams of leather couches were lined against mirrored walls, which nearly circled the entire club. Round tables, which were fastened to the floor, crowded the space between the couches and the stage; they also served as platforms for dancers to perform.

The inside of the club was alive with activity. A tall, thick-bodied female with cocoa colored skin and long, stringy, black hair stood atop the stage, gyrating to a popular go-go song. She was squatting with her back facing the audience, flexing and popping her firm rear end to the rhythm of the song. The multi-colored lights from the stage on which the dancer performed illuminated the clear, spike-heeled shoes with a brilliant spectrum of colors. Thugs, pimps, business execs, and family men alike, all filled the club. Women of every shape, size, and complexion, all of them beautiful and in great physical shape, busied themselves with customers. Some of them danced sexily atop their individual tables, while others straddled their patrons, simulating the most lewd sexual acts one could imagine. For the right price, a customer could easily get what was so teasingly flaunted in front of his face.

Jamil was a regular customer at Coco's, while Sadon only visited occasionally. Nearly every dancer, whether with a customer or not, acknowledged Jamil's arrival as he and Sadon traveled throughout the club and towards an open couch, which was at the rear. It seemed a pure stroke of luck that they found a seat that just so happened to be directly beneath one of the club's air vents.

Sadon took a moment to make himself comfortable, as Jamil, with a handful of twenty-dollar bills, signaled for a pair of dancers. Peaches and Cream were identical twins that have clearly taken the concept of "sisterly love" to an entirely higher level. They shared everything from clothing to men, even each other if the price was right. Both Jamil and the twins were great fans of each other's work. Jamil's lust for their sexual prowess was just as strong as their lust to enjoy his company and his money; the latter being the greatest attraction.

Knowing Jamil's routine, both Peaches and her twin sister, Cream swayed seductively toward his couch, each of them carrying a bottle of champagne in their hands. Their skin was the color of caramel; their eyes were sharp, and attentive, matching well with their slim noses and full, fleshy lips. They smiled while nearing Jamil and Sadon, their thigh and stomach muscles twisting and flexing as they approached. Everything, from the thin strands of thread, which was struggling to hold their breasts in place down to the finger-wave style of their hair, was exactly the same. The look in the twins' eyes, along with their sly, seductive grins, promised a night that would be well worth remembering.

Sadon and Jamil were having the time of their lives. Peaches and Cream had long ago slid their thongs to the side and allowed the two young thugs to find their way inside them.

With one hand griping a bottle of champagne and the other gripping the dancer's ass, both Sadon and his partner settled back to enjoy the ride.

The pressure now building from within Jamil's loins was now beginning to reach its peak. Feeling himself nearing an orgasm, he leaned forward and spread Cream's butt cheeks wide apart while digging deeper and deeper inside of her. Cream, too, felt her climax soon approaching.

"Shit," she groaned while fighting to match Jamil's intensity. "Come on, baby, yuh."

Jamil growled and groaned as he ejaculated, noticing a familiar face strolling about the club as he did so.

"Yo, nigga!" he said in a hushed, but urgent tone, while at the same time punching hard on Sadon's leg. "There go that fuck-nigga right there!"

Sadon was relaxed against the cushions of the couch, totally engulfed by the feeling of Peaches' sexual expertise. She sat facing Sadon with her arms wrapped tightly around his neck, working as hard as she could to satisfy him. Peaches ever so skillfully slid up and down his erection, twisting, popping and pulling on his penis with her vagina as she rode him. It was a feeling Sadon never wanted to end. A forceful jab from Jamil, which knocked the bottle of champagne from Sadon's grasp, was enough to snap him back into reality.

"...right there, dawg!" he finally heard Jamil say. "There go that fuck-nigga right there!"

Sadon was now at full attention, spotting Rod and one of his cronies mingling about the club; he immediately understood Jamil's sense of urgency. "Wait. Daddy," said Peaches when Sadon tried to rise up. "I'm about to cum." Sadon tossed Peaches hard onto the cushion beside him, and then rose to his feet. He then tossed the used condom on the floor.

"I ain't payin" to make yo' ass cum," he growled while hurriedly fixing his clothes.

Peaches remained silent. Jamil smiled as Cream watched her sister with uncertainty. Without bothering to say another word, Sadon turned and left.

Fortunately for Sadon and Jamil, there was only a little more than an hour until the club closed, which left them with plenty of time to plan their attack. The parking lot was filled with cars. The absence of activity seemed to make it look more like an abandoned car lot. They sat inside the convertible Oldsmobile, this time with the roof up, waiting impatiently for Rod to exit.

"There he is!" Jamil exclaimed, happy to see his target leaving earlier than expected. "There go that nigga right there!"

Rod was stone drunk. Dressed in a pair of black denim shorts, a white tank top, and a button up shirt, which was opened and exposed a huge, platinum necklace, he leaned heavily on his partner's shoulder while making his way through the parking lot.

Jamil took a moment to check his double-barreled, sawed-off shotgun before exiting the car and following behind Sadon, who was armed with a nine-millimeter handgun. Rod, who lay in a drunken stupor as his henchman fumbled to stick the key in the car's ignition, never saw them coming.

Sadon made his way to the passenger side of the car and smashed the butt of his pistol hard against the side of Rod's forehead. The force of Sadon's blow knocked Rod far to his left side, blood splashing all over his designated driver, who was shocked. The feel of Jamil's double-barreled shotgun jammed against the man's temple transformed his sense of shock into pure terror.

Sadon reached inside the car to get a firm grasp of Rod's tank top and then yanked him close toward the window.

"You like tellin' niggas to suck your dick, nigga?" Sadon asked. "Tellin' me to suck your dick, nigga? Nigga, is you fuckin' crazy?"

Rod could only stare with confused eyes, his mind still struggling to make sense of what was now happening. Blood seeped profusely from the wound on his forehead, trickling down his face as he fought to recognize his attacker. With the pain pulsing about his torn and bloodied face, came a sudden realization.

"Sadon," Rod sputtered. "Sadon...homey, listen..."
"Nigga, shut the fuck up! Sadon barked while striking Rod with his pistol once more.

Jamil smiled at the crunching sound of Rod's nose being crushed beneath the weight of Sadon's blow. A fist full of shirt still clenched in Sadon's grasp keeping him from falling backward.

"Guess whose gon' be suckin' dick tonight, mutherfucker," Sadon remarked.

Rod's eyes went wide with shock and then disbelief. Jamil smiled as if reading Sadon's mind, he then ordered Rod's partner to unbuckle his pants; the man complied without argument.

"Suck that nigga's dick," Sadon commanded.

"C'mon, dawg," Rod whined. "I ain't tryna to suck no nigga's dick, dawg."

"You got three seconds to put that nigga's dick in your mouth, fuck-nigga," Sadon coldly replied.

Rod immediately leaned over and took his partner's penis into his mouth. He couldn't believe that he was actually placing his mouth on another man's genitals. The very thought of him doing such a thing was sickening. He nearly vomited when feeling it slide past his lips and into his mouth. Rod's companion was just as disgusted and felt ashamed, even more ashamed as he grew. Tears trickled down his cheeks while enduring this gross humiliation.

Jamil had been standing guard for nearly five minutes. It felt strange for him to have his weapon trained on someone for so long without using it, and finally, he'd given in to his impatience.

One of the barrels of Jamil's sawed-off shotgun exploded with a thunderous roar. The victim's head jerked away violently; blood and chunks of flesh splattered the car as he slumped over. Sadon, without hesitation, took aim and began to fire. Rod looked just in time to see the brilliant flash of his enemy's gun barrel. Jamil emptied the second barrel into his victim as Sadon continued pumping slugs into Rod's lifeless body. The car was illuminated with the brilliance of gunfire; in a brief matter of minutes, the thick mist of gun smoke soon clouded the sight of what they'd just now done.

Satisfied, with the deed being done, both Sadon and Jamil turned and walked swiftly away. The patrons of the strip club were just about gone; the huge parking lot was relatively empty. There was a mixture of both fear and adrenaline, which coursed through their veins as they entered inside Jamil's car.

"Hold up, dawg," said Jamil while exiting the car.

"What?" asked Sadon. "Where the fuck?"

His question fell upon deaf ears. All that was left for Sadon to do was insert a fully loaded magazine into a now empty pistol. If by chance, they were to encounter the police, then, Sadon wanted to make sure he was prepared to go all out.

Jamil returned moments later with a portion of Rod's platinum necklace dangling from inside his pocket.

"I couldn't leave empty handed, dawg," Jamil said with a smile. He then began to start the car. "Let's get the fuck up out of hur."

Thinking of the arrangement he'd made with a real estate broker in Brooklyn, New York, not even a week ago, Sadon couldn't have agreed more.

Chapter Two

Sadon stared out the window of the taxicab, observing the change of scenery as he traveled from John F. Kennedy Airport to Brooklyn, New York. Long gone was the sight of Carol City's, one-story homes, palm trees, and customized, old model cars with hydraulics and things of that sort. New York was a huge city filled with busy streets and high-rise buildings. Even while inside the taxi, Sadon could feel the intensity of the city's inhabitants. Like those living in Carol City, New York City, dwellers traveled about with an acute sense of urgency, but New York's, jam-packed and bustling environment greatly increased the need for one to be serious about their business. The gangsters, criminals, and thugs of Carol City may indeed be every bit as vicious and as dangerous as those in New York. But in "The Big Apple," the cycles of aggression seemed able to come full circle at a much more rapid and fierce pace; not just among strangers, but more so within their own factions.

After a little more than thirty minutes, Sadon arrived at the front of just one of a cluster of high-rise buildings. A gang of thugs stood huddled around the entrance of its lobby. Sadon eyed them more so out of curiosity than apprehension.

Why the fuck is they wearin' boots in ninety-degree weather? He asked himself.

"Welcome to Marcy Projects," said the driver while returning Sadon's change. "Don't get yourself killed out here."

While hauling is luggage out of the trunk of the taxicab, Sadon made sure to keep an eye on the local thugs who were, in turn, watching him closely. Suddenly, someone broke away from the crowd to approach him. Sadon turned around to face the stranger; it was a smooth, almost graceful movement, enabling Sadon to position himself into a fighting position without warning a would-be attacker.

"What's poppin', Baby?" the stranger asked. "You movin' in?"

Sadon eyed him coolly. The man now standing before him was tall and somewhat stocky; his complexion was as black as Jamil's. His hair was cut close and waved up, his hairline trimmed to perfection.

"Yuh," Sadon replied, his deep, southern accent ringing loud and clear. "I just came from down bottom, dawg. Miami."

"Word up?" the man remarked. "That's what's up. I'm North."

The two of them shook hands. Behind the whites of North's eyes was the gaze of a stone-cold killer; it was the same homicidal look Sadon recognized in Jamil's eyes. North smiled as he shook Sadon's hand. Reading how the genuine show of North's hospitality matched his poorly hidden lust for violence, Sadon judged that North was more or less a standup guy. How they'd get along in the near future had yet to be determined.

"Let me help with ya shit," North offered.

"F' sho," Sadon replied.

With the last of his luggage now out the trunk, the cab skidded off and into traffic.

While holding a suitcase in each hand, Sadon took one last moment to observe his surroundings before starting inside the building. The streets and sidewalk were littered with garbage. Empty bottles of beer, weed bags, and various articles of trash were noticeable all around the neighborhood.

Shayom Patterson a.k.a. "North," "Shay," and even "Shay-North," was the son of a dope fiend and a bank robber. His father was serving a triple life sentence in prison before North had even been conceived, and his mother died of a heroin overdose when he was just seven years old. He'd spent a great majority of his childhood in and out of youth homes and orphanages, selling any type of drug he could get his hand on in between times. With a short temper and a vicious fight game to match, North managed to gain quite a reputation throughout the projects where he'd been spending his time. He'd grown to be no more than a local thug with little ambition for the drug game; still he was thoroughly respected by drug dealers both in his project buildings and others.

North may not have been all that serious about making it big in the drug game, but he was definitely strict when it came to being respected.

The stares Sadon received from the thugs in front of the building were every bit as hostile as the glares of Carol City thugs, when observing a stranger in their midst. With that in mind, Sadon was far from at ease with North's abrupt hospitality. It could easily be a set up for him to be robbed. With his head held high and holding a suitcase in each hand, Sadon stared evenly at the thugs while walking through one of the double entrance doors that North was holding open for him.

To Sadon's immediate surprise, the inside of the project building was far filthier than the streets outside. The smell of garbage, alcohol, stale weed, and urine, together, was unbelievable. Bullet holes and graffiti covered and scarred its grimy walls; the floor seemed as if it hadn't been scrubbed in years. With hopes of escaping this unbearable stench, Sadon followed close behind North as he turned into the elevator; he was sadly mistaken. Every filthy stench and stain Sadon had encountered while in the hallway now seemed concentrated into the tiny, but extreme confines of the elevator.

In a few minutes time, North and Sadon reached the fourth floor. To Sadon's relief, the hallway of his own apartment floor was dirty, but nowhere near as filthy as the first floor. When finally reaching Apartment 417, Sadon placed his luggage down by his feet, and then took a moment to light himself a cigarette before retrieving the door key from inside his pocket.

"Home sweet home," he announced out loud while opening the door.

Sadon was utterly shocked and appalled by what he now saw. His studio apartment was every bit as filthy and as trashy as the streets outside. Bags and bags of clothing, some of them overflowing, were scattered around the apartment. The floor was littered with garbage, leftover food, and dirty dishes. The tiny twin-sized bed which, had only two of its four legs, reeked of urine.

"This red-neck cracka don ganked me, dawg!" Sadon exclaimed. "I can't believe this shit, dawg."

Sadon was teeming with rage. His temper had gotten the best of him, causing his country attitude and mannerism to surface and show its true colors. Despite the seriousness of Sadon's displeasure, North couldn't help but to feel a touch of humor about the situation.

"Yeah," he remarked while exhaling a stream of cigarette smoke. "Welcome to the projects. You smoke trees, my nigga?"

Still trapped in his own world of disappointment and rage, Sadon took a moment to calm down before answering.

"Yuh," he finally replied. 'Hell yuh, I smoke, dawg."

Although he barely knew Sadon, North could sense something good about the stranger from Miami. He had the strangest feeling that him and this "country kid" would somehow be doing great things in the future.

"I'ma take you to my home girl's crib," North declared. "And we gon' smoke some good shit to get ya mind right you heard me?"

Sadon was still very much upset, and his true, down-south manner had yet to subside. His answer of "hell yeah" sounded more like "hail yur." With that, Sadon allowed North to leave first and then closed the door and locked it behind him before heading toward the elevator. After a long, tiresome and disappointing first day in New York, for Sadon, a fat blunt was a good remedy.

***

The door to Apartment 307 was finally opened by a short, brown-skinned woman with long hair and gorgeous facial features; the sight of her physique was just as pleasing. She stood in the doorway dressed in a pair of denim shorts that rode high above a set of sculpted, well-defined thighs and a skintight half-shirt. Her eyes were soft and inviting. The smile she wore promised Sadon a very, very good time.

"Damn, Maria!" North barked. "Can a nigga get in the crib or what?"

Maria? Sadon thought to himself. He could have sworn the name of the girl North described as being the closest thing to family he'll ever have, was a Puerto Rican girl named Nina.

Maria only continued to stare at Sadon. She'd never been so attracted to a man so quickly before in her life. She looked past North and stared him up and down, liking everything about the tall stranger with smooth skin and cute, reddish-brown dreadlocks. Not only was Sadon a new face in the projects, but the bright, almost neon-colored clothes he wore told of him being from somewhere other than New York.

"Man, what the fuck is you doin'?" North growled while pushing past Maria. "That's my nigga, 'Don from Miami, and we about to get fucked up."

Sadon remained still at the doorway, waiting to be formally allowed inside.

"Miami?" asked Maria while flashing a smile.

"F'sho," Sadon answered with a slight smile of his own.

A mouth full of gold teeth, too? Maria thought to herself. *Damn, this nigga is exotic.* "Come in, cutie," she said while widening the door for Sadon to enter inside. "You're nothing like rude-ass North."

The confines of the third floor, one-bedroom apartment was almost too small for Sadon to bear. The living room was meticulously clean, and despite the mismatched, old-fashioned furniture, there was still a particularly cozy feel to the place. North took a seat on a sofa, which was directly across the room from a large, but old model television. Maria walked past Sadon with the most seductive strut she could muster, and made sure to bend all the way over while turning on the radio.

The most attractive sight to Sadon's eyes, however, came in the form of a young woman standing in the doorway of the bathroom, combing out her long, jet-black hair. Although dressed in an oversized tee shirt, baggy pants, and gym sneakers, Nina Nuñez was remarkably beautiful. Even from a distance, Sadon could see her prettiness. After taking the time to wrap her hair into a tight little bun, she started walking toward Sadon who was standing in the same spot he'd been, since entering inside the apartment.

Sadon was captivated from the very first glance. Despite her plain hairdo and conservative style of dress, there was no denying Nina's beauty. Her facial features were sharp and well pronounced; her nose was slim, her lips plump and reddish in color. Her eyes were a bright colored hazel, which helped provide a sexy, but down-to-earth type of stare that went well with her smooth, banana-yellow complexion.

Nina approached Sadon slowly, thoroughly measuring him as she drew closer. Finally, the two of them were now standing face to face. Sadon introduced himself while accepting and kissing the back of her hand.

"I know who you are," she replied, seemingly unimpressed with Sadon's showoff chivalry. "I heard Shay tell my girlfriend your name."

Noticing Sadon's obvious attraction to her best friend, Maria immediately rolled her eyes when realizing his interest. It was far from the first time that Maria had lost a potentially good man to Nina. *Good luck, nigga,* she thought to herself while turning her attention back to the Play Station 2 video game system.

"So," Nina asked. "What brings you to New York?"

"A better life," Sadon replied. "I'm tryin' to leave a lot of bullshit behind and start a new life off on the right foot. Ya heard me?"

"A 'do-right' nigga from Miami? Ha!" North laughed out loud while fiddling with the stereo system. "This nigga done came all the way to Marcy Projects talkin' about nine-to-fivin' it!"

Nina remained stone-faced while staring at Sadon. Her eyes, however, revealed that she was impressed with his aspirations.

After starting a cassette tape filled with hip-hop instrumentals and twisting a blunt, North bobbed his head to the music while searching his pockets for a cigarette lighter. He lit the blunt, took a few tokes, and then passed it to Sadon, who seemed just as pleased with the music as North.

"You spit (rap), my nigga?" North asked.

"A lil somethin'," Sadon replied in between tokes.

"Lemme hear something' then, nigga," North encouraged. "Don't be actin' all 'scurred' and shit."

Sadon only smiled at how North poked fun at his Florida accent. After taking another toke of the blunt, he immediately began to rap.

Everyone in the room, including Nina, was shocked and impressed with Sadon's talent. His style was different; his southern drawl was heavy on each word he spoke, and it only reinforced his rhyme scheme to reach its maximum level. His skill was near perfect; the pictures he painted with his lyrics were all-too vivid. North, Nina, and Maria listened intently as Sadon illustrated his experiences with love, hate, death, and violence.

Nina fought not to smile when hearing Sadon rap about how pretty she was and how someone like her could help him do right in life. To Nina, getting high and running the streets went hand in hand, making her a bit disappointed to see Sadon smoking weed. But to hear him display his feelings for her in such an earnest and impressive fashion lightened her heart.

After nearly five minutes of listening to Sadon's freestyle, North couldn't help himself. He cut into Sadon's rap with an impressive freestyle of his own, his skill being every bit as fierce as Sadon's. North accepted the blunt from his newfound friend from Miami, not missing a single beat as they smoked and rapped at the same time. Individually, both Sadon and North were undoubtedly worthy of a record contract; the two of them together were phenomenal.

With the freestyle over and done with, North and Sadon were now seated beside each other on the couch sharing a blunt. In the back of Sadon's mind, he too began to see great things coming about from dealing with North.

A little more than a month had passed since Sadon's arrival in New York, and he had yet to find himself a job. A great deal of the money he'd brought along with him was nearly spent on improving his living quarters. Directly in front of his king-size waterbed was an expensive entertainment center, which stood nearly four feet high and was fitted with a huge fifty-four inch screen television. The bent, scratched, and stained wooden floor panels were straightened, cleaned, and then covered with a plush, light-gray carpet; the walls, too were scraped and repainted white. The condition of the apartment, along with his wardrobe had undergone a tremendous change more fitting for a "New Yorker." But now the need for money seemed a far greater burden than ever before. With only a few thousand dollars left to his name, and the bills yet to be paid for this month, things looked grim to Sadon. The fact of him being turned down by nearly every job he'd applied, only increased his frustration.

He sat on the edge of his bed staring around the room at a number of framed photographs, which were hanging on the walls. They were all pictures of Sadon and his homies from Carol City. There was one picture in particular that Sadon cherished most. It was a poster-size photograph of Sadon and Jamil in an abandoned house, surrounded by a group of their pit bulls. They stood face to face with their machine guns drawn on each other; the snapshot even captured the mist of marijuana smoke as it seeped from out their mouths and nostrils. It was a striking pose.

Sadon sighed while staring at his beloved photograph.

Damn, dog, he said to himself. *I miss you nigga!*

North entered inside Sadon's apartment a few days later without bothering to knock, this time accompanied by an attractive lady. She was short with a caramel colored complexion and appeared to be at least in her early twenties. The skin-tight Roc-A-Wear jeans and tank top she wore exposed a full set of breasts, a flat stomach, and a firm, shapely rear end. Her hair was cut short and combed backward; her eyes seemed tired, but alert, alert and hungry.

Sadon lit the blunt he had just finished rolling and watched as North pulled out a bundle of coke vials from inside his pocket. The hunger he saw in the girl's eyes intensified when seeing his handful of drugs.

"You ain't put no cut on it, right, North?" she asked.

Sadon was surprised at the tone of desperation he recognized in the girl's voice. With her pretty face, up to date clothing, and sexy body, he would never have believed her to be an addict.

"Maan! Listen Nicole, that's my nigga, 'Don," said North, completely ignoring her question.

He then eased two bottles from the cluster of cocaine vials, which were held together by a rubber band before replacing them back into his pocket.

"You gon' take this raw shit and let me and my nigga do whatever we wanna do to that sexy ass, right?" North asked while offering the vials. She nodded in agreement while accepting the cocaine and then began to strip.

"Y'all can do whatever y'all wanna do to me," she replied meekly. "Just don't be too rough."

Sadon couldn't help but laugh when hearing her request. He stepped off to the bathroom and returned to find that North had wasted no time with Nicole. He'd positioned her on the side of the bed, where she remained on her hands and knees with her backside arched high into the air, struggling to withstand the pain of North plunging himself deep inside of her. Contrary to the painful grimace etched across Nicole's face, North smiled brightly as he pounded her womb from behind, even smoking a blunt as he did so.

Sadon returned to the foot of his bed, pulling out his erection as he approached. With one hand gripping the base of his rock-hard penis and the other grasping a handful of Nicole's hair, he twisted the poor girl's head upwards and then shoved his penis deep into her mouth. The sounds of Nicole gagging and struggling to accept him down her throat only added to Sadon and North's excitement. They now stroked in unison, having their way with Nicole's body from both ends. Sadon and North made eye contact with each other while ravaging Nicole. With smiles on both of their faces, they reached over and celebrated the moment with a quick hand-clap.

As lewd and as disgusting as the scene may appear to the average eye, Sadon and North's actions were typical of what goes on in the 'hood. From the east coast to the west coast, from north to south, the exploitation of one's needs and desires was commonplace in the ghettos of America. In the back of Sadon's mind, at that very moment, he was back home in the slums of Carol City.

With the end of the weekend came another Monday morning, which for Sadon meant the beginning of another series of him trying in vain to find a job. He was half-dressed when learning that his iron had suddenly conked out. In a rush, he hurried down to Nina's apartment to borrow hers.

Nina was barely dressed when she answered the door. Her breasts bubbled against the hem of a towel, which teasingly hugged every curve of her voluptuous body. After nearly two months of conversation, she and Sadon were nearing the possibility of having a relationship. Still, they weren't the least bit intimate with each other. This was the first time Sadon had ever seen Nina so scantily dressed; the bulge now beginning to swell from inside his pants verified as much.

"Yo, girl," Sadon said while turning away. "You ain't got no business openin' the door like that! You act like you don't know what you be doing to a nigga!"

"Boy, please," Nina replied while combing out her silky black hair.

She took a moment to gaze into Sadon's eyes before seductively staring him up and down.

"You shouldn't come down to my apartment half-dressed, either."

With that, Nina turned around and started off, leaving the door open for Sadon to walk inside. He stared lustily at Nina's rear end as she headed toward the bathroom, admiring the shape of her chunky butt cheeks and thick hips as they pressed ever so teasingly against the damp fabric of her bath towel.

"I need to borrow your iron, sexy," Sadon announced while starting toward the closet.

"I see how hard you've been trying to find a job, Sadon," Nina shouted from inside the bathroom.

Her voice was barely heard above the noise of the blow dryer.

"You gotta stick with it baby. It'll pay off sooner or later; you know it will."

"I'm funna go to an interview right now, sexy," Sadon replied. "These crackas be actin' like they ain't tryin' to hire a nigga, though. I be close as hell to sayin' 'fuck it' sometimes, you know what I'm sayin'?"

Nina walked up on Sadon while still dressed in nothing but a towel. Her hair was now dried and combed straight down the sides of her face. She grabbed him by the hands, and then stood up on her toes to reach and kiss Sadon softly but intently on the lips. Sadon was stunned. It was the first time they'd ever gotten physical.

Yo! Sadon thought to himself with surprise. *Shorty is really feelin' a nigga. Shit, it's about fuckin' time.*

Against the urge to have his dreadlocks styled backward in cornrows, Sadon instead wore them in a tight ponytail. He was dressed in a black pair of khakis, a crème-colored button-up shirt, which was the same color as the casual style Timberland boots he wore. Nina dubbed it his "lucky outfit," but right now, while on his way inside McGillan's Warehouse and Supply Shop, Sadon wasn't feeling the least bit lucky. This was his eighth interview this month, his 15 in all, each one eerily seeming the same as the last.

The manager was a huge, barrel-chested white man with quick, blue eyes and thinning blonde hair. He stared at Sadon for a few minutes before extending his hand.

"How are you?" he asked. "My mane's John Rafton."

"Mitchell," Sadon replied while shaking the manager's hand. "My name's Sadon Mitchell."

As soon as Sadon opened his mouth, John Rafton's face went slack, his eyes portraying a mixture of both awe and uncertainty. It was an expression Sadon recognized on the faces of those intimidated by his very presence.

"My!" John Rafton remarked. "You must not be from around here. Those teeth almost blinded me, buddy!"

You act like ain't no niggas in New York walkin' around with gold teeth, Sadon thought to himself. "Yuh…" he said out loud, trying not to sound as agitated as he felt. "I wish I could take'em out, but unfortunately, they're permanent."

"I see," John Rafton said. "Look, I have to ask if you've ever been convicted of a felony as a juvenile or as an adult."

Man, I knew this shit was a waste of time, Sadon said to himself. "F'sho, dawg; fa'sho," he replied, not caring to let his country gangster show a little. "Listen, man, I'm funna just get on up and out your face, man."

With that, Sadon rose up out of the chair and started out the office. In all actuality, he had long ago given up on trying to find a job. He looked too much like a thug, spoke too much like a thug, and carried himself too much like a thug to get a job in the white man's world. In fact, it became extremely clear to Sadon that he, himself, was too much of a thug to want to work for the white man anyway. He was now beginning to feel like a fool for ever trying to change who he was. Sadon was a thug; he was a thoroughbred, and thoroughbreds made their way in the streets of the ghetto.

⚜⚜⚜⚜⚜⚜

Nina watched as Sadon entered her apartment without saying a word; the expression on his face said more than enough.

"Yuh," he finally said while taking a seat on the sofa. "I ain't get the job, man, but fuck it. You know a nigga's use to this shit by now; it's all good."

Nina stood by the threshold of the kitchen, feeling terrible for Sadon. To see him having such a hard time trying to do right made her feel bad; her heart definitely went out to Sadon. She slowly approached him, stripping out of her sweatpants and hockey jersey before making her way to the sofa. Nina's body was far more spectacular than Sadon had ever dared to imagine. She had a perfect hourglass figure; her breasts seemed to almost burst from out of her sheer black bra, which matched her see-through bikini underwear. She stared seductively at Sadon as she approached, the muscles of her abdomen and lower body flexing and twisting with each step she took toward him.

Sadon was speechless. He stared dumbly at Nina as she straddled herself on top of him. He traced the curves of Nina's firm, meaty rear end with the palms of his hands, surprised at how large, shapely, and firm her buttocks actually were. *Goddamn!* He thought to himself. *How the fuck could she have been hidin' all this ass?* Nina wrapped both her arms around Sadon's neck and then leaned forward and kissed him passionately on his mouth. She broke away soon afterward, allowing Sadon the chance to look into her eyes and realize the intentions she had in store for the both of them.

He scooped Nina up in his arms and then proceeded to carry her into the bedroom. Once inside, Sadon eased her onto the bed before clicking on the stereo; the sounds of R. Kelly instantly filled the room. Nina watched with hungry eyes as Sadon began to undress. It had been a little more than two years since she'd been anywhere near intimate with a man; the sight of Sadon's erection now opened the door to a heightened sense of passion she never before thought existed. Nina gazed up at Sadon's body as he neared the bed. With the exception of a bullet scar on his right shoulder, Sadon's golden-brown complexion was smooth and without blemish. Every muscle in his body, including the one between his legs, was taut and well defined. She was eager to receive him.

Knowing of Nina's celibacy, Sadon figured her womb would be entirely too tight to accept him, so he opted to make sure she'd be ready. He kissed Nina softly on the lips, and with the tip of his tongue, licked his way down to her firm, ample breasts. Nina sighed with passion as he nibbled and pinched her nipples with his teeth. After taking a good moment to thoroughly service her breasts, Sadon then began kissing and licking his way down between Nina's legs.

Again, Nina sighed as Sadon began probing the inside of her. Nina's tunnel was tight, but slick with her own juices, making it easy for Sadon to slide his erection all the way inside. The walls of her womb were tight; the heat Sadon felt blazing from inside Nina's vagina was unbelievable. He extracted his penis all the way to its tip and then slid all the way inside her once more.

"O-o-h-h!" Nina moaned. She lay flat on her back with her legs cocked wide open, shaking her head from side to side with closed eyes. Her expression was one of pure ecstasy. Sadon maintained his pattern of stroking, feeling the tightness of Nina's vagina bringing him close to his own orgasm.

He quickened his pace, watching Nina's firm, yellow breasts jiggle and bounce around as he stroked. Nina's breath began to increase, as did his. Sadon pushed and pounded, digging deeper into her womb as he neared his climax. Nina bucked her hips to his rhythm, fighting to reach yet another orgasm. They stared into each other's eyes while giving it their all; and finally, it happened.

Nina closed her eyes even tighter than before as she climaxed. Sadon only furrowed his brow and growled, digging as deep into her womb as he possibly could, while feeling his own self explode. He then collapsed on top of Nina, obviously spent of all his energy. He never in his life felt such an intense moment of relief. Sadon rolled over onto his back and allowed Nina to snuggle up close to his body.

"I love you, Sadon," she said honestly. "I really do."

"I love you, too," Sadon replied without thinking.

He silently cursed himself for revealing his feelings so quickly. In fact, he cursed himself for having these feelings at all, but just couldn't help it. Sadon was all too used to dealing with treacherous, conniving, and money-hungry women. Nina was the first female that he could seriously consider being "wife material." He'd never felt this way about a woman before in his life. He wanted to make Nina happy; he wanted take her places she'd never been before and buy her all types of things she'd never had before.

Nina was one of a kind, and Sadon was determined now more than ever, to do what he did best. *Look out, New York,* he thought to himself. *Here I come.*

Chapter Three

It was a bright, sunny afternoon when Sadon made his way outside the project building, looking for North. He didn't have to look far. North was sitting on top of a milk crate making a drug sale flanked by a group of hustlers; all of who were either drinking liquor or smoking weed. Sadon made his way through the crowd and barged past North's customer with the same manner that an impatient coke addict would have.

"Dawg", Sadon said with a strong sense of urgency. "I need to holla at you about somethin', my nigga."

The serious look on Sadon's face made North agitated with how long the addict was taking to buy his product.

"Hurry up, mafucka!" he barked. "You got all the money or not? You see me and my man over here got somethin' to talk about. Hurry the fuck up, man, goddamn!"

After what seemed an eternity, the exchange had been completed. With the money he'd just received from the drug sale now added to the rest of his cash roll, North led Sadon a safe distance away from the radar-like ears of the other hustlers; Sadon didn't waste anytime.

"Listen, dawg," he began. "This job shit ain't doin' shit for me…"

"What?" North interrupted. "You ready to get out here and get this money?"

Sadon's face remained serious.

"F'sho, my nigga," he replied sharply. "If a nigga can't bubble no drugs, then I'm funna get mine in blood, feel me, my nigga?"

"Nah, nah, baby," North laughed. "Calm down, baby. It ain't even that serious. I knew you'd come around sooner or later. Talkin' bout you was getting a job; you was straight buggin'!" he scoffed. "But yeah, you caught me at the right time 'cause I was just getting ready to re-up."

North then took a moment to stare up at the sky as if he was trying to gather his thoughts.

"How much doe you got put up?" he asked.

It was now Sadon's turn to look up at the sky and take a moment or two to think.

"Man, I got like thirteen hundred," he finally answered.

"All right, cool," North replied. "Meet me here in like thirty minutes with twelve hundred, and I'm gonna match that twelve with twelve hundred of my own; then we'll go meet my connect together. Fuck it. Yo, we gon' cop like four ounces of raw and then take it from there, feel me?"

With all of the time North put into the streets, one would think that he'd be a major drug dealer by now. However, North was the exact opposite. The fifteen hundred, sometimes two thousand dollars he'd make from the streets each week would usually disappear as quickly as it came. Like most common criminals of the inner city, North lived for the basic pleasures of ghetto life; weed, alcohol, name brand clothing, and fast women.

Sadon, on the other hand, was a completely different story; he was a natural hustler. He was always sharper and much more aggressive than the rest. If he hadn't wasted his time looking for a job, Sadon figured, he'd surely be making big money in these streets by now. The environment may have changed, the slang and style of dress may be different, but when it came to the ins and outs of the criminal underworld, all 'hoods were practically the same, and Brooklyn, New York wasn't the least bit different from Miami, Carol City.

⁂

Almost an hour later, North and Sadon made their way out of the subway station and were now standing at the corner of 183 Street and Amsterdam in Manhattan. The sidewalks were every bit as busy and as jam-packed as the traffic in the street. Scores of people filled the sidewalks, traveling this way and that way beneath the fifteen and twenty-story buildings, which loomed from the skies above. It was a surreal sight for a country boy like Sadon, who was used to the one and two story buildings spread around his hometown in Florida.

He followed North across the busy street to a well known drug area, which was only a few yards or so away from the corner. After traveling through a narrow passage between two fifteen-story buildings, they found themselves directly in front of another building. It was a huge apartment building with a tough looking group of Dominican hustlers congregating on the front steps where two "lookouts" stood posted on both sides of the building. All of them wore state-of-the-art headsets with microphones attached to the earpiece, which kept them all informed of every moment in and outside the perimeter of their territory. Sadon was a bit leery, but definitely impressed with the entire set-up.

A well dressed, but rugged-looking Dominican man with dark skin, hard eyes, and long, oily hair greeted North with what seemed to be a forced smile.

"North," he said with a thick, Latin accent. "It seems like I just saw you yesterday. Ready to re-up already?"

"Somethin' like that Mike. You know who I'm trying' to see," North replied while exchanging hugs and handshakes with the rest of the bunch, "Let him know that I'm here"

Mike raised a finger as if to tell North to wait a minute while stepping away and pressing into the earpiece of his headset, while speaking in Spanish. After a moment, he nodded in conformation as he approached the crowd.

"He'll take care of you, Papi," Mike said while rejoining his entourage. "Just sit tight for a minute."

North understood perfectly well what was going on. The homie whom North spoke of was a smoother, easy going and older Dominican man named Johnny, and he was in charge of this entire operation. Aside from the armed guards positioned on the front steps, lookouts were posted both outside and inside the building as well. Everyone communicated with one another by way of the hi-tech headphones they wore; nothing moved without Johnny's say-so.

After nearly five minutes of waiting, Mike nodded and called inside for a Dominican man known only as "Uno" to lead them to their destination. They started through a narrow passage between two buildings. This route seeming to be more of an obstacle course than anything; the tiny alley was cluttered with trash and garbage bags, which Sadon and North had to maneuver around in order to reach a side entrance.

The door of the side entrance opened to the sight of a brick wall; to the left was a staircase, which led straight down into the basement. The light of day was now beginning to disappear with each step they took down the stairs. Uno clicked on a flashlight just before it had grown pitch-black in the cellar. Their journey stopped short at the bottom of the stairway, where a huge, wooden door now stood before them.

Uno spoke rapidly into his walkie-talkie and then banged impatiently on the door, to which the sound of a huge bolt being unlocked was now being heard from the other side. The door then seemed to open with a suctioned sound. The offensive odor of raw cocaine was recognized almost instantly.

The heightened show of security showed just how close they were getting to North's Dominican "homie;" Sadon felt himself growing impatient. Uno disappeared back into the darkness of the stairwell, leaving both North and Sadon in the company of two armed guards, and a thin, well-dressed Latino, wearing a dark pair of sunglasses and a headset to match. One of the guards gave then both a rough and thorough pat down before allowing them to continue on.

What Sadon now saw was unbelievable. He had never before in his life seen such an airtight operation. The basement was dank and barely lit; the off-white colored paint on the walls was cracked and peeling. A team of seats, which seemed to have been ripped from inside of a van, served as couches for a number of workers busying themselves with counting, rubber band wrapping, and marking huge amounts of cash. North and Sadon walked into another room where a group of workers each stood before a huge turkey pot, which was set on top of a large, rectangular cardboard box. They all wore paper oxygen masks and plastic gloves in order to protect them from the potency of the cocaine they were chopping and packaging.

Standing beside a huge, digital scale and a compressing machine used for packaging cocaine was a slim, sharp-eyed Dominican man who, despite his plain, almost raggedy style of dress, possessed an air about him that reeked entirely of money. His hair was salon-styled; his glowing, sun-tanned complexion contrasted sharply with the wrinkled, stonewashed jeans and skin-tight tee shirt he wore. It wasn't hard for Sadon to guess this was the man in charge.

Jonathan "Johnny" Vega was one of the biggest cocaine dealers in Manhattan; so big, in fact, that he felt untouchable. He was a sometimes overly aggressive individual and was known for making decisions based more so on how he felt rather than rational thinking. Besides fast cars, and pretty women, Johnny's arrogance was undoubtedly one of his greatest vices. There was no way in the world a drug dealer of his stature, should have been anywhere near a manufacturing detail such as this; that's what his captains and lieutenants were hired for. Yet Johnny felt invulnerable and was always inclined to prove it; henceforth, his acquaintance with North.

There was no way a low-level dealer like North should have ever been allowed into this urban fortress, but Johnny prided himself in having the power to break such cardinal rules of the business. The least he could do, Johnny figured, for North tipping him off about an impending raid by New York City's Drug Task Force, was to allow the struggling black drug dealer inside his building to grant him a few requests. North was a straightforward guy who hadn't once overstepped his boundaries. With that in mind, Johnny allowed North to bring Sadon along with him.

"Good to see you, my friend," Johnny said while giving North a heartfelt handshake and a hug.

After taking a moment to introduce both Johnny and Sadon to each other, North got straight to the point and told the older Dominican drug supplier of his and Sadon's plans to form a partnership. Again, Johnny was impressed. Not only was North once again coming with straight cash, instead of asking for a handout, he brought along someone who appeared to be a stand-up guy. For North to bring him along, was an indication of just how great an asset he may be. Sadon locked eyes with Johnny, who stared curiously at him while embracing North.

Yuh, mafucka, Sadon said only in his head. You lookin' at a real ass nigga from down bottom, pussy and me and my nigga funna go straight to the top!

***

For Sadon, the trip back to Marcy Projects seemed an eternity. Upon their arrival, he eagerly agreed with North to chop and bottle the cocaine at his studio apartment. Sadon had never in his life dealt with anything other than crack-cocaine and was more than curious as to learn how North would measure and bottle the powder. They set a large, glass dish atop the bed, and with razors in hand, began cutting the compressed cocaine into chunks. It was only when Nina entered his apartment unannounced that Sadon had suddenly realized why he was a bit hesitant to handle his business at home. In a gesture to substantiate their relationship, Nina and Sadon both made duplicates of their house keys and gave them to each other. It was an act that Sadon somehow knew he'd come to regret. She froze at the very sight of North and Sadon sitting on the bed bottling what she knew was powder cocaine.

Sadon was just as shocked and at a loss for words as Nina; the two stared at each other with genuine horror. Nina's eyes began to bubble and tear.

"Nina…," he finally found the voice to say. "Nina, I'm…"

Sadon was never given the chance to finish. Nina turned and stormed out the apartment, slamming the door behind her as she went. Not really knowing what to say, North only shook his head from side to side. He fully understood Nina's heartache when realizing Sadon had chosen to revert back to his old ways just as much as he knew how hard it was for Sadon to admit to himself, let alone to Nina, that he wasn't meant to live the life of a regular, working-class citizen. North didn't bother to watch as Sadon leapt from the bed to chase after Nina and instead kept focused on the ounces of powder he was now cutting apart. The street life was North's only love, and his friendship with Sadon only added spice to that relationship.

He'll be back, North thought as he busied himself with his razor. *Regardless of what, I know he'll be back. We got big plans baby, big plans.*

<hr>

Nina stood in front of the closed doors, feverishly pushing the button while hoping it would open sooner than she really knew it would. Sadon stood quietly behind her, desperately searching to find the right thing to say. Nina had long ago told him of her parents, who were both up and coming drug dealers, and how they were killed by rival competition when she was just a child. She told of how, after being bounced around from one relative to another, she finally landed in Marcy Projects where she met North, whose childhood was nearly just as traumatic as hers. Deep down inside, however, Sadon knew there was no sugar coating his intentions. He'd given the honest life a try, and it didn't work for him. Sadon was never one to sit around without a dollar to his name, struggling to make ends meet. There was money to be made in the streets of New York, and he was determined to make it. He wanted to reach out and touch Nina, to turn her around and look into her eyes as he spoke, but decided against it.

"Listen hur, baby girl," Sadon began. "You know how hard a nigga's been tryin'. But how long did you expect me to keep bussin my ass out hur without supporting myself, huh? I got bills, too, baby. I got bills to pay, too, Nina. I got rent to pay. And a nigga gotta eat."

Nina turned to face Sadon. Her eyes were wet with moisture; a single tear had now begun to trickle down her cheek. Sadon's heart melted at the very sight of it.

"Let me tell you the truth about my mom and my dad, Papi..."

"I know, I know..." Sadon interrupted. "You already told me, baby. Listen, Nina, you ain't gotta..."

"Just be quiet and let me talk," Nina snapped.

Sadon was taken aback by the manner in which she had just spoken. He searched Nina's face for the sweet, tenderhearted woman he'd come to love, but found no such thing. Her eyes were as cold and as crisp as her demand for Sadon to be quiet. It was the first time she had ever spoken this way. Seeing that Sadon had begrudgingly given her the floor, Nina began revealing her secret.

"My father was a big time drug dealer in the Bronx, and when I say big time, I mean big time. He sold drugs to the people that sold it to the street hustlers. I was barely ten years old, but I remember. I remember how everyone respected my father; they worshipped him. I lived better than the rest of the kids and they hated me for it. They hated me with every fiber of their beings, but were too scared to express it for fear of what my father might do. I had no friends, Papi. No one wanted to play with me; the kids in my neighborhood didn't even speak to me. All I had was my mother."

Nina took a moment to reflect on the relationship she once shared with her mother.

"She was beautiful; I mean she won beauty pageants and everything. What I didn't know then, was that my father was steadily feeding her heroin. He was treating her real bad, too. Beating her and cursing her out all the time, it was such a shame. She started losing weight and looking terrible. It got to the point where she'd never even leave the house.

"For some reason, I woke up in the middle of the night and found my mother stretched out in the middle of the living room floor. I ran straight to her and shook her and tried to wake her up, but she didn't respond; she just laid there with her eyes half open. I swear to God, I thought my father had killed her. I cried and I cried, calling her name and begging for her to get up and say something. I don't know how long I sat there going through all of that.

"And then I saw the powder sitting on top of the coffee table. And even though I didn't really know what it was, I knew it was drugs. I knew this was the stuff that my father was selling, and it didn't take a rocket scientist to figure out what happened. Papi, you can't imagine how I felt; I mean, my mother was everything to me. She was the only friend I had. She was the only friend I had in the whole world, and now she was gone; she was gone because of that 'shit' my father was giving her."

Nina's face was blank; a slight glimmer in her eyes was now her only show of emotion.

"I stared at my mother thinking that she was dead. You can't imagine how it feels to think the only person in the world that truly cares about you is suddenly taken from you. She was the only thing that mattered to me, Papi. All I knew was that if she was gone, then I wanted to be gone, too. If she was dead, then I wanted to be dead, too. I took that poison and I sniffed, Papi; I sniffed it and then laid down beside my mother. And I began to feel so bad that I just knew I was dying. First, my nose started to burn, and then my head started to hurt; my brain felt like it was on fire. I was throwing up like crazy.

"It was the first time that I realized just how bad drugs were. I couldn't believe that my father was actually feeding this shit to my mother. After seeing him curse her out and beat her so many times in the past, I figured that he had somehow used that shit to kill her, and since I thought he had killed my mother, I made up my mind to kill him. I can't explain what I was actually thinking at the time, but I just knew I was about to die, and I at least wanted my father to pay for what he'd done.

"I was so tired, Papi. It was a struggle for me to even get up on my feet, but I did. My vision was so blurry, I could barely see. I went into my parents' bedroom where my father was fast asleep, and I got the gun that he kept hidden on the top shelf in his closet. I can't remember what kind of gun it was, but it was big and it was heavy. I didn't want to kill him while he was sleeping; I wanted him to be awake. I wanted him to look me in the eyes as I squeezed the trigger.

"I tapped him on the head with the barrel of the gun and called him over and over again. He opened his eyes slowly at first, but the sight of the pistol being aimed directly at his face woke him right up. His eyes got big, but he didn't move. He laid still on his stomach, staring at me from the corner of his eye. He called my name out and asked if it was me, and I told him to turn over and look at me. Instead of him doing what I told him to do, he tried to reach and grab for the gun. I stepped back and squeezed the trigger. The first shot hit him in the shoulder, turning him all the way over on his back. The sound of the gunshot was the loudest thing I've ever heard in my life. The kick of the gun almost knocked me off my feet, but I stood firm and kept it aimed at my father. I squeezed the trigger two more times. The whole back of his head exploded; blood had gotten all over the place, even on me.

"I just stood there staring at him. I couldn't feel anything. I thought my mother was dead, Papi, I really did, but she wasn't. She stumbled into the bedroom all high and what not. I guess the sounds of the gunshots were loud enough to wake her up from her 'dope high.' She went crazy when she saw what I did. I just stood there holding the gun, watching as she ran back and forth between me and my father, screamin' and askin' me what did I do. I thought she was dead, Sadon. I thought she was dead, and I thought she was dead because of my father; that's the only reason why I shot him. When seeing my mother come into the bedroom, I was too hurt to even shed a tear.

"Mami took the gun out of my hands, and then gave me a real big hug; then told me to go dial 9-1-1 and say that my daddy got shot and then hang right up. I ran and did exactly what she told me to do. Then out of nowhere, 'BOOM' I dropped the phone and ran back into the bedroom to find that my mother had stuck the gun into her own mouth and blew her brains out.

"The cops never found out what happened, but my family somehow pieced things together and treated me like shit because of it. I spent the rest of my childhood bouncing around from one relative to the next, all of them treating me badly and blaming me for what had happened. I finally landed in Marcy Projects where I met Shayom. He's been through a lot, too. I didn't even have to explain anything to him for him to show me love and respect. He's the closest thing I'll ever have to a brother, and I really mean it."

More shocking than the story Nina had just told him was the cool, almost emotionless manner she displayed while telling it. Sadon was totally speechless.

"I never would've guessed," he finally said. "I'm sorry to hear that shit, ma, for real."

"Now do you understand why I didn't want you to be involved with that shit?" she asked.

Sadon sighed.

"Yo, I'm sorry about what you went through, and I can see why you ain't feelin' a nigga sellin' drugs" he began. "But I gotta eat, ma. If I could get a job tomorrow and make things right with you, I would, but shit ain't workin' out for me like that, baby. I'm thousands of miles away from home, my cash ain't lookin' right, and if I don't come up with somethin' soon, I ain't gon' have a place to live. What, you want me to go back down bottom and leave you behind? What do you expect me to do?"

"I didn't ask you for no fuckin' sob stories, Sadon," Nina replied flatly. "And I didn't ask you to make no excuses for why you're out there doin' what you're doin'. I asked you if you understood why I didn't want you involved in the drug game."

She then looked Sadon square in the eyes. "Do...you...understand?"

Sadon only stared at Nina. His urge to contend with her venomous sarcasm thwarted by his shock at how cold and impersonal she appeared. Sadon had murdered quite a few people in his time, and had kept company with many who'd done the same. But never before had he met someone able to carry such vivid memories of death without the slightest hint of psychosis; it flashed from within her eyes as she now stood face to face with him.

Sadon fished a cigarette from inside his pocket and placed it into the corner of his mouth.

"Yuh," he said while setting fire to it. "Yuh, I understand."

The two now stood in silence, the quietness suddenly proving to be uncomfortable for both of them. Sadon only stared at Nina as she turned her gaze away from him to peer down the hall. To both Sadon and Nina's relief, the doors to the fourth floor elevator had finally opened. Nina stepped inside without bothering to say a single word. Sadon only watched as the doors began to close, still not knowing how to react to Nina's abrupt change in demeanor. After a moment or two of contemplation, he cracked a wide, gold-toothed smile.

I got myself a gangster bitch, Sadon thought to himself while finishing the rest of his cigarette. *Nina's a bona fide gangster bitch, and she don't even know it.*

Chapter Four

North and Sadon's method of conducting business was simple. One would serve as a lookout for both the stick-up kids and police while the other sold directly to the addicts, their duties alternated with the beginning of each new day. Sadon possessed a work ethic unlike anyone North had ever seen. The country boy from "down bottom," to North, was a true thoroughbred. From bottling up the product, to how to deal with the coke fiends, Sadon proved himself to be a natural born hustler. He lived and breathed the drug game. Sadon's approach to the game was a strong enough inspiration for North to get serious about what he was doing in the streets. He began toning down his spending habits and was now saving himself a pretty penny because of it. Both North and Sadon now spent their nights hustling until the break of morning, making their presence felt amongst the other dealers in the projects. Word of how good their product was and the decent manner in which they handled their customers was spreading fast.

Sadon had always been an exceptional drug dealer, even while hustling in Carol City. He always managed to seem a step ahead of the rest. In New York, however, he had become even more aggressive. The urge to visit strip clubs or spend his time and money on basic pleasures of the body had all but disappeared. The desire to hangout and "shoot the breeze" with so-called homies no longer existed, and he had no patience for anyone who wasn't as serious about making money as he was. Sadon was all of a sudden on a level far beyond the other drug dealers in his project building, and he had Nina to thank for it all.

The only thing more disturbing to Sadon than the eventful day in the hallway with Nina was the way she carried herself since then. It was as if she had never killed her father and provoked her mother to commit suicide; it was as if she hadn't suffered and endured more than ten years of guilt or mental anguish at the hands of her own relatives. It was if she had never told Sadon the truth of what had happened; it was if it never happened at all. The cold, near emotionless personality, which commanded Sadon's total attention was gone, now replaced with the sweet, tenderhearted girl he'd first met almost three months ago. Her smile was always bright, and she was always attentive to his needs; there was no trace of the woman who'd forcefully demanded for him to be quiet as she revealed her murderous tale. That woman was no more than a ghost in Sadon's mine. Questioning his ability to make it big in the streets of New York; while at the same time taunting him for fearing Nina's ability to somehow switch off the pain of what she'd experienced during her miserable childhood. It drove Sadon to hit the streets with a vengeance.

His determination didn't go unfounded. Sadon and North's operation was going smoothly. Addicts were literally falling in line to buy their product, and as a result, the four ounces they started with soon turned into six, and the six ounces quickly turned into nine. From Johnny, there was nothing but praise. He applauded North's change in attitude, and he was even allowing Sadon to enter inside his fortress to do business without North's presence. Sadon and North were a team, and in their minds, there was nowhere to go but up.

※※※※※※※

It was two o'clock in the morning as Sadon stood in front of the building lobby with a few hustlers who refused to allow the frigid, pre-winter winds to chase them indoors. They all stood around dressed in Timberland boots, heavy jeans, and over-sized coats. Although it was only the middle of October, it felt like the middle of January. A boom box was placed on a stack of milk crates, which completed the circle of drug dealers now spending their time taking turns rapping to a hip-hop instrumental. Sadon, as usual, dazzled the audience with his foreign style of rap and amazing wordplay. His skill with rhyming words was now just as well known as his skill for making money; once again, he and North proved to be a dynamic duo on the microphone as well as on the streets.

Everyone huddled closer together when it was Sadon's turn to rap. They listened intently as he rapped about the fight he'd gotten into last month and how he had beaten his enemy to a bloody pulp. He rapped about how thorough a hustler he was and how he was determined to get rich or die trying. He swore on the knots of money now bulging from his socks and his pockets that it was only a matter of time before becoming a millionaire. Even North, who was watching out for the police from a short distance away, traveled down the street to listen in.

There was one hustler amongst the crowed, however, who wasn't impressed with Sadon's lyrical skill; in fact, he didn't like Sadon at all. J.T. was a local thug, who had just come home after an eighteen-month stay at Riker's Island, to find North and Sadon standing in the way of his plans for success. For North to deny J.T. the chance to get down with his business was bad enough, the fact that he'd joined hands with this "country outsider" instead of a fellow Marcy Projects native only added insult to injury. He'd been outside and in front of the building all night watching Sadon dominate a great majority of the drug sales that came through. Seeing Sadon break away from the rap session for another two hundred dollar sale was the last straw.

"Man, fuck that!" J.T. exclaimed. "What's up with your mafuckin' peoples, North?"

It was a loud and sudden outburst that snapped everyone from the good time they were all having. They all stopped and stared at J.T., the music from the boom box being the only sounds between them. North stared at J.T., masquerading his rage at J.T.'s nerve for complete ignorance.

"Man, what the fuck is you talkin' about?" he asked.

"You know what the fuck I'm talkin' about, nigga!" J.T. barked. "That country-ass nigga ain't even from around here, and y'all niggas is out here lettin' him lock shit down. This nigga's makin' all the money around here and right in front of y'all faces, too! He's even rapin about that shit! Man, fuck that nigga!"

Everyone in the projects, including J.T., knew that North and Sadon were partners, which meant that whatever applied to Sadon applied to North as well. J.T. was inadvertently challenging both of their right to make money in the projects.

North stared over J.T.'s shoulder and at Sadon who was slowly approaching them from behind. The fire North saw in his eyes was proof enough that his partner in crime had heard a great deal of J.T.'s comments. After seeing Sadon kneel down to pick something up from off the ground, North amped up his attitude to keep J.T.'s attention.

"What, nigga?!" he flared. "What the fuck is you talkin' about?"

Standing only a few inches shy of six feet, J.T. wasn't nearly as tall as North, but he was broad-chested with bulking shoulders; his muscles flexed against the fabric of his army jacket as he now prepared for combat.

"Fuck you, nigga!" Sadon exclaimed from behind.

J.T. turned halfway around only to meet the edge of a brick which landed square on his temple. There was a loud, hollow thud as the rock met its mark. It was a sickening sound. J.T.'s head almost twisted off his neck as he turned and crumpled onto the street. North only smiled as Sadon proceeded to stomp J.T.'s broken and unconscious body. His anger had now taken full surface; he raged and cursed wildly while stomping J.T. in the face, shoulders, and all over his back.

The beating Sadon was laying down on J.T. was indeed a terribly gruesome sight. It took a few moments for the others to get over their shock of what just happened. They stared dumbly as Sadon continued to brutalize his victim, and then rushed to intervene before taking the chance of allowing their drug spot to be transformed into a murder scene. Sadon was out of control. It required an incredible amount of strength for all of them to pull him off J.T.'s near lifeless body; he was still cursing and raging at J.T. even as his fellow hustlers forced him off and into their building.

Only North remained outside, staring down at J.T.'s bloody and broken body while smoking a blunt. *This nigga's got a lotta fuckin' nerve trying' to play me and my peoples the fuck out,* he thought to himself. *Well, he 'had' the nerve.* North took a moment to smile at his own sense of humor.

"We always gon' be gettin' money around here, nigga," he said out loud with his foot now pressed against J.T.'s blood-soaked and swollen face. "You're the one that can't get no more money around this bitch, you and anybody else that tries to get in our fuckin' way."

Meaning to punctuate what he'd just said, North spat a huge globe of mucus onto J.T.'s face. He then squatted down and bent halfway over to whisper into the poor man's ear.

"If I see you out here again, I'ma push you, That's a promise."

With that, North rose to his feet, and started back toward the building.

"Oh, yeah," he said before stopping and returning to the place of the brutal stomping. North then took a second to pluck a few ashes of his blunt over J.T.'s body.

"Thanks for the weed, you faggot-ass nigga."

Chapter Five

North and Sadon sat side by side in the backseat of a taxicab bubbling with anticipation. Inside their backpacks was everything they'd been working for: a half kilo of cocaine apiece. They spent every dollar they had on this one purchase; it was an all-or-nothing leap of faith with nothing but high expectations for what was to come.

There was nothing but silence between them as the taxicab pulled over in front of their project building. North and Sadon both slung their backpacks over their shoulders as they exited onto the street. It was a typical day in the projects. Clusters of drug dealers were spread about the area smoking, joking, and partaking in the everyday activities. Addicts mingled around the area, anxiously waiting for Sadon and North to package their product and then proceed to open up shop. It was North's turn to hustle; his eagerness to get things going was evident by the way he looked up, down, and around his surroundings as the taxicab pulled away. Fellow hustlers acknowledged Sadon's and North's arrival with a raised fist. Fiends did so with a simple nod; their hunger to get high was every bit as strong as North's desire to serve them. He was desperate to get things underway.

Sadon, however, wasn't as enthused. There was something in the air that had automatically tripped his silent alarm. While appearing cool on the outside, he was a nervous wreck on the inside. Ever since arriving back to the projects, Sadon had suddenly become apprehensive. He couldn't explain what it was that made him feel this way, but it didn't matter; he and North were only a few feet away from the safety of their own homes, and it was imperative now more than ever to get there. *Get the fuck inside, dawg,* Sadon said to himself while starting toward the front door of his building. *Let's get the fuck inside, bag this shit up, and then make it happen.*

And then, suddenly, it happened. In the blink of an eye, the entire street was swarming with Narcotics officers. Plain-clothed officers had instantly began to materialize from the crowds of pedestrians walking to and from with their guns drawn, screaming for everyone to 'get the fuck down on the ground." Black vans with tinted windows suddenly raced onto the scene from both directions of the building with officers dressed in all black hopping out the side doors before its tires ever had the chance to finish coming to a screeching halt. They wore large helmets with face shields attached and full-length body armor; their handguns and assault rifles seemed like something seen only in a science fiction movie.

There was sheer pandemonium in the streets. Both drug dealers and drug addicts alike were now scrambling to escape. 'New York's Finest' was all over the place and knee deep in the midst of the scuffle; slamming, tossing, and even tackling suspects who were now trying their best to get away. Sadon had barely managed to place one of his feet inside the building before being tackled hard onto the ground, losing a great deal of his breath in the process. He got halfway back to his feet only to be grabbed by the collar of his coat and flung back down to the concrete, this time knocking all the air out of his lungs. His back exploded with pain when feeling the knee of a policeman crash down hard between his shoulder blades.

In less than a minute, Sadon found himself handcuffed and sitting beside North who unfortunately, had met the same fate. They sat against the wall of their project building with their hands cuffed behind their backs and watching as two members of the Narcotics Task Force began inspecting the contents of both their backpacks. Neither North nor Sadon bothered to acknowledge the look of satisfaction shining from the eyes of the detectives now discovering the two half kilos of cocaine. In the midst of a routine drug raid, the police had unwittingly scored big time. Sadon and North continued staring straight ahead, not wanting to watch as the cops celebrated their act of intercepting and destroying everything they had hustled and worked so hard to accomplish.

♦♦♦♦♦♦♦♦♦♦

Not only was Stephanie Welch a prominent lawyer and a member of an illustrious legal firm in Brooklyn, New York, she was also just one of North's many "on-again/off-again" love interests. It was Stephanie that had provided North with the tip about the impending raid on Johnny's territory, but unfortunately for North and Sadon, there was no forewarning for them in their dilemma; not only that, but there was nothing she could do for them now. The state's case against North and Sadon was airtight; being foolish enough to even attempt going to trial would undeniably do them more harm than good. Stephanie's advice, before leaving them in the bullpen, was to accept the four-year plea bargain before it was yanked away and replaced with something harsher than the first deal.

With Stephanie long gone, both North and Sadon sat together in the cramped bullpen absorbed in their own individual thoughts. Everything Sadon had worked so hard to acquire; the apartment, his clothes, the half kilo of cocaine, everything, had all gone up in smoke. Nina was all that he had left; and it tore him inside to imagine how she'd react when learning of his and North's arrest. Sadon turned to look at his crime partner now turned co-defendant. North sat with his back straight against the wall staring into nothingness; he seemed broken by the entire experience.

"What's up, dawg?" asked Sadon.

"You know what it is, my nigga," North replied.

He then turned and looked Sadon straight in the eyes before continuing his response.

"The longer the setback, the stronger the comeback," he replied. "Let's take this ride up state and bang this shit out."

Sadon could only smile at his partner's fortitude. North matched Sadon's smile with an arrogant half-grin of his own, and just like that, their determination to get rich or die trying was renewed; prison was nothing but an obstacle, and a small one at that. While sharing a bench in the tiny bullpen, North and Sadon reaffirmed their commitment to each other with a heartfelt, ghetto-style handshake; while staring into each other's eyes, they both agreed that nothing, not even prison, would keep them from realizing what they knew to be their destiny.

Months had passed by since North and Sadon's arrest; still, Nina was numb all over by the news. Ever since learning of Sadon's intention to hustle, she expected this day to come; yet she was surprised to find out just how much of an impact it would have on her life. Never before had Nina learned to love a man as she did Sadon; it shook her to think she couldn't love someone as much as she had once loved her mother. No, it did more than shake Nina; it scared her to death. Nina loved her mother to death, so much so that it didn't matter if she'd die with her or for her. How could she have let Sadon get into her heart like this?

No matter how scrambled Nina's thoughts may have been, not once did she ever express, or give into the confusion that constantly racked her brain. On the outside, she was everything Sadon expected her to be and more. She visited him nearly every week at Nap Nap State Penitentiary and even brought Maria along to visit North. She kept Sadon's mail coming on a regular basis and accepted his phone calls whenever she had the chance to do so. The toughest task for Nina was getting Sadon to accept the money orders she tried to send every month. Knowing that he and North were both locked up and doing their time together, however, gave Nina the advantage. She used Maria to send North a few extra dollars, which she knew would help contribute to him splitting everything fifty-fifty with Sadon.

For Nina, her relationship with Sadon was about more than love; it was about trust, honesty, loyalty, and respect. If it was all about how they felt about each other, then she would have definitely felt some type of way about him not telling her when he was due to be released. After all, what woman wouldn't be upset at the notion of her man keeping such valuable information a secret? Nina Nuñez, that's who. As it was said so many times before, Nina stood upon the virtues of trust, honesty, loyalty, and respect. Not once while Sadon was running the streets, did she ever bother to questions his actions, and with that being the case, she found no reason to start questioning him now.

With the years that quickly passed, what mattered most to Nina was that she had an idea of when he may be coming home. Sadon and North were partners; they split everything, including their crimes, straight down the middle, which meant that his release date couldn't be too much longer than North's, and with North due to come home tomorrow, Nina knew that it wouldn't be much longer before she was reunited with the love of her life.

It was a gorgeous summer day, perhaps the best so far for the month of August. The sun shone brightly above from clear, blue skies; the feel of an easy summer breeze added to the comfort of the eighty-degree temperature. The final gate that had barred North from the outside world for more than three years had finally begun to open. He didn't bother waiting for it to open all of the way and slipped outside at the very first opportunity he was given. Nina and Maria stood outside the prison, smiling as North boldly made his way towards them.

Although Nap-Nap State Penitentiary had an open recreational yard, which enabled its inmates to get fresh air, the oxygen he now breathed while standing outside the walls of prison felt entirely different than on the side.

Finally! I'm mafuckin' home! North thought happily to himself while exchanging hugs and kisses on the cheek with both Nina and Maria. *Well, halfway home,* he thought to remind himself when thinking of Sadon, who was due to be released thirty days later.

"Damn, nigga!" Maria said. "Step back and let me check you out for a second!"

North smiled while taking a step backward, giving Maria a full view of his body. During his three-year stint in prison, he and Sadon had been working out in the weight room faithfully, and it showed. North's back and shoulders were wide and seemed to almost stretch the fabric of his tee shirt. Maria became even more excited when he stripped it off to show his bulging chest and stomach muscles. Nina, on the other hand, gave an almost insignificant nod of approval, her smile seeming more cosmetic than anything.

Nina's style of dress hadn't changed one bit. She stood leaning against the driver's side of her old model Honda Civic hatchback with her arms crossed, wearing a knee-length tee shirt, a pair of over-sized gym shorts, and sneakers. Her long, silky black hair fell down from beneath a fitted baseball cap that she wore backwards on her head.

Maria was dressed in her usually smutty attire. Her breasts bulged against a tank top that was every bit as skintight as the thigh-high cut off denim shorts she wore; she was also sporting the clear-colored, spike-heeled shoes made famous by the whores that worked in the strip clubs.

Same ol' Nina and Maria, North thought to himself with a smile.

Suddenly, North wasn't in such a playful mood; he was ready to get as far away from this God forsaken place as humanly possible.

"Let's get the fuck outta here," he grumbled. "This ain't no fuckin visit!"

Maria, who was still caught up in the moment of playfulness, pulled a loaded .38 revolver from the small of her back and aimed it directly at his stomach.

"Yeah, nigga," she said with a smile. "Put your fucking hands in the air."

North was far from amused. He recognized the .38 that Maria was now playfully aiming to be one of the pistols he'd left stashed away at her house before getting arrested and shipped out to prison. His face went tight, his eyes now blazing with rage.

"You forgot where the fuck we're at?" he asked angrily. "Get the fuck in the car before you get us all locked the fuck up."

Although shocked and hurt by North's heated reaction, Maria completely understood. North had done a lot of growing up during his incarceration, and he was far from the reckless, fierce-hearted young boy with something to prove. Nina was silently impressed.

Maria climbed into the backseat of the car and allowed North to sit in the front with Nina.

"Gimme that pistol, too," he said as Nina started out of the prison's parking lot.

North took the pistol and tucked it into the waistband of his jeans. No one bothered to say another word as Nina's tiny car raced back toward what North silently described as home sweet home.

⁕⁕⁕⁕⁕⁕⁕⁕⁕⁕

While on his way back to Marcy, North was overwhelmed by a tremendous sense of eagerness. He'd only been away for a little more than three years, but it seemed an eternity. Everything seemed so different; even some of the thugs now huddling around the door of his project building were a bit diverse. Of the dozen or so hustlers now occupying his old stomping grounds, there were maybe three or four that he recognized. There was one face in particular that he was definitely happy to see.

Rah-Rah was in his teens when North and Sadon were home; he couldn't have been more then sixteen or seventeen years old when they were in the projects trying their best to make a name for themselves. North could remember Rah-Rah quite clearly; how could anyone forget him? He was a short, stocky-built, and brown-skinned kid with hard eyes and a seriously chipped tooth. Like most kids in the projects, Rah-Rah had endured a pretty rough childhood, but what separated him from the rest was the respect he commanded from everyone around him.

Everyone knew that even as a kid, Rah-Rah was not be taken lightly. His boxing skills were every bit as sharp and as explosive as his temper, it was a combination that helped make him very well known while at the same time placing him in good favor with North and Sadon. It was North, however, that had always taken a greater liking to the young, up and coming street thug. Rah-Rah reminded North very much of himself in his younger years; consequently he showed Rah-Rah a great deal more attention than the others.

The look in Rah-Rah's eyes when recognizing North as he cruised by in the passenger seat of Nina's car was proof of him not forgetting those days. He stood in a crowd of hustlers dressed in a black pair of basketball shorts, a white tank top, and a red on white pair of Nike sneakers. Rah-Rah threw up both of his hands in acknowledgement of North's arrival.

"What's poppin', my nigga?" he hollered out with a grin.

North couldn't help but absorb some of Rah-Rah's happiness to see him free and back on the streets.

"Yeah, nigga, yeah!" he exclaimed out of the car window. "The kid is home, baby!"

Rah-Rah met North in the parking lot as he exited from the car. After exchanging handshakes and bear hugs, the two now sat against Nina's car sharing a blunt.

"Damn, homie!" Rah-Rah commented after noticing North taking an extra long drag of the blunt. "You ain't been home in a minute, dawg. You better get used to the weed before you start hittin' it like that."

North smiled while letting out a stream of smoke.

"Man, this shit ain't about nothin'. You know Maria had that good shit for me just about every visit."

"Word? Damn, time flew my nigga. It's been like three years, right?"

"Yeah, but it was nothin', though, my nigga. I had to poke a nigga up when I first went down, but after that, it was pretty much smooth sailin'. On some real shit though, you know what it is; you know it's about to get ugly."

"I heard. Ay, yo," Rah-Rah said while pulling a stack of cash from inside his shorts pocket. "I'm gon' be the first nigga to cushion those pockets for you. Take this, my nigga."

He split his cash roll in half and handed one of the stacks to North.

"Shit," North said while accepting the money. "You must be out her touchin' it, huh?"

"Touchin' it out here?" Rah-Rah remarked with a genuine look of disgust. "Man, I don't sell no drugs. These niggas out here is pussy! Ever since you and Sadon got bagged, shit done changed. I be straight leanin' on these niggas out here."

Mentioning Sadon's name caused Rah-Rah to stop and reminisce on the memory of Sadon nearly beating J.T. to death.

"Yo, you remember when Sadon beat the shit out of J.T.? That shit was funny as hell! Yo, when the fuck is my nigga comin' home, anyway, man?"

North remained stone-faced. He didn't quite understand what Rah-Rah meant when he said, 'shit done changed'.

"Yo, what the fuck do you mean shit done changed ever since me and Sadon got bagged?" he asked. "What's poppin'?"

"Man, these niggas out here is straight bitch," Rah-Rah answered. "You act like you ain't heard."

In all actuality, North didn't hear. Maria could only see but never know what was going on in the streets. Like any other hoochie North ever knew, she took everything on face value and was always impressed with what hustlers had and never how they got it. In other words, according to Maria, Marcy Projects was still off the hook, and hadn't changed one bit.

"Man, listen," Rah-Rah began. "Since it looks like you don't know what's goin' on, I'm gon' break shit down for you. All these niggas out here is hustlin' for that nigga, Rock from Fort Green Projects. Shit, why do you think I be robbin' these bitch-ass niggas out here? These niggas is scared as hell of that mafucka, for real. Don't nobody out here sell shit unless it's Rock's." North stood still while finishing the rest of the blunt, fighting not to show the shock he felt when hearing how bad things have gone for the hustlers in his building.

How the fuck could shit come to this?

"You gotta be fuckin' kiddin' me," North grumbled out loud, not meaning to speak his thoughts.

"Yeah, nigga,' said Rah-Rah. "That's what it is around here; shit just ain't the same. But listen, my nigga," he said while glancing at his wristwatch. "I gots to go meet up with this bitch real quick, ya heard?"

"I heard," North replied. "I heard."

They both gave each a handshake and another heartfelt hug.

"Stop lookin' all stressed the fuck out, nigga," Rah-Rah said while backing away. "I know you gon' get shit poppin' in a hot second. Take your time, my nigga. Holla at me when you need me."

With that, Rah-Rah turned and started around the corner, leaving North alone with his thoughts. He was still struggling to deal with the news of how bad things had gotten. It seemed like yesterday when thinking of how the hustlers in his project building controlled their own destinies, but now, all of that has changed. As angry as North may have been about the situation, he knew enough not to do anything rash. What Sadon did to J.T. three years back was a shining reminder of what happens to thugs who come home from prison thinking they can bully their competition.

Sadon.

The very thought of Sadon coming home in thirty days was enough to force North's lips into a wicked smile. *Thirty days,* he thought to himself. *Thirty mafuckin' days until my nigga comes home, and then it's on and poppin'.*

Chapter Six

Much to everyone's surprise, North's return home from prison was a rather uneventful occasion. He hadn't kicked up any dust or displayed any animosity towards any of the drug dealers who'd been hustling for Rock; he didn't even attempt to sell a single drug. On face value, North didn't want any part of the street life. He distanced himself from nearly everyone he had a previous history with, busying himself more so with females that lived on various floors in his project building and smoking weed. After his first moth of being home, the apprehension of the local thugs had all but disappeared; it was back to business without entertaining a single thought of North being any type of threat.

Contrary to everyone's misconceptions, North was far from being "scared straight" and was instead doing what the military described as "gathering intelligence" on his enemies and rivals. Women always seemed to have a stranglehold on all the gossip, and "cuddle time" after sex always proved to be the best time for North to milk them dry of anything they'd have to say. Although his disdain for the "new jacks" in his building played a major part in why North kept a safe distance away, it was also because he wanted to monitor their movements without appearing too suspicious; while smoking blunt after blunt, North observed the scenery to determine which rumors were the closest to being the truth.

In a month's time, North had managed to learn all he needed to know. There were a few independent drug dealers sprinkled about the building, but the greater majority of hustlers sold either crack or powdered cocaine for Rock, and he was making a killing. Rock was a big time hustler from Fort Green Projects and was in control of quite a few drug areas. It was more so, on the strength of his family ties rather than Rock's own reputation that he commanded so much fear and respect.

Rock was a first cousin to a pair of brothers whose deeds and acts of violence gained the respect of all five boroughs in New York. Although now locked away and serving multiple life sentences, the Jenkins Brothers still held an incredible amount of influence in a few Brooklyn neighborhoods. With his infamous family as a shield and sizable amount of drug and money behind him, Rock proved to be a very intimidating person to go up against.

After a careful and scrutinizing investigation, North had come to the conclusion that "intimidation" was all Rock really turned out to be. Rock's 'muscle' didn't compose of the bloodthirsty criminals responsible for making every project building in Front Green a virtual deathtrap for strangers. But mostly of stragglers and lackies who'd gladly snitch or switch sides to save their own necks. Rock's careless and shamelessly flamboyant demeanor only added to his vulnerability. It didn't take a rocket scientist to figure out that being flashy and most of the time intoxicated, was an extremely dangerous equation. In a mere matter of weeks, North had learned a great deal of Rock's habits and many hangouts. The fact that he traveled with an ensemble of street soldiers only when doing business made him an easier target. All one needed was patience. It was a wonder to North that someone hadn't killed Rock already.

⚜⚜⚜⚜⚜⚜

It was nearing the end of September, yet it was remarkably warm; the season was what many old-timers called an "Indian Summer." Dressed in an army green tee shirt, black denim jeans, and beige Timberland boots, North sat on top of a milk crate, which was a short distance away from the local thugs, smoking a blunt all by himself. Except for Rah-Rah and very few others, no one bothered speaking to North, which didn't bother him one bit, for North had decided not to speak to them since the very first day he came home from Nap-Nap.

While nearing the end of his blunt, North suddenly caught notice of someone blending in and out the approaching crowd of pedestrians from up the street. There was no mistaking the cocky, wide-shouldered prison bop that he'd recognized from the time spent in Nap-Nap; the glossy, reddish-brown dreadlocks were a dead giveaway. The time had finally come and North was beside himself with joy.

Sadon, while dressed in a tee shirt, a pair of sweatpants and a plain pair of white Nike sneakers, strode toward North with an air only worn by ex-convicts. His facial features seemed a stone carving, the hardened gaze in his eyes told of years of him plotting, planning, and scheming to make things happen in the streets.

North rushed to greet his best friend and partner in crime with a heartfelt bear hug.

"Damn, nigga!" he laughed as North rushed to embrace him. "What's poppin'?"

It wasn't until that very moment that North realized that Sadon seemed to have lost his southern accent.

"What's poppin'?" North remarked excitedly. "What's poppin'! This, nigga!" he finally said while pointing to Sadon as well as himself. "We home. Me and you is what's poppin'!"

"What's good with all these niggas out here, though? I could sense the bullshit already, dawg," Sadon remarked while peering down the street as he spoke.

"Yeah,," North replied distastefully. "Fuckin' unbelievable."

"What happened?" Sadon asked while accepting a freshly lit blunt.

"Man, these nigga out here is straight bitches…"

North went on to explain how Rock, a big time drug dealer from Fort Green, was all but forcing the hustlers in their building to hustle his product and his product only. Sadon listened intently as North went on about the strengths and weaknesses of nearly everyone in the building.

After learning all there was to know about the 'hood, Sadon remained quiet while smoking and staring down at the crowd of hustlers as if they didn't belong there. North tried to explain why he didn't have enough money to welcome Sadon home the way he really wanted to, but was cut short.

"That shit don't matter, my nigga," Sadon interrupted as they started down the street and towards their project building. "We gon' get what's comin' to us; believe me when I tell you."

With North walking by his side, Sadon moved easily past the crowd of drug dealers, acknowledging those he knew with a simple nod of his head while totally ignoring the rest.

Nina was still at work when Sadon arrived, but North had the keys to her apartment, which had now automatically become Sadon's as well as Nina's. As happy as Sadon was to finally be home, he couldn't help but to feel a bit dismayed to see that everything in the apartment was the exact same as it had been three years ago. The furniture was still old and mismatched and situated in front of the same small screen television set and old model stereo system. It was his hope for Nina to improve the apartment, which compelled him to argue against her urge to send him any money. Looking around the tiny, one bedroom apartment, Sadon could clearly see that it was all or nothing.

This shit is gonna change, baby, he said to himself. *This shit is gonna change, big time.*

"Yo, my nigga," North began. "I ain't tryin' to sound like I'm bein' impatient, dawg, but a nigga's hungrier than a mafucka. When you wanna get shit poppin' out this bitch?"

Sadon collapsed against the cushions of Nina's sofa chair and took a moment to enjoy the difference between the couches at home and the steel benches at Nap Nap State Penitentiary.

"Don't even wet that, my nigga," he finally replied. "First, I gotta spend the night fuckin', suckin', and smokin', and then, first thing in the morning, I'm gonna holla at a few people. Before the week is out, we'll be coppin' from Johnny without havin' to worry about this chump-ass nigga, Rock. Trust me."

Knowing that Sadon was a man that was true to his word, North only smiled at the prediction given to him by his right-hand man.

Nina was undoubtedly in for the shock of her life, this time when she came home from work. She stood frozen in her tracks, staring with disbelief at the very sight of Sadon standing directly in front of her.

"Hey, girl," he said with a bright smile. "What's poppin', Ma! Can a nigga get some love, or what?"

Nina raised both of her hands to her mouth still staring at Sadon in silence and then instantly rushed forward to wrap her arms around him.

"Oh, Papi," she said hoarsely. "I missed you so, so much."

Nina gently held Sadon's face with both of her hands and then began showering him with kisses, her overwhelming show of affection was enough to distract both North and Maria from the video game they were playing.

"Damn!" Maria exclaimed teasingly. "Go get a room for goodness sakes!"

Just as Maria began to stress the need for Nina to cook Sadon something to eat, Rah-Rah barged inside the apartment without bothering to knock.

"Why the fuck do I gotta be that last mafucka to find out that you just touched down?" he asked while tossing North a plastic bag full of the most exotic weed around.

Rah-Rah then rushed forward and gave Sadon a strong, meaningful hug. With the weed now being smoked in abundance, it was only right for the liquor to figure into the picture; and soon, Nina was the only one inside the house whose system was completely free of both alcohol and marijuana.

In a few hours' time, Nina and Sadon found themselves alone and in the bedroom. North, Maria, and Rah-Rah had all went their own separate ways long ago, leaving the newly-reunited couple, with the chance to finally do what they've waited three long years to do. The love they made was fierce and turbulent; the pent up passion they truly and sincerely felt for each other only added to the intensity of it all. After the fourth or fifth orgasm they shared, Nina and Sadon now lay on the bed together fighting to catch their breaths.

"Listen, Ma," Sadon finally began. "It's about to go down. I'm about to turn it up on these pussies, you hear me?"

"Hold on, Pa," Nina interrupted. She then turned Sadon over onto his stomach and began massaging his back. He couldn't help but to sigh when feeling how Nina squeezed, rubbed and kneaded the muscles between his shoulders.

"Like I was sayin'," Sadon continued. "I know how you feel about me bein' in the game, but listen baby, I ain't your average nigga. I ain't tryin' to make no career out of this shit. I'm tryin' to stick and move, get this cash right quick, and be done with it."

"You don't have to say anything else, Papi." Nina interrupted. "I'm with you."

Sadon was shocked. He turned over onto his back and found Nina staring at him with the same loving gaze she held in Nap Nap's visit hall when saying "yes" to his proposal to get married. Despite her wanting to get married right then and there, Sadon instead, chose to wait until he returned home and made something of himself before settling down and starting a family. Nina leaned over and kissed him ever so softly on his lips.

"Anything you want, Papi," she said while slowly kissing her way down his neck and chest. "As long as we're together, it's me and you against the world. We ride together; we die together."

Sadon felt his breath began to quicken as Nina's tongue trailed past his stomach and down into his public hairs.

"Hold…one more thing," he said in a strained voice.

"Anything," Nina huskily replied while kissing and licking his penis back into a full erection.

"I need you to help me, Ma….I need you to start using your sex appeal," Sadon declared.

Nina's blood went cold when hearing Sadon's request, but not once did she exhibit or show her unease. She continued licking and stroking his penis, occasionally taking the tip of it into her mouth to further arouse him.

"That ain't gonna be necessary," Nina replied. "Now's not the time for me to move like that, Pa. Not yet."

She then straddled the tip of his rock hard penis, taking her sweet time and allowing it to fully penetrate into her womb. Sadon could only gasp at the feeling of him sliding up into the warmth and the wetness of her vagina; it was a struggle for him to even continue his argument.

"Listen, Ma," he said softly. "You're sexy as hell with a body that most bitches would kill for, and you're smart as hell. All you gotta do is look, walk, and talk as sexy as you could, and I guarantee, we can make it to the top without ever havin' to get our hands dirty."

It was all Sadon could manage to say. Nina began with a long, teasing mount, raising all the way up, leaving nothing but the head of his penis inside her, and then sliding down slowly to deliberately intensify the feeling she was giving him. Nina now began to quicken her pace, twisting and pulling at this erection while talking. Sadon, with his eyes closed, only gripped her buttocks with both of his hands as she rode him.

"Now's not the time, Papi," she said while riding him. "You gotta believe me. We gotta take it slow, baby. Please, let's just get things started first; you'll have plenty of time to play the pimp role later."

Sadon open his eyes and stared up at Nina when hearing what she had just said. Once again, she had managed to surprise him with an attitude far too uncouth, and far too gutter for his liking; it seemed to surface from out of nowhere.

Feeling himself nearing another orgasm, Sadon momentarily dismissed his urge to have Nina dress up and show off her "assets." His greatest concern right now was how she'd react to his proposal of being the one to pick up the product from Johnny. Nina seemed hell-bent on being a part of what he and North were setting out to accomplish. And as much as Sadon disapproved, he knew she'd play an invaluable part by acting as a middle man between them and Johnny. From his experience with the Cubans in Florida, Sadon felt that all Hispanics treated each other with a bit more regard than blacks, and Nina would definitely receive a much warmer reception than he and North. Sadon's more immediate problem, however, was Rock. The hustler from Fort Green had to be dealt with before any moves were made, and it had to be done as soon as possible.

Burger King was normally a busy place of business, but today, it seemed exceptionally crowded. Nearly every stool and every booth in the vicinity was filled. There was a flurry of activity inside the lobby; customers moved back and forth, some getting in line to order while others left with their trays full of food. The doors on both sides of the fast food restaurant, including the walkway towards the restroom was filled with movement. Even while in the midst of such activity, Jamil stood out strikingly from amongst the crowd. North was automatically reminded of when Sadon first arrived from Miami. The brightness of Jamil's clothing, which contrasted his jet-black skin complexion, was near blinding.

Once spotting both Sadon and North already seated at a dining booth, Jamil took a seat across the table from them.

"Long time, no see, dawg" said Jamil in a nonchalant, yet cool manner; each movement of his lips giving hint to a mouth full of gold teeth.

"Hell yuh! It's been a minute, my nigga." Sadon replied.

North was utterly surprised when hearing Sadon switch his pitch and speak with such a heavy southern accent. It seemed as if he'd never, ever left Miami. Seconds after Sadon introduced Jamil to North, Jamil retrieved a sealed envelope from inside his pocket and then placed it on top of the table.

"That's five grand," he said while sliding it toward Sadon "Get yo dick out of the dirt, nigga, ya heard me?"

It wasn't hard for Sadon to believe that Jamil was now a killer for hire. Murder was something Jamil had always seemed to be exceptionally good at, and with the payment for murder, along with the act of committing it being much more immediate, then why not get paid for it?

Sadon wasted no time in explaining his dilemma. Jamil listened intently while helping himself to some of Sadon's French fries; his entire demeanor seemed both impersonal and somewhat detached. After ten or so minutes, Sadon had finally finished. Jamil only smiled, his teeth every bit as bright and illuminant as his attire.

"Damn, dawg," Jamil remarked with a mouthful of fries. "You ain't changed a bit."

<hr>

Totally impressed by Jamil's style, North had absolutely no qualms with being asked to drive him around Brooklyn, which in all reality meant showing him where Rock lived after first taking him shopping for a more New York style of dress.

Jamil, too, was equally impressed with how thorough North carried himself. While driving through the streets of New York, both North and Jamil exchanged stories of their experience in the streets with Sadon. It was surprising to both of them when learning just how much they actually had in common. They laughed, joked, and shared blunts while reminiscing about the "good old days," while at the same time hoping that neither one would ever try betraying Sadon. As the two killers drove around New York enjoying each other's time, they both silently hoped that they'd never have to meet each other under those circumstances.

<hr>

Jamil sat inside his rented Toyota Camry, watching Rock's apartment building with the eyes of a hawk. The sky was pitch-black, which lent an eerie feeling to the sight of the infamous Fort Green Projects. Jamil bobbed his head while humming a tune to one of his favorite rap songs in order to pass the time away; staking out his victims for the kill was perhaps the most unsavory part of his profession.

It was just after midnight when Jamil saw the shiny, jet-black Hummer 2 pull into the parking lot, its huge rims spinning and sparkling as it went.

That's gotta be him, Jamil thought to himself as he perked up against the steering wheel. *Yuh! That's him f'sho!* He silently confirmed as the short, heavyset man exited the truck; he was a perfect match to the photograph North had given him earlier.

As Rock busied himself with exchanging handshakes and hugs with the thugs standing in front of his project building, Jamil took a moment to check both his pistols and to adjust the bulletproof vest he wore beneath his shirt before exiting the car. The hit didn't call for him to carry such a heavy arsenal, but Fort Green Projects had a notorious reputation for its hostility towards outsiders; Jamil didn't want to take any chances. Jamil, himself wasn't too fond of New York. He much more preferred the warmth of his hometown in Florida, but this time, New York's chilly October climate proved useful. He strolled past the glares of Fort Green's local thugs with his army coat zipped up and covering the bulge of his bulletproof vest and two guns.

By the time Jamil reached the ninth floor Rock had already made his way inside his apartment. Once again, Jamil found himself having to wait. He stood by the entrance of the stairwell, pretending to use his cell phone each time a resident would so happen to surface. He stared around the hall as he waited, feeling every bit as repulsed by the filth of the building as Sadon had been when he first arrived from Florida.

Shit, if I knew I had to wait in this dirty ass mutherfuckin' spot to get rid of this nigga, I would've had to charge 'Don. Jamil thought to himself with disdain.

Close to four hours had passed since Jamil followed Rock into his ninth floor apartment; his impatience was starting to get the best of him. Just as he began to contemplate whether or not to enter inside, Rock had suddenly appeared out the front door.

Jamil's heart nearly skipped a beat; he'd been waiting for this moment all night.

Rock had just locked the door behind him and started towards the elevator, paying little attention to the man who while arguing with someone on his cell phone, was slowly approaching from the opposite end of the hall.

"I told you; I have to pay the rent with this week's paycheck," Jamil argued to no one. "The trip to Atlantic City is gon' have to wait, baby."

Broke-ass nigga, Rock thought to himself. *What kind of nigga...*

Jamil had suddenly smashed his cell phone against Rock's head; he recovered from the blow only to receive another, this one being from the butt of Jamil's chrome-colored Glock. He snatched Rock by the neck to prevent him from falling over and then forcefully shoved his pistol into the fat man's mouth, breaking some of his teeth in the process. He stared at Jamil with wide, terrified eyes; then gun, which was now shoved deep and lodged into his throat, muffled his pleas for mercy.

"Shut the fuck up, nigga!" Jamil growled. "If you don't wanna die, nigga, then shut the fuck up and don't say shit!"

Rock instantly obeyed Jamil's command. His lips, which were now wet with the blood that oozed from the wounds of his scraped gums and broken teeth, had abruptly stopped moving and now slightly trembled as they remained wrapped around the barrel of Jamil's gun. He only stared at Jamil, hoping that he was truly a man of his word, but unfortunately, in Rock's case, he wasn't.

Jamil retrieved a syringe filled with cocaine from inside his pocket and then quickly jabbed it into Rock's heart; he smiled while imagining how fast the drug was now coursing through his victim's bloodstream.

"I lied, you bitch-ass nigga," Jamil said. "Yuh, how that feel, nigga, huh? Live by it; die by it. That's what we say down bottom, nigga."

The terrified expression of Rock's face froze as the cocaine filled his heart; the whites of his eyes were now showing as he began to convulse and fall to the floor.

"Yuh," said Jamil while lighting a cigarette. "That's your brain on drugs, nigga. That's for my nigga, 'Don."

With that, Jamil turned and walked swiftly from the ninth floor to the eighth before taking the elevator down the rest of the way.

Chapter Seven

Nina sat beside Sadon on the living room couch, stunned beyond belief at what he was now asking her to do. North sat on a chair opposite to them, silently smoking a cigarette. His eyes were sharp and attentive, studying the conversation between she and Sadon with the utmost concentration. It was obvious to Nina that he and Sadon had already discussed the matter before confronting her with a proposal to be the one to go between them and Johnny. Nina was angered by the thought of them using her to carry the drugs instead of selling them. She would have settled for simply looking out for the policy. The fact that North and Sadon seemed to have considered this without first consulting her only added insult to injury.

While listening to Sadon's plan to buy eight ounces of cocaine for five thousand dollars, Nina couldn't help but to reflect on the conversation she had with him when he'd just came home from prison. She recalled the combination of lust, love, and passion they shared, the energy that burned from within their bodies as they shared one another.

Anything you want, Papi, she remembered saying. *Anything you want, Papi. As long as we're together, it's me and you against the world. We ride together; we die together.*

It was more than just a promise that she'd made to Sadon while in the midst of heated passion. It was a promise that Nina had made to herself three years ago, when first hearing Sadon being arrested. Staying true to the oath she had made to herself is what helped Nina through the most trying of times, and she was determined more than ever to remain true to it now. Aside from reaffirming her resolution to ride with Sadon to the end, was

Nina's promise to never, ever allow herself to be left out in the dark again; she would be in control of her own destiny.

❦❦❦❦❦❦❦❦

Neither North nor Sadon liked the idea of having Nina go between them and Johnny, and silently hoped that she'd somehow find a way to back out of the plan, but she didn't. As reluctant as they may have been to involve her, they both agreed it would be a rather grand advantage if she agreed to do so. More important than her being an unlikely target of police surveillance was her Puerto Rican heritage. Despite Johnny being Dominican and Nina being Puerto Rican, they were both Hispanic, which meant a far greater chance of her being more well-received by Johnny and his employees. Sadon's misgivings about involving Nina in his business were lightened by his expectations of needing no more than six or so months to acquire the amount of money they'd need to get up and out to the game for good.

The arrangements had been made. Nina dropped North and Sadon off at the corner of 183 Street and Amsterdam Avenue, and then parked a short distance away. She met them at the alley, which would in turn, lead them to Johnny's concrete fortress. Sadon couldn't remember the last time he had ever felt so nervous. He looked into Nina's eyes, searching for any signs of fear or apprehension, which may have given him a reason to send her home, but he found none.

"You okay?" he asked.

"I'm good," Nina replied. "You're the one that's lookin' a little spooked."

Sadon's jaw stiffened. North suppressed a smile while observing their exchange; he too was a stranger to this rigid and seemingly fearless side of Nina and was thoroughly pleased with her display of hardiness. Sadon blinked away his anger.

"Let's go," he said plainly.

On the outside, Nina may have appeared without fear, but inwardly, she was scared to death; however, that only made her more determined to go through with the plan. She followed North and Sadon through the narrow passage to the same group of Dominican hustlers that had been there three years ago. Mike stared Nina up and down, while giving North and Sadon their welcomes. The procedure hadn't changed one bit. Nina, Sadon, and North patiently waited for their arrival to be confirmed and then cleared to go. In a few minutes time, they'd all received the okay and again, were lead through a maze and down to a great wooden door, where they finally made their way inside.

Everything was exactly the same as it had been three years ago. A host of workers sat on top of their makeshift couches, paying strict attention to the money they were sorting, counting, and wrapping in rubber bands. Not a single soul bothered to look up and acknowledge Sadon, Nina, and North's sudden entrance. Johnny was busy stuffing huge stacks of money into a set of duffel bags when they arrived. He dropped one of the bags onto the floor and then turned to find that his guests had finally arrived. Johnny took a moment to fix the collar of his shirt before extending his arms to both North and Sadon.

"I missed you fucking guys, man!" he announced while flashing his patented smile. "How the hell have you been?"

"Shit, we all gotta pay our dues one way or another; you know how it is," North replied as he freed himself of Johnny's embrace.

Johnny was making a grand spectacle of their reunion, which didn't affect the concentration of his money counters one bit. They continued sorting the dollar bills and running them through the electronic money counters as if totally oblivious to the commotion Johnny was making.

"Johnny," Sadon said while wrapping an arm tightly around his fiancée. "I want you to meet wifey; this is Nina."

While still in Sadon's embrace, Nina leaned forward to shake Johnny's hand. There was something about Johnny that she didn't like. His smile was too bright, his eyes too inviting.

"It's good to meet you, mamita!" he said. "You're Puerto Rican, VERDA?"

His eyes took an instant appraisal of Nina as he asked her.

"Si," she replied while trying not to show the disdain she felt for Johnny; the way he ogled her was quick and unassuming, but Nina noticed and was sickened by it.

"Yeah, Johnny," North interjected, trying to do away with the sudden sense of discomfort he was now feeling by getting straight to the point. "Like I was sayin' earlier, we're tryin' to turn it up a notch, but we got niggas out here that hate us, man. That's why we wanna get my homie's wife to pick the shit up from now on."

"Sure! No problem, North! No problem at all!" Johnny remarked, seeming a thousand percent more comfortable than when the idea was first proposed to him. "Just make sure she calls and makes the arrangements in advance. I just wish we could go out and celebrate... seriously, man. I'm glad you guys are home now. I'm a bit caught up, but we'll get together some other time, definitely. Just make sure you guys stay out of trouble. Now, let me get out of her before I miss my appointment."

With that, Johnny turned and yelled out a command to one of the drug packers in the next room over. Although it was spoken in Spanish, Sadon and North could tell it was an order for the merchandise to be delivered. A thin, young Dominican man wearing nothing but a pair of shorts, latex gloves, and a paper oxygen mask hurried into the room and handed North a package of what they knew was raw cocaine. North passed it to Nina, who in turn, placed into the pocket of her jacket. Nina, Sadon, and North then said their goodbyes while beginning to make their exit.

※

Nine drove straight home while North and Sadon took the subway; they were all in pretty good sprits when arriving at the apartment.

"That was so easy, Papi!" Nina said while rushing to give Sadon a hug and a kiss. "We make a great team!"

"I know," Sadon replied. "You did good, baby, you really did."

North went into the bedroom and returned with the vanity mirror that had once been attached to the dresser and placed it on top of the dining room table. Sadon retrieved the lactose (synthetic cocaine) from inside the kitchen, along with a box of single-edge razor blades and a box of empty cocaine vials. The very sight of Sadon dumping the cocaine on top of the mirror prompted Nina to hurry and remove the photos of Jesus and a host of other saints, which were posted on the walls all throughout the house. North and Sadon sat across the table from each other, laughing at what Nina was doing.

"What's so funny?" she asked.

"Come here, Ma," Sadon said to Nina. "Come sit on my lap."

He then pulled out his chair a little bit so they could both have room to sit down.

"Listen, Mommy; I made up a prayer for God, and I say it to him all the time, too, It goes like this:

Damn, God, can I get a turn, can I actually live?
Feel me Lord, and understand what I did.
I mean, can you blame me for tryin' to eat?
So young and native growin' up in these streets;
You would've did what I did if you lived like I live.
Growin' up one of many strugglin' ghetto kids.
But if you think not, then give it a shot.
Be born where I was, and be raised on the block.'
I can tell you like this…
When the sun goes down, the guns come around,
And ladies in blue? Ain't no nuns in our town.
So can I get a turn? Can I actually smile?
You know who I am, please love your Ghetto child…"

It was the first time that North had ever heard Sadon's prayer, and he was terribly excited. He jumped to his feet and began throwing a flurry of punches into the air.

"That's what the fuck I'm talkin' about! You heard that shit, God?!" he screamed up at the ceiling while still jabbing at the sky. "That's my nigga, 'Don, talkin' to you!"

He then turned to Sadon and gave him some dap.

"Word up, man. That's what's up," North said as he began to calm down.

"Iy…whatever, Pa," Nina replied with a sigh. "I ain't tryin' to go there with you. Let's just get this over with; teach me how you turn a profit with this stuff."

The next few hours, for Nina, were long and exhaustive. North and Sadon took turns explaining to her the ins and outs of the game, punctuating each lesson with examples of what they've been through while hustling. Nina listened carefully, soaking up every word of their lectures. She watched and took note of how they handled the product, noticing what amount of lactose they applied, and what they expected to make before bottling it up; she studied the process of it being bottled up and even took the liberty of packaging a few hundred dollars of capsules herself. With this all being said and done, the profit would be a few dollars shy of what she first thought it to be.

Not a bad estimate for a first timer,   Nina thought to herself, inwardly sharing some of the excitement that North and Sadon were now feeling and expressing.

She too was anxious for them to get the show on the road.

※░※░※░※░

Most of the hustlers from Marcy Projects didn't know how to act with the confirmation of Rock's death. Those who'd been working for Rock now found themselves with packages of their own to sell, while the hustlers who originally worked for themselves now found it a bit easier to make a few dollars. Many so called hustlers were actually acting like they were celebrating the death of Rock. Sadon and North were sickened by everyone's energetic and seemingly senseless gossip, yet they couldn't help but to celebrate Rock's death as well. With the best product around and no formidable competition, North and Sadon had sold the eight ounces of cocaine they'd bought from Johnny in record timing; there was now no place for them to go but up.

ıΔΛΔΔ

Nina stood at the passageway between the two buildings, staring down its tiny alley while trying as best she could to steel her nerves before going to make the exchange with Johnny. With Sadon and North by her side, seemed an easy task to accomplish, but now she was all by herself and was feeling a bit nervous. She took one deep breath and then started on her way. Mike, as usual, was standing in front of the building surrounded by his team of goons. Despite the exaggerated looks of appraisal given by his tough looking henchmen, for Mikey, it was business as usual. He greeted Nina with the same sense of welcome he'd shown North and Sadon, and then made her wait for the okay before leading her to and down the main corridor. She stood nervously in the dark stairwell waiting for the door to open, and entered inside where one of the armed guards seemed to enjoy himself while overzealously frisking her. The door shut behind Nina with a boom; she jumped at the very sound of it.

Johnny stood a few feet away from Nina, acting as if he was too busy helping the money counters to notice her arrival. Contrary to the usual "working man' wardrobe he usually wore, Johnny was dressed to a tee. He donned a flashy, tailor-made suit with his hair greased and slicked to the back. He wore a top-of-the-line Rolex watch on one wrist, and a gold and diamond-studded bracelet on the other; his neck and fingers were every bit as flashy as his wrists. Johnny intentionally dropped a roll of cash on the floor while pretending to just now notice that Nina had arrived. Knowing that Johnny was merely putting on a show, one of the money counters fought not to smile while reaching down to gather the loose bills, which were now scattered around on the floor.

"Oh, nooo, Mami," he said with a rueful smile. "I can't believe that he actually went through with putting you up to this."

Even while standing across the room from Johnny, Nina could smell his expensive cologne, it seemed as if he had taken a bath in it. She stared at Johnny as he approached, not liking the vibes she now felt surging from within him.

"What are you talking about, Johnny?" Nina asked warily.

Johnny had gotten a little too close.

"What am I talking about?" he was with a mixture of both confusion and humor. "Not only are you my Latin sister, but you're beautiful. This kind of work is not what's best for you."

They now stood only a few inches apart from each other. The heavy smell of Johnny's cologne was beginning to irritate Nina's eyes and nostrils.

Oh, no the hell he didn't! She thought to herself while fighting not to take a step backward.

Johnny's face was smooth, his smile easy, yet his eyes were ablaze with hunger. He had now revealed what Nina had seen in him since they very first time she met him.

I can't believe this shit! Nina said to herself. *How the hell is he gonna find the* nerve *to come on to me like this?! BASTARD!!*

"Easy, big fella," she said. "I have a job to do."

Knowing how important it was not to strain the relationship between Johnny and Sadon, Nina forced a smile onto her face as she fought not show her disdain. It was an awkward, out-of-place grin that failed to match the hardness of her eyes.

Johnny matched Nina's smile with one of his own and then turned to order for one of the runners to deliver their product. Nina took advantage of Johnny looking somewhere else to quickly wipe the sweat from off her forehead.

"Here you go, Mami," Johnny said while handling Nina the cocaine.

She accepted the package and then quickly stuffed it into her coat pocket.

Although dressed in a simple sweat suit, running sneakers and a lightweight, waist length jacket, Nina's beauty and well-built physique wouldn't be denied. Johnny allowed her to turn around and start out the room then took a moment to look Nina over before calling her back into the room. He couldn't help but lick his lips with lust as he stared at the switch of her rear end through the fabric of her sweat pants.

"Mira, Mami, Mira," he called out.

Nina sighed under her breath as she stopped and turned around to see what Johnny wanted.

"I look forward to doing business with you. You'll get what you come for every time, pero, whenever you're ready to be treated like the Boriqua princess that you are, you just let me know."

Damn, this motherfucker's got balls, Nina thought angrily to herself.

She looked over at Johnny, her total disgust for him only surfacing as a neutral purse of her plush, fleshy lips.

"I'll keep that in mind, Johnny,' she replied.
Johnny's smile widened when hearing Nina's remark. Nina gave him a nod and then started on her way out the door.

Now in the car with another eight ounces of cocaine, Nina reflected on how badly Johnny was flirting with her and Sadon's reaction if she was to tell him about it. He'd go ballistic, which meant that either Sadon or Johnny would end up dead. Giving thought of the wealth and power Johnny possessed, Nina was sure that Sadon would die, even if he did somehow manage to murder Johnny, and that was something that Nina knew that she wasn't prepared to deal with; not now, not ever. With that in mind, Nina decided not to let Sadon know about the incident. Although caught off guard by Johnny's indiscretion, she was far from surprised most men tend to go crazy and even betray their most trusted comrades for their lust of a woman.

Nina decided to tell Sadon only if things were to get out of hand; until then, she'd put up with Johnny's flirting ways.

After all, Nina thought to herself. *I've been through worse.*

Chapter Eight

North and Sadon's climb to the top of the criminal food chain was going smoothly. In a little less than a month's time, they were only a few thousands dollars short of buying a half a kilo of cocaine, They could have stood to make much more than what they currently had, but this time, Sadon and North both agreed to go slow and take a different approach. This time around, they decided to spread a little love and employ a few local thugs whom they knew were thorough and had a promising future in the streets. Rah-Rah was one of those soldiers. However, he was more than just a common street worker. Rah-Rah was fierce in heart and deathly loyal--he was definitely an asset.

With North and Sadon employing a few hustlers on their own while still struggling with four and half ounces between them, things were definitely a strain; not to mention the size of their bottles were huge, which consequently shut down all competition. The domination of their drug trade was the only bright spot in North and Sadon's strategy, and it was precisely what they intended. Sadon and North's clientele was now to the point where the addicts wanted absolutely no one's product but theirs. And with there always being someone on the streets selling their cocaine, Sadon and North's stranglehold on their building's illegal income was only tightening.

<hr>

It was an early October morning as Sadon, North, and Rah-Rah sat perched on top of their milk crates in front of their project building. It was a bit unusual for any one of them to be out just after nine o'clock in the morning. But being less than a few hundred dollars short of having what they needed to buy a half of a kilo was more than enough inspiration for them to keep hustling past the rising of the sun. Rah-Rah was simply hanging out to keep them company, enjoying the chance to smoke every blunt they lit up.

The autumn weather was uncompromising. The temperature had dropped a few degrees during the night and had maintained its chill throughout the morning. North was dressed in a knitted skullcap, a tee shirt with a black army jacket, navy-blue jeans and black Timberland boots. Rah-Rah was dressed in a thick, black sweat suit with red lettering to match his red on black Nike sneakers. Sadon sat against the wall of the building dressed in all navy-blue with a tan-colored goose down jacked that matched his Timberland boots.

All three hustlers sat tiredly on their milk crates, sharing a blunt while listening to rap songs, which boomed from the speakers of a large, portable stereo. North looked up the street and spotted a scantily clad female standing at the far end of the parking lot getting ready to use the payphone. The very sight of her large, busty chest squeezing against the short, one-piece dress she wore instantly brought him to life.

"Yo, look at shorty over there in that little ass sundress," North said while smoking his blunt.

Sadon and Rah-Rah leaned forward on their milk crates to see what had suddenly captured North's attention. Sadon frowned when noticing her so skimpily dressed.

"Damn! Shorty's thick as hell. Look how she's dressed, though, straight hood rat," he remarked with distaste.

"Man you act like hood rats ain't fuckable, my nigga!" North said while rising to his feet. "Let me find out you on some new shit since you started fuckin' with Nina!"

Rah-Rah couldn't help but to laugh. Sadon only halfway smiled at North's remark.

"Let me go handle my business," North said while handing Sadon the blunt. "I'm bout to go bag this bitch.

Sadon took a moment to smile, his gold teeth flashing ever so brightly from its contact with the sunlight. North returned his best friend's grin with one of his own before turning and starting up the street toward the girl at the payphone.

"That nigga's crazy as hell!" Rah-Rah said, roaring with laughter. "For real, North's a funnay ass nigga!"

⚜⚜⚜⚜⚜⚜

North was so busy conversing with the young lady who'd introduced herself as "Tonya," that he failed to recognize the black, nineteen eighty-nine model Cadillac DeVille creeping down the street towards Rah-Rah and Sadon. After pulling into the parking lot beside North and Sadon's building, two men, dressed in all black and wearing ski masks, exited the car and crept slowly around the corner of the building. One held a sawed-off, double barreled shotgun, the other a nine millimeter handgun.

Rah-Rah was the first to spot the armed robbers, and by instinct, motioned for the nine millimeter stashed inside the milk crate that he was sitting on.

"Get your hands up, mafucka! Don't move!" One of the robbers barked. "Y'all know what it is, where the paper and the drugs at? Don't make this a homicide, nigga!"

Rah-Rah froze. Being as experienced in the art of stick-ups as he was, Rah-Rah saw no future in testing the stick-up kids' courage to squeeze their gun triggers in broad daylight; after all, he himself had shot quite a few people in the middle of the day.

"All right, all right," he said with his hands raised. "Y'all got the drop on a nigga. I respect it."

Sadon, however, remained seated. He continued smoking the rest of his blunt as if totally oblivious to the man now holding a pistol to his head.

Man, ain't this a bitch! Sadon thought to himself, noticing that he was now facing the same types of weapons that he and Jamil had used to kill Rod and his partner in the parking lot of the strip club back in Florida. He thought of the fear in their eyes as he and Jamil aimed their weapons and fired upon them; it was the same fear that had compelled Rod to take another man's penis into his mouth.

Sadon remained still, taking his time with the blunt. The tokes he took seemed longer than usual; it was as if he was taunting the stick-up kids, goading them into squeezing their triggers.

Rah-Rah, with his hands still in the air, looked into the eyes of the man who was now aiming the shotgun to his chest. His gaze was every bit as calm and as steady as his grip on the sawed-off, twelve-gauge shotgun. It was the look of an experienced stick-up kid who wholeheartedly believe in the "nobody moves-nobody gets hurt" method. The man holding his nine-millimeter to Sadon's head, however, was the exact opposite. He was all too anxious and extremely irritable.

"Sadon…" Rah-Rah said, trying to call his attention to what was now happening.

Sadon took another toke of the blunt before staring up at his robber, his eyes being a combination of both rage and disgust.

"Nigga, what type of niggas you think you fuckin' with? You high or somethin', mafucka?" Sadon boldly asked.

Rah-Rah's mouth fell open.

"Sadon..." he began to plead. "Respect the game, my nigga. Give these niggas what they came for, man. You know it's nothin'."

The man holding his gun to Sadon's head was livid.

"Who the fuck you think you talkin' to nigga?! Huh, you think you can't get it?!" he asked with his hand now shaking while holding the pistol.

"Nigga, who the FUCK you think you talkin' to?" Sadon barked back, then plucked his blunt to the floor, and reached for his 'loaded and ready' forty caliber handgun, "you think you can't get..."

His words were cut short by a shower of gunfire.

※※※※※※

Tonya was thoroughly enjoying the conversation she was having with North, but the sight of the two hustlers who were about to be robbed while sitting in front of their own building, was a much more interesting spectacle. Curious to what was now grasping Tonya's attention, North turned around just in time to see the man open fire on Sadon.

North's blood froze. Everything seemed to be happening in slow motion. First, there was the brilliant flash from the gun barrel. Sadon's head sort of twisted away from the light as his body lurched backward; North didn't see the second shot, but he definitely heard it. Both Rah-Rah and the killer's accomplice jumped from the sudden burst of gunfire. The robber then gathered his wits in an instant, knocking Rah-Rah to the ground with a gun butt to the head and began to flee.

Tonya stared down the street with wide, disbelieving eyes.

"Oh...my...God", she whispered with her hands now raised to her mouth in shock.

She couldn't believe what she had just seen.

"Oh shit! Oh shit!" North cried as the man squeezed the trigger. "Oh shit, that's my nigga, 'Don!"

He pulled the .357 Magnum Revolver from the waistband of his jeans and opened fire on the gunman as he ran forward. The two men took immediate cover behind a parked car before returning fire, forcing North to seek shelter as well. It was enough time for them to enter inside the Cadillac.

North squeezed the trigger once more as the Cadillac hurriedly backed out of its parking space, shattering its rear windshield and punching holes into the rear of the car as it sped out of the parking lot. The man on the passenger side of the car stuck his pistol outside the window and immediately opened fire, sending North behind another parked car to escape the volley of gunfire.

With the stick-up kids now gone, North emerged from in between the parked cars and rushed down the street toward what he knew, but didn't want to accept was a murder scene. Rah-Rah was on his knees, holding Sadon's now lifeless body in his arms.

"I told him to just give'em the money," he cried out loud to North. "I told him to give'em the money, man. What the fuck, man?! What the fuck?!"

The .357 Magnum, now being spent of all its rounds, seemed like nothing more than dead weight; it slipped from off of North's trigger finger and fell onto the concrete with a hard, metallic sound that only a large, steel handgun could make. North could only stand still and stare at Sadon's lifeless body; his heart starting to sink further and further as he neared the reality of what had just happened. His eyes were now beginning to bubble with moisture, and then suddenly began to burst with tears, some of which were spilling onto the body of his now deceased best friend.

⁂

Nina had just finished getting dressed for work when she heard the shots. Even while in her bedroom and a great deal of distance away from the window, she heard them. She heard them, and she felt them. The shots were loud and thunderous; she nearly jumped out her skin with each time she heard it, and then she felt cold all over. It was a sickening feeling, which forced Nina to sit down on her bed and try as best as she could to relax the bubbling sensation she now felt gnawing at her stomach. She sat on the edge of the bed with both of her arms wrapped tightly around her stomach; and then she heard it: the gunshots, the shouts and the hollering and then the squealing of car tires, which was just as soon followed by another succession of gunfire.

Nina soon found her herself rocking back and forth at a most furious pace; the front and back of her shirt had grown wet with perspiration. And then suddenly, it came to her. Something was wrong; something terrible had happened, and it happened to someone she loved. Now worried for Sadon, Nina, as if possessing the supernatural power of speed, hopped to her feet and raced out the door without bothering to shut it behind her.

The elevator just wasn't fast enough. Flaming with impatience, Nina turned and ran down each flight of stairs. She burst through the double doors of the building and into a crowd of bystanders, all of them staring down at Sadon who lay sprawled out on the pavement in a pool of his own blood. Rah-Rah had long ago disappear with their guns, leaving North still standing in the same place he'd been since realizing what had happened.

It was now Nina who found herself standing still in her tracks. Her shock was instant and overwhelming. North could only stare down his own feet, unable to look at either Nina or Sadon.

"Nina…" he struggled to say. "Nina…I…I'm…"

Realization had just now set in on Nina's mind.

"No…no…"

It began as a whisper, but got louder and much more animated with each time she spoke.

"No…No, Sadon, no!"

Nina was now crying and screaming uncontrollably.

"Nooo! Papi, no!"

Nina fell to her knees in tears, crying hysterically.

"I love you, Papi; I love you so much," she cried while cradling Sadon; she was now stroking and straightening out his dreadlocks. "I'll never forget you, Papi. I swear to God, I won't."

Nina continued on this way until the police arrived to drag her away form her beloved fiancée, kicking and screaming as she went.

Chapter Nine

Two Weeks Later

The atmosphere inside Nina's apartment was every bit as sobering and as noiseless as a tomb. With the intentions of being there to console Nina, North and Rah-Rah basically lived in her home, leaving out only to buy weed or to make a few dollars here and there. Their attempts to comfort Nina and to provide her with some support through these trying times seemed all in vain. For, she was slowly slipping away from the outside world. Nina hadn't been to work in almost two weeks; in fact, she rarely left from inside of her bedroom. North and Rah-Rah spent the majority of their time smoking weed and playing video games, neither one of them really wanting to give into the grief they felt over losing Sadon. It was a great enough struggle for them not to be overtaken with sorrow, let alone comfort Nina's tears. They were both silently ashamed to feel somewhat grateful that she kept to herself most of the time. Maria showed every day after work to try her best in soothing Nina, but often would she end up just as emotional and aggrieved as her best friend. It was the very situation that North and Rah-Rah fought so hard to avoid.

<hr />

North and Rah-Rah were seated on the living room couch, playing against each other on a video game. As usual, Nina had secluded herself inside the bedroom, leaving them alone and with the burden of not giving into the grief of losing their beloved friend. There was a depressing silence between them. The only sound in the apartment came from the sound effects of the video game they were playing. Nina entered into the living room dressed in an over sized pair of sweatpants, a tee shirt which hung down to her knees, and a pair of slippers.

When compared to how she normally looked during this trying period of her life, Nina appeared to be in a slightly better state of mind.

"Hey, Nina," North said when noticing her standing beside him.

Nina's eyes were still glossy and a bit puffy, but she was relatively a bit easier to look upon. He instinctively scooted over to give her room to take a seat on the couch beside him. The silence in the living room seemed more disturbing now than ever before. Rah-Rah shuffled uncomfortably as he played the video game while North fought even harder to concentrate on battling the enemy aliens on the television screen.

It was Nina who first broke the silence.

"Shay-North," she said emotionally. "Listen, I need you to roll somethin' up for me; for real, man. I'm goin' through this shit somethin' terrible. I need to get my mind right."

Rah-Rah's eyes were wide with shock. North only stared in disbelief.

"Word is bond?" he asked, unsure of what he'd just heard Nina say. "You really tryin' to, smoke something?"

"Yeah, North," she honestly replied. "This shit's tearin' me up inside. I can't handle feelin' like this anymore."

"Yeah, I know what you're talkin' about," North solemnly replied. "I'm gon' roll somethin' up, right now."

With that, he pulled a plastic bag full of weed from out his pants pocket and a few cigars from out the other. He tossed one to

Rah-Rah and immediately began to roll Nina her very first blunt to smoke.

With exception to that fateful night between Nina and her parents, she had never touched a single drug in her life. She absolutely abhorred cocaine and heroin, and to Nina, weed and alcohol were nearly just as distasteful. Since childhood, everyone in Nina's life either sold drugs or used them; some people even did both. She'd observe people drunk or high on weed, watching with distaste as they seemed to be in their own little comfort zone, letting their personalities loose and what not. Nina even hated for Sadon and North to smoke and drink the way they did; she only tolerated it because she loved them both.

Sadon. The very thought of him haunted every waking facet of her thinking; his smile, his scowl, the sound of his voice, the way those gorgeous, reddish-brown dreadlocks fell over his shoulders and down his back...everything. God, she missed him. She missed everything about Sadon, and it hurt. With each blink of Nina's eyes, and with every breath she took, it hurt. In the midst of all her misery, Nina thought of how relaxed Sadon and North would be during some of the most stressful of times after smoking weed. With that in mind, she wanted to smoke; she wanted to try it. Nina wanted nothing more than to escape these horrible feelings that were shredding her from the inside out. It was worth a try, she figured. To be free of the pain she was struggling to endure, Nina would try almost anything.

North had just finished rolling and drying the blunt with his cigarette lighter.

"You sure you wanna smoke?" he asked after setting fire to it.

Nina only stared at the blunt, it was long and thick. The green leaf of the cigar wrapping North had used to roll the blunt with seemed barely able to contain the weed that was filled inside. Rah-Rah and North watched as Nina stared at the blunt, both of them still doubting that she'd actually smoke with them. Finally, Nina opened her mouth to speak.

"Gimme," she said with her fingers outstretched. "Let me hit it."

The video game was on pause, its character on the television screen frozen in their individual battle poses.

"That's a fat-ass blunt," North warned. "Take it easy when you hit it."

Against North's caution, Nina closed her eyes and inhaled deeply. The smoke was thick and consuming; it nearly clogged her throat while traveling down to her chest and filling her lungs. Nina's reaction was instantaneous. North couldn't help but to smile at the sight of her coughing and choking off the weed smoke. She had never smoked marijuana before, which meant the coughing fit she'd just now experienced would guarantee a strong high.

She passed the blunt back to North and laid back against the cushions of the couch as he continued to smoke with Rah-Rah. The immediate effect of the weed was torturous. Her breathing was labored; her eyes were teary, and her head was raked with the thoughts of going through it all. With each second Nina spent catching her breath came the euphoria she was seeking. The oncoming rush of relaxation was sudden and overwhelming. Nina sat back against the couch, totally consumed with serenity.

Her body felt totally free, her mind now illustrated with the most beautiful and happiest of memories. She saw herself as a little girl, smiling and enjoying life as only an eight-year-old child should. She thought how happy her parents were back then. She reminisced on how dapper her father looked in his thousand dollar suits, slicked-back hair, and smooth shaved chin. Nina, like her mother, was so happy and proud to have him in their lives.

Oh, her mother was so beautiful, so graceful, and delicate. Her high-yellow complexion, bright eyes, and sparkling smile was all so vivid in Nina's mind; her sweet, melodic voice and words of encouragement rang ever so clearly.

Keep your head up, Mamita; never let them see you down in the dumps because that's what they want. For women like us, Mami, strength and beauty are one and the same. Make them respect you just as they admire you.

Nina then thought of Sadon and how much they loved each other. In her mind, right before Nina's eyes, Sadon was standing and smiling right in front of her, his gold teeth glistening as he whispered "I love you." She was shocked by his sudden appearance and far too stunned to utter a single word. She could only sit and stare back at him, overjoyed that he'd come back to her. Nina's elation, however, was cut violently short when hearing Rah-Rah's voice.

"Ay, yo! Yo, North!" she heard him say. "Look at her, yo! She's fucked up!"

"Fucked up" was a term Nina hadn't ever used to classify anything, but now as the images of those she loved began to take a grim and painfully realistic turn for the worse, "fucked up" couldn't have been too far from the truth. Visions of Sadon's peaceful and beautiful face were instantly replaced with memories of him lying dead on the sidewalk with a bullet hole between his eyes. Nina remembered how she felt while holding him, feeling what she guessed to be his brains nearly hanging from a hole in the back of his head.

Was this how Mami felt when seeing what I had done to Papi? Nina asked herself. *My Papi, our Papi.*

She remembered the shock that registered in her father's eyes when seeing her aiming the pistol at him. The shock turned into curiosity and then fear after being shot in the shoulder.
Fear. Yes, fear.

Sadon, said only in her mind. *My sweet sexy-ass Sadon.*

"Fuck that, Nina!" North exclaimed while jumping to his feet. "I gotta get this doe, man!"

Nina half-opened her eyes to find North standing at the window staring down at the streets below. "What did you say, North?" she asked.

"You know what it is, Nina," he replied heatedly. "You ain't been to work in like two weeks, which pretty much means that you KNOW you ain't got no job. You know I'm gonna make sure you all right and shit, but ain't no bills getting paid around here, so I gotta keep on keepin' on; straight like that! Ain't no way around it, baby girl."

Of course, Nina knew there was no way around it. Life for her was, as the term goes, "fucked up" since she'd murdered her own father and drove her mother to suicide. She recalled the whispers of the many different relatives she lived with. All of them at one point in time agreeing that she'd always be cursed for what she had done; that Nina had indeed come from a long line of criminals, and that murdering her parents was proof enough of her being doomed to live the life of an outlaw. Wholeheartedly believing Nina was a black widow in the making, they all treated her as if she had the plague.

Throughout the worst of times, including now, her mother's words of advice constantly echoed in Nina's head.

Keep your head up, Mamita. Never let them see you down in the dumps because that's what they want. For women like us, Mami, strength and beauty are one and the same. Make them respect you just as much as they admire you.

Never before this particular moment did her words make as much sense to Nina than right now.

"Listen," Nina said after taking another moment to smoke some more of the blunt. "How much money did you and Sadon have altogether?"

"Say what?" North remarked while staring at Nina with reddened eyes.

It was obvious that he didn't feel the least bit comfortable about discussing anything dealing with money.

Nigga, you got some nerve, tryin' to be secretive with me! She raged only in her mind.

The thought of him trusting Nina enough to run back and forth between them and Johnny, but not enough to tell her how much cash he had stashed away only aggravated the fire inside Nina's heart. Despite it all, she remained cool.

"What?" Nina asked while matching his gaze with a hollowing stare of her own. "I refuse to believe that you don't trust me."

It wasn't what Nina had just now said, but the cold, half-accusing, half-arrogant manner in which she said it that made North's face tighten with emotion. She sat with her legs extended and crossed at the ankles, staring at North while awaiting an answer.

"Man, like six grand...and about three ounces of raw," he replied while silently blaming the weed for Nina's abrupt and sudden change of demeanor.

Nina immediately sat up and folded her hands together while resting her elbows and forearms against her lap. It was as if she was preparing to offer the proposal of lifetime.

"All right, look," she began. "Forget about what's left over in raw, but go get the money while I get dressed. We gon' hit the mall and..."

Nina stopped in mid-sentence when noticing the look of unsurety on North's face; it was evident that he was doubting the concept of giving her whatever was left of his and Sadon's money, especially when it was close to all that was left.

She stared North in the face with a look of seriousness that seemed too hard and too intense for a face as pretty as Nina's.

"North, please" she said seriously. "You gotta trust me. You need money, and I need money. WE need money, and trust me, we're gonna get it. I'm gonna get it. I'll explain it to you. Right now, you just need to get that cash."

⚜⚜⚜⚜⚜

After sending Rah-Rah off to sell the rest of the cocaine, North and Nina drove to the mall in silence. They hadn't once bothered to look at each other. Nina kept to herself while driving, desperately trying to figure out how, after all of the hustling North and Sadon had been doing, they'd only acquired six thousand dollars in cash and a few ounces of cocaine to split between the two of them.

Six thousand dollars? Nina thought to herself angrily. *All of this violence and heartache for six thousand dollars?! I lost Papi over a few measly thousand dollars?!*

It was a perplexing, yet enraging concept for Nina to ponder; it had an amazing effect on her psyche. She remained cool, almost cold while at the same time burning with unimaginable anger. Her mind feverishly fought to make sense of what had happened and why. Then, suddenly, in her mind, everything was beginning to make sense. Sadon's death wasn't behind him struggling to make six thousand dollars; in fact, it had nothing to do with money at all. Sadon's death, as Nina saw it, held a far greater purpose.

She was now awakened to the truth behind the whispers of her relatives and now understood their fears of her. Sadon, before being murdered, had unwittingly groomed Nina to be strong enough to accept her destiny. Not only did she learn how to buy and package cocaine, she knew the measurements, what to dilute it with, and what profits to expect after doing so. More importantly, Nina had become familiar with a great variety of personalities involved with the drug game. From low-level workers to big time coke suppliers like Johnny and everyone else in between. No one was to be trusted. The slightest mistake, and BOOM; it's all over. The sight of her beloved Sadon's lifeless body sprawled out on the pavement was a testament to this understanding.

North remained quiet as they parked the car and headed into Macy's. He, too was distraught over Sadon's death and wholeheartedly sympathized with Nina, but giving her six thousand dollars in blood money to go shopping?

What the hell kind of scheme is she up to? Fuck it; it don't matter, North thought to himself while following Nina into the woman's department. Nina was his heart, and he loved her to death. Even if the scheme somehow backfired and North found himself without a dollar, he'll hustle even harder to get back on his feet or die trying. With Sadon gone and Nina going halfway crazy, death didn't seem all that bad of a thing.

Once inside the department store and surrounded by what seemed an infinite amount of clothing and accessories, Nina found herself in a dilemma she didn't expect to be in. After years of trying as best as she could to conceal the beauty of her face and body, Nina was confronted with the fact that she didn't know much about dressing sexy; she was now forced to rely on North to teach her about what was "in" and what wasn't.

Seeing the dejected look upon North's face, as he sat listlessly on the bench beside the dressing rooms, made Nina a bit hesitant to consult him.

"Come on, Shay," she said using his childhood nickname to soften him up. "I need to get rid of these big-ass clothes. Let me see your work; help me pick out some outfits and a few dresses that'll make me look sexy."

North cocked his head to one side and stared at Nina with sharp, suspecting eyes.

"Sexy?" he fixed his lips as if to question her motives, but then thought against it.

All traces of anger and suspicion disappeared from North's face; he now assumed a look of resignation.

"Man, it don't fuckin' matter," he sighed while laying backing against the bench. "Just get whatever the fuck you gon' get, so we can hurry up and get the fuck up out of here. Word up, yo' I got too much shit on my mind."

<hr>

With a dazed and near-blurry vision, North watched as Nina ran back and forth from the shopping area to the dressing room. Finally, it had all come to an end. What North now saw before his eyes was enough to clear his mind in seconds. He sat straight up in his chair, staring with disbelief at Nina's transformation.

She stood before him dressed in a pink Donna Karen cat suit with black, spike-heeled boots. The one-piece stretch-suit Nina wore was skin-tight and sheer, its fabric hugged every square inch of her body, revealing certain aspects of her physique North had never before seen in his life. She had a perfect hourglass figure with large, shapely breasts that bulged and fought against the straps of her outfit. She looked like an entirely different person. Nina's hair, which was now free of its ponytail, now fell flat against the sides of her face and past her shoulders.

"Well?" she asked while doing a slow twirl. "How do I look?"

Every nook and cranny of Nina's body could be seen through the fabric of her outfit. She had one of the largest, most firm behinds that North, of all people, had ever seen.

Caught off guard and ashamed of his reflex to stare lustily at Nina's body, North had instantly gotten upset.

"What the fuck is this?!" He asked angrily, making sure to keep his glare focused on Nina's face and not her shapely physique.

Nine stared down at North with her hands fixed on her ample hips; the outward curve of her knees told of her being bow-legged as well. North rolled his eyes while shaking his head.

"Yo, what the fuck are you doin', Nina?" he asked. "You're fuckin' me up right now, you know that?"

This was the first time that North had ever seen Nina dressed in this fashion. He fell back against the cushions of the bench, closed his eyes, and sighed. It was imperative that he take his eyes off of her figure as quickly as possible.

I don't know what the fuck she thinks this is, he thought to himself. *Man,* this is some straight bullshit.

Nina stooped down in front of North and caressed his face with both of her hands.

"I know it's tough for you Shayome," she began. "It's tough for me, too, but you gotta trust me. I know it's hard for you to look at me like this, but you have to. You're all I have left, Shay, and I need you now more than ever. I need you to toughen up, Shayome. Can you toughen up for me, Shay? I need you to show your true colors."

Nine looked North directly in the eyes as she spoke. The smooth, soul-soothing manner in which she spoke seemed to ease through the cracks of North's mind and abled him to speak.

"I got you, Nina," he replied. "Let's just get this shit over with, all right?"

"Now," Nina said while rising to her feet. "Tell me how I look."

She took a few steps back and posed for North once more. Taking Nina's speech into consideration, he eyed her beauty with sharp appraisal.

"Yeah," he honestly had to admit. "I can't even lie, I ain't even know you was that sexy. There ain't a nigga in the world that could say 'no' to you, especially when you dressed like that. What the fuck is you up to, Nina?"

"I'll explain everything to you later," she replied. "But right now, we still got some shopping to do."

♦♦♦♦♦♦♦♦

Not only did Nina and North spend the rest of the day shopping, but they also ventured to a beauty salon where she paid to get both her hair and nails done; they even shopped on Canal Street in Manhattan for a fake diamond necklace and matching earrings.

It was late in the evening by the time Nina and North arrived home in Marcy. Rah-Rah and a bunch of hustlers that surrounded him outside had no idea that the woman who was walking beside North, was Nina. Nina gave everyone a quick smile and simple nod as she strolled by, but the second that North realized everyone was staring at Nina with lustful eyes, he sucked his teeth and hollered, "What the fuck is y'all niggas lookin' at?!"

Rah-Rah quickly followed his comrades' lead by shouting some remarks of his own.

North was more than eager to hear Nina's explanation for everything that had taken place today.

"All right, Nina," he said while tossing the bags on the couch. "Tell me what's poppin': I've been patient with your ass all day. What's really good?"

The first thing Nina did was take off the spike-heeled shoes she'd been wearing; sporting heels was a totally new experience for Nina, and she was more than happy to relieve herself of the irritation. She then took North by the hands and guided him to the couch. They were seated side by side. Nina looked away as she began to speak.

"I never told you or Sadon because I didn't want any trouble. I know how y'all two can get, and…"

"And what?" North interrupted while rising to his feet. "Come on, man, spit it out."

North's face was a mask of frustration; Nina knew she had to be delicate with what she was getting ready to tell him.

"Look," she began. "Every time I went to Johnny's spot to pick up the coke, he'd make it his business to be there, too." North was paying strict attention to what Nina was saying with the feeling that he was not going to like what she was now about to say.

"He was always talkin' that "Latinos need to stick together' bullshit, talking about y'all are niggers and that niggers don't care nothing about their own kind, let alone me. He was always talkin' about how I should be with my own people, which really means that I should be with him."

North exploded with anger.

"What!?!" he hollered out loud. "Why the fuck you ain't say nothin'! Nah, man, nah; fuck that! What the fuck was on your mind, Nina? Why the fuck you ain't say somethin'?!"

Nina arose to her feet and forcefully took control of the conversation.

"This is why, Shayome!" she yelled. "Look at you, all emotional and shit. And Sadon was just as bad as you are!"

North hadn't seen Nina's temper flair up in years; his momentary silence was evidence of just how stunned he was. Nina took full advantage of the lapse in their argument and moved quickly to talk some sense into him. She gripped North by his shoulders and looked directly into his eyes.

"He never crossed the line and tried to put his hands on me, Shay." Nina said. "And more important than that, we needed him. The tables are turnin' though because now he's gonna need me."

North's anger was rekindled in an instant. He snatched away from Nina's grasp with a genuine show of disgust.

"What?!" he asked, seemingly angry enough to strike her down with his hands, which were now balled into large, trembling fists. "This is why you had me spend forty-five hundred dollars? To seduce some slimy-ass Dominican motherfucker that don't even like black people? You mean to tell me this is your fuckin' plan?"

Nina remained quiet, allowing her own anger to build as North vented his. She wouldn't engage in a screaming match, nor would she wither beneath his rage. She waited patiently as North carried on, and after seeing that he'd finished, began to speak her case.

"I remember when Sadon was tryin' to talk me into dressing all sexy and shit, but I wasn't trying to hear it at the time. His argument was that we could go straight to the top without ever getting our hands dirty; my argument was that it just wasn't the time. I know what kind of body I got, and I know the type of niggas I'd attract if I dressed like this; that's why I never did it. You and Sadon ain't need that type of trouble, especially when y'all always goin' through some bullshit, but now's the time, North. Now's the time for us to take the streets over, if not for ourselves, then at lest for Sadon; he died for this shit. Now's the time, North; now's the time for us to get what's rightfully ours."

She stepped backward to give North a full view of her marvelous physique.

"Now's the time for us to go straight to the top without, getting our hands dirty. What better motherfucker to cross than the nigga that tried to play us against each other from the beginning?"

North understood exactly where Nina was coming from, but still he didn't like it. The very thought of his best friend's woman flashing and flaunting and dealing with their enemy was nearly too much for him to swallow; still, it made perfect sense. As if reading his mind, Nina griped North by the shoulders and stared in his eyes once more.

"Look at me, Shay," she said. "Shay, look at me."

North forced himself to look into Nina's eyes, and again, he didn't like what he was now seeing. She had the look of someone that was very, very, dangerous. It was something like the gaze of those he remembered from inside the maximum-security section at Nap-Nap State Penitentiary. It was surprising, yet unnerving to know that she possessed such a stare.

"Listen to me, Shay," Nina said once again. "That nigga ain't getting none of this, you hear me? I would never disrespect Sadon by fucking one of his enemies. This game is a motherfucker; it took my mother, my father, and now my fiancée. All we have is us; all I have is you, and all you have is me. We're gonna get what's rightfully ours, but I can't do it without you. I need you to soldier up, Shay."

"Soldier up?" North remarked. "What the fuck you mean, 'soldier up'? I was born a soldier, and I'll die a soldier. Don't get it fucked up just because I'm goin' through somethin' right now. Shit, you just sprung this shit on me out of nowhere. How the fuck was I supposed to react?"

"I know, I know, and I'm sorry," Nina replied before giving him a hug and gently caressing his face. "But now it's about this money, and I'm ready to get it. Are you with me?"

North stared Nina evenly in the face.

"Let's make it happen," he replied. "Let's get it."

Chapter Ten

To this day, Nina couldn't quite figure out why she kept the phone number Johnny had given her one time during his many attempts to seduce her. The guilt she felt for accepting it only multiplied after Sadon's death; ripping up the paper it was written on and setting it on fire did little to sooth her conscience. Now, a little more than two weeks later, Nina was ever so thankful that she'd somehow managed to remember the once dreaded piece of information.

Johnny didn't appear the least bit surprised when Nina called him; in fact, he seemed rather smug. The conversation they had was short and to the point. Nina said hello, and Johnny returned her greeting. She claimed to have wanted to see him, and he immediately gave her a time and a place. Johnny, while on the phone, gave the impression of him being much too busy to talk, almost uninterested; his offer of condolences felt fake.

Bastard, Nina thought to herself.

Johnny had proven just how much he cared for Sadon long before he'd been murdered, and now it was almost as if Johnny was grinning and singing "I told you so, Mami? I told you so?" It made Nina more determined than ever to be the cause of his downfall.

Despite North's promise to support Nina's scheme, she could tell that his heart wasn't truly into it. North, for the first time in years, was now keeping his emotions in check. He and Nina rarely spoke, and even when they did happen to talk, the conversation between them was terribly strained. Nina completely understood the misgivings North felt about her plans, for Nina too, was still in mourning. Sadon's body hadn't been in the ground for a month yet and she was already dressing sexy and using her looks to reel in a major player in the drug game. Not only was Johnny a player, Nina constantly reminded herself, but he was a player who'd made the mistake of trying to play her against the two men she'd ever loved in her life. With the phrase "You have to pay to play," embedded deeply in her thoughts, Nina reasoned that Johnny had played long enough, and it was now time to pay. He would indeed pay, and it would cost him dearly.

◆◆◆◆◆◆◆◆

If someone were to tell North three years ago that he'd witness Sadon being killed in broad daylight, he would never believe it; Nina dressing as sexy as she possibly could to win the heart of his enemy was even farther beyond his imagination. Even now, days after Nina's startling revelations, North found himself bewildered by the weight of the entire situation. After learning of Johnny's blatant disrespect toward Sadon, there was no way in the world that North would buy any more cocaine from him. It didn't matter if it was the best product in the projects. His decision to boycott Johnny's business was every bit as costly as it was honorable; with Rah-Rah only a few sales away from being completely sold out, North's grip on the project's illegal drug flow was beginning to look grim. Something had to be done, and it had to be done fast.

Realizing just how badly he needed Nina to meet success with her plans to manipulate Johnny made North feel truly ashamed of himself. He felt like a low-level pimp who needed his whores more than his whores needed him. It was demoralizing for North to even compare his relationship with Nina to that of a pimp and a whore in the first place. Adding insult to injury was the fact that it was North who felt like the whore. It was now Nina and not North who'd be dealing directly with Johnny. North's plan was to simply follow the two of them around until the opportunity to commit murder presented itself, but Nina would hear none of it. It was a genuine show of love for North to downplay his own murderous desire and abide by Nina's wish for him not to do anything rash until she gave the word.

"Johnny's got the best coke in New York," she argued. "Why kill him and rob him for a few thousand dollars when he's worth so much more? Only a fool would allow his pride and his emotions to prevent him from getting what's rightfully his."

As biting and as calculating as Nina's words may have been, it was the look in her eyes while speaking that proved to be the most striking. Her face was hardened and seemed to almost bunch up into one of the coldest scowls North had ever seen. Her eyes reflected just how serious she was. Nina's overall demeanor was icy and cold-blooded, leaving North with no choice but to admit that she just might have what it takes to pull it off. With his product soon to be all sold out his desire to "get up, get out, and get something" felt as if it would soon spin out of control. He was in a rush for Nina to show and prove something and do it quickly.

※

Nina walked into the living room wearing a blue, one-piece, strapless dress with a matching waist length jacket and high-heeled shoes. Her bright, hazel eyes beamed out from the glossy shine of her jet-black hair, which was combed out and falling straight down the sides of her face. North did his very best to concentrate on the video game he was playing as she entered. The sight of Nina being all dressed up and looking drop dead gorgeous set his mix of emotions into high gear. The grief of losing Sadon, the frustration of not avenging his death, the anger when learning of Johnny's sleazy intentions, and the need to make some fast money were all festering deep inside North's brain. There was an ever-existing whirlwind of thoughts that seemed only to intensify when seeing Nina dressed in such a provocative way.

Nina looked down upon North as he faked as much as he possibly could be too into the video game to notice as she entered into the living room. He sat with the control panel in both of his hands while leaning towards the television, diddling with its buttons at an almost feverish pace. Nina recognized North's pitiful ploy, but chose not to force the issue. Again, she understood completely.

I know, Shay. This shit is killin' me too, Nina said only in her mind. *We gotta stay strong, though. The game's just beginning, and it's gonna be a rough ride. But, best believe it's on and poppin', so don't bitch up on me now, Shay, because I need you.*

With that, Nina turned and started out the door, pretending not to notice North who, in turn, was pretending not to notice her.

<hr>

Instead of meeting at his drug spot, Johnny was waiting further up the street in front of a ratty-looking Chinese restaurant. In fact, the entire street was Johnny's territory, but he wanted the chance to show off the fact that he'd color coordinated his expensive wardrobe with his brand new 600 Series Mercedes Benz. He was dressed in a navy blue, pinstriped suit with a silk, sky-blue shirt and tie, which, in turn, matched the dark blue Mercedes Benz with sky blue interior.

All the drug dealers in this particular area knew Johnny, and knew enough not to bother with him while he was out in public. His very presence was nothing but an inspiration for the young, Hispanic hustlers to get serious about their business. They had nothing but respect for their boss who was now leaning against an impressive, up-to-date luxury car with the Rolex watch on his wrist glistening as brightly as the large rims on his Mercedes.

Johnny flashed a bright, million-dollar smile and waved as Nina drove past him in her old model Honda Civic.

I dios mios, he thought to himself while watching Nina exit her car. *I can't believe how sexy she is.*

Nina took her time strolling up the street, making sure that he'd taken in every inch of her body as she approached. Johnny licked his lips as she drew near, trying his best not to display just how enticed he was with the way Nina's young firm, hourglass figure twisted and turned against the fabric of her outfit as she walked.

"Nina," he said while taking both of her hands inside of his. "It's good to see you again."

I'm sure it is, you fucking snake, Nina replied only in her mind while masking her hatred for Johnny by flashing a sly, girlie-like smile. She then leaned forward to kiss him softly on the cheek.

After playing the perfect gentlemen by showing Nina to the passenger side of his Mercedes, Johnny spent the entire time offering his condolences and explaining that his advances toward her as nothing more but an expression of sheer concern for his Latin sister. Nina remained silent in the car, completely numb from the inside out while trying her best to appear as naïve and as compliant as possible. She felt a slight sense of relief as they pulled into the parking lot of an extravagant and expensive Dominican restaurant. At least then, while eating dinner she'd be a little bit further away from him. Her stomach went tight at the very thought of kissing him.

They both entered inside the restaurant arm-in-arm it was as if she were a contestant for a beauty pageant being ushered onto the front stage. Everyone inside, both customers and employees alike, knew Johnny and greeted him with the utmost respect. Hearing him introduce her to everyone as his "lady" only sickened Nina more. A slim, big-busted waitress with large, dreamy, bedroom eyes appeared just as soon as they were seated. After ordering for both Nina and himself, Johnny then proceeded to retrieve a large wad of cash from inside his jacket pocket.

'Mira, Mami," he said as if Nina hadn't been watching as he placed a stack of dollars bills on top of the table. "I want you to have this. It's just a little something…"

"What?!" she remarked with an animated show of offense. "Are you trying to play me like some cheesy, easy-ass slut or something?"

Johnny stared across the table at Nina with a look of genuine shock.

"Mira, Nina," he stammered. "I'm just…"

"I called you because I need someone to talk to, and you're trying to play me like a cheap slut. Is that what you think of me, Johnny, a cheap slut?"

Nina stared at Johnny with an expression that held a perfect combination of fear, pain, and humiliation. In an effort to appear as convincing as she possibility could, Nina allowed just a sliver of her truest emotion to show. A film of liquid had almost instantly glazed over her eyes, and her lips were now beginning to tremble ever so slightly. Nina's façade worked like a charm. Johnny's face went slack; it seemed as if he were on the verge of crying himself.

"Iy, Mami," he said softly while stuffing the money back into his jacket pocket. "I was just trying to help. Please believe me, Nina, I'm sorry. Don't cry, Mami, please."

Nina was thoroughly surprised at how effective she'd been with her deception. Empowered by her newfound emotional advantage over Johnny, Nina pressed on.

"You want to be here for me, Johnny?" she remarked smartly. "Be somebody I can talk to. Be someone I can trust and depend on. I'm pretty sure you have enough money to take care of me, but I need more than that. I need somebody who can...who can treat me better than Sadon ever could."

It was hard enough for Nina to even speak of Sadon, let alone speak ill of him; the act of doing so was more than enough to bring tears to her eyes. Johnny was undoubtedly moved by her feminine show of emotion. With the urge to use it for the tears he felt beginning to well up in his own eyes, Johnny pulled a silk handkerchief from inside his pocket and used it to dry Nina's eyes.

"Iy, Mami, I'm here for you," he earnestly replied while blotting Nina's cheeks. "I'm here for you, Nina. I can be more of a man to you then Sadon ever could, just give me a chance."

Every emotion Nina felt running wild in her body froze when hearing Johnny's last remark.

More of a man than Sadon ever could?

Even when giving into his pathetic sense of sympathy, still Johnny couldn't let go of his feeling of being superior. It was a sobering reminder to Nina of what the game she was playing was really all about.

Nina's date with Johnny was far more of an emotional drain that she had ever expected it to be, but in the end, it would undoubtedly prove to be time well spent. With Johnny being just as weak for a cute, innocent-looking face, as he was flashy and arrogant, Nina figured that avenging her fiancée's honor would be much easier to do than she previously thought.

Eager to relieve herself of the torture of wearing high heeled shoes, Nina walked swiftly down the hall towards her third floor apartment. The thoughts and plans of what to do next were racing at a much faster pace than the steps she was taking. She entered inside her home to find North sitting on the couch staring at a photo album. Trapped in his own world of memories, North was oblivious to the sound of Nina opening the door, he tried in vain to wipe the tears that feel from off of his face and onto the large, eight by ten photo of him and Sadon, which was taken many years ago.

Damn it, Shay! Nina cursed silently while walking past, pretending not to see North desperately fighting not to show that he was crying. *I miss him, too.*

In a matter of minutes, Nina returned dressed in her normal attire: an oversized sweat suit, gym sneakers, and her patented ponytail-styled hairdo. She sat down beside North who had now replaced the photo album he was once holding for a large, freshly rolled blunt. His eyes were dried, but reddened more from grief rather than the weed he was now smoking.

Nina sat down beside North and then wrapped both of her arms around his neck before kissing him softly on the cheek.

"I know, Shayome, I know," she said gently. "I miss him, too. I miss Sadon so much."

She then freed North of her embrace and allowed him to follow his toke of the blunt with a swallow from his fifth of Hennessy.

"I'll tell you what," she said while rising to her feet. "Let's go see him."

North looked upward at Nina as if failing to comprehend what Nina had just said.

"Say what?" he asked. "See who? You mean go to Sadon's grave?"

"Yes," Nina replied. "Let's see him one last time. Shayome. I think we both still have a little more to get off our chests."

After a moment of consideration, North finally agreed. He took another swallow of cognac and then followed it with another long drag of the blunt before taking another gulp from his bottle of cognac.

"All right, Ma." North said while rising to his feet. "Let's go see my nigga."

<hr />

It was well into the evening when North and Nina drove through the gates and entered into the burial grounds. The skies were pitch-black; the darkness of night had settled down upon the cemetery, giving a rather grim, hollowing aura to the entire scenery. North sat in silence, observing the mountainous tombstones that marked a great majority of the graves they passed, Nina too hadn't bothered to speak. Unlike North, her mind wasn't occupied with the event now about to take place, but more so focused on the course of events, which were due to happen in the very near future. She was now about to embark upon a most dangerous and near impossible mission to betray and maybe even kill one of New York's biggest cocaine dealers. One of the few things more dangerous than a broken hearted and vindictive man, Nina figured, was one with as much money and as much power as Johnny. In order to prove herself successful, Nina needed North to return back to his "I don't give a fuck, ride or die" frame of mind. Hopefully, their trip to Sadon's grave would do the trick.

Nina's Honda Civic had finally come to a halt. The silence between her and North had grown even more intense as they both sat inside the car acting as if neither of them wanted to exit. North had long ago finished his first blunt and was now smoking another.

"Well," he said after finishing off the rest of his Hennessy. "Let's go, Nina."

Nina sighed and then exited the car along with North. They walked side by side through a short maze of headstones and gravesites until finally reaching the place where Sadon was buried.

North stared around the cemetery, noticing a wide variety of tombstones and noted how beautiful and distinguished most of the headstones were. Some were as tall as five feet high; others were merely a few feet tall. There were even some that were fitted with beautiful sculptures of angel and crucifixes. He spotted a group of people who had gathered around someone's grave; its tombstone was huge, probably the largest in the entire cemetery.

North looked down upon Sadon's grave with a mixture of both anger and regret. A small block of granite with Sadon's name and lifespan in scripted on its face was his only marker; it was all that North and Nina could afford.

Nina stood close to a foot behind North, watching with her arms crossed against her chest. Although she only had view of North's back, she didn't need to see the front of him to imagine what was going on through his mind as he stood over his best friend's grave, smoking a blunt. She's known North long enough to figure how his emotions worked.

We ain't even give my nigga the burial he deserved, North thought angrily to himself. *Man, what the fuck?*

He then turned around and marched toward the car, informing Nina that he'd be right back as he passed her. Nina took advantage of North's momentary absence by approaching and kneeling before Sadon's gave and offering a prayer. After begging God to forgive not only Sadon for his sins, but also for hers and North's as well, she rose back to her feet to find North standing beside her holding a full bottle of Hennessy.

"This for you, my nigga," he said out loud while emptying the entire bottle of liquor onto Sadon's tiny headstone. "I was on some bullshit for a minute, but I'm back. You ain't die for nothin', my nigga. Me and Nina bout to do our damn thing down here, and it's all for you, my nigga."

North's resolution was brief and to the point, ending with a final drop of liquor that spilled from the now empty bottle. North, as Nina had come to know, was officially back. She blinked back a tear while fighting not to smile at the joyous sight of seeing North's rejuvenated sense of street prowess. With North now standing behind her one hundred percent, Nina felt as confident as ever. North rolled two more blunts, one for him and the other for

Sadon, and then buried Sadon's in the liquor soaked soil before following Nina to the car.

While driving back to Marcy, Nina wasted little time with telling North every detail of her dinner date with Johnny. North listened intently as she stressed how weak Johnny was for her and how, if things went according to plan, North and Nina would get their revenge plus much, much more. It was only at the end of Nina's conversation that North saw the need to object.

"Hold up, hold up," he said while exhaling a stream of blunt smoke. "How the fuck am I supposed to follow this nigga day in and day out? You ain't got no job, and I ain't got no coke, which means that ain't NOBODY payin' the bills. How the fuck are we supposed to pull that off?"

"Listen," Nina said intently. "My grandmother down South Jersey has a couple of dollars. It shouldn't be a problem for her to lend me enough money to hold us down for a minute. The most important thing is that you keep a close eye on Johnny. You can't even let Rah-Rah in on what we're trying to do. This is a solo mission; feel me? I just need enough time to get Johnny where we need him, but until then, you can't do nothin' else but follow him. To hell with hustling, and fuck hanging out with them niggas out there in the projects; fuck all of that shit."

Nina kept her eyes on the road as she spoke, but still North could read the degree of seriousness from the side of her face. Nina appeared totally different from the grieving, near-hysterical woman he knew from only a few weeks ago. She seemed smarter, colder, more calculating, and deathly determined to get rich.

"Can you promise that, Shayome?" she asked.

Nina glanced over and into North's eyes as she questioned him. Her gaze was cold, yet blazing at the same time. It was an eerie, but comforting sight for North to behold. With a sly grin, he gave Nina a nod of affirmation.

Even though North wholeheartedly agreed to play the game Nina was setting up to play, he was still a bit unsure if it would actually work. Johnny was one of the biggest drug runners he knew, and North had heard more than enough stories about the gruesome details of what happens to those who had tried, but fell sort of killing or robbing the crafty and treacherous Dominican drug lord. Whichever way the ball bounces, North figured, he'd ride with Nina all the way to the end. He'd die with Nina, and he'd die for her. In North's mind, it didn't make too much of a difference which scenario would have his name on it.

Chapter Eleven

Any criminal who deems himself thoroughly experienced in the craft of robbery and murder is quite familiar with the task of stalking out their victims. North was very much experienced in this matter, but still he found keeping track of Johnny to be an exercise in futility. The crafty Dominican drug dealer moved about as if he knew he was being watched and followed. He'd weave in and out of the busy New York traffic and disappear into side streets and alleys. The bastard even switched cars on a frequent basis while enroute to his destinations. After three painstaking days of frustration, North had all but given up on the stakeout. The only chance he had of successfully clocking Johnny's movements was when he'd keep company with Nina, which was the only time Nina made clear that she didn't want him to be followed.

After losing sight of Johnny for the "umpteenth" time, North was now sitting in his old model Pontiac Grand Am, burning with frustration. He'd followed Johnny deep into the heart of Brooklyn and into one of the city's countless Dominican bodegas, where he spent hours waiting for Johnny to exit only to see a total stranger exit and drive off in Johnny's black Acura.

"Man, what the fuck?" North screamed out loud while finishing the last of his cigarette. "Man, Nina better be doin' way better on her end that I'm doin' on mines, 'cause this shit ain't workin' at all!"

Now imagining how easy it would be to just blow Johnny's brains out of his head the very next moment he had the chance, North started his car and began heading back to 183 Street and Amsterdam Avenue, where he'd wait to see if Johnny would eventually resurface.

"Back to square one," he muttered out loud. "Back to square one."

♛

Not even a week had passed since Nina's date with Johnny, and he was already calling and literally begging for her to accompany him on a four-hour drive to a warehouse in Maine to visit a business associate. He refused to accept any of her excuses to join him and had even offered to compensate Nina for the time she spent with him. The fool was literally throwing money at her. The only problem Nina faced, again, was what to wear. Her transformation from a "tomboy" to a "glamour girl" wasn't a natural occurrence; even with a multi-thousand dollar wardrobe, Nina was still struggling to find something acceptable to put on.

Maria was sitting on a chair, which was in the corner of the bedroom, watching as Nina frantically tried on one outfit after another.

"Puñeta!" Nina sighed out loud while collapsing backward onto the bed. "This shit is driving me crazy!"

Having seen enough of her best friend's suffering, Maria thought it was time for her to intervene and save the day.

"Girl, get up," she said while rising from off the chair and heading towards the mirror, which was attached to Nina's dresser. "Come here."

Nina rose from off the bed and made her way beside Maria, the both of them now staring into the mirror.

"Look at yourself," Maria began to lecture. "Your body's as bad as mine, if not better; plus you got all those fly-ass clothes sittin' in that closet."

Nina only continued to stare pointedly at her own reflection, visibly unimpressed with all of Maria's compliments.

"Let's see what you got in here," Maria said while walking towards the closet before Nina could find the chance to respond.

"Shayome doesn't think it's gonna work," said Nina, not bothering to follow behind Maria; she instead remained in front of the mirror, staring at her half-dressed reflection. "I can tell by the way he acts. I mean, he doesn't really say much', but still, I can tell."

"Girl, that's how niggas are," Maria replied after taking a moment to suck her teeth. "They swear a woman's gotta fuck a man to get somethin'. It's all a mental thing; fucking him just gets you more than what he was gonna give you in the first place. I never met Johnny before, but from what you've told me about him, shit, he'd probably bend over and let you fuck him in the ass!"

Nina's feeling of depression had broken; she couldn't help but to crack a smile and giggle at Maria's candid remark.

"Bitch, you're crazy!" Maria said while spreading out a number of Nina's outfits across the bed. "Look at all of this shit! You got Prada, Louis Vutton, Gucci, and the whole shit! Ain't no way in hell you need to be in here stressin' over what to wear for that pussy hungry ass-hole."

After years of arguing with Nina about her need to dress a bit more provocative, Maria had at least gotten her way. Not only was she finally allowed to play "dress up" with her closest friend, but she'd be doing it with top of the line clothing; Maria couldn't help but to feel a bit overexcited. She stared at Nina's half-naked body with eager and excited eyes.

"Now," Maria said with the giddiness of a high school student. "Let's get this party started."

⚜⚜⚜⚜⚜⚜

Johnny's jaw fell open when noticing Nina making her way towards him. With her white, skin-tight Parasuco pants and matching fur jacket which contrasted with her black string-strapped blouse, and black, open-toed high heel shoes, she looked more like a cover girl model. The black sunglasses Nina wore, along with the Gucci purse dangling from her arm, only added to her look of sophistication.

"Coño, Mami," was all that Johnny could utter while escorting her to the passenger side of his pearl-white Jaguar.

Once inside the car, Johnny immediately engaged in conversation while starting into traffic.

"Mira, Mami," he began. "My mother's birthday is coming up, so before we hit the highway, I want to know if you would help me pick out something nice for her. "Tato?"

Nina was all too familiar with the "can you help me buy a gift for so-and-so" game, which was played by nearly every hustler in the world. She was sickened by Johnny's cheap and predictable stunt; still, she refused to let her feelings show.

"I don't know, Johnny, she replied with her best "confused little girl" expression. "I doubt if my taste is as good as yours. I mean, we're shopping for your mom for God's sake!"

"Nonsense!" Johnny remarked, half-feeling himself. "Pick a store – any store."

Broadway was one of the most jam-packed and commercial areas in Manhattan, New York. Stores and small businesses of every kind were lined up and down both sides of the large, traffic-filled street. Determined to test the weight of Johnny's wallet, Nina pointed out an extravagant and well-known jewelry store.

"Right there!" she exclaimed with an exaggerated tone of excitement. "Get your mother some jewelry. Nothing says 'I love you' like diamonds!"

In a matter of minutes, both Nina and Johnny were inside the jewelry store, browsing around. Nina had intentionally focused her attention to what she figured might have been the most expensive piece of jewelry in the entire store; it was a V-shaped necklace, clustered with huge, multi-colored stones, which could easily outshine the gold in Sadon's mouth on its darkest day. The uncomfortable feel of Johnny closing in on her from behind immediately broke Nina's attention.

"Oh, that one right there, Pa!" she said, fighting not to shrink away from his touch. "Your mother would love it!"

Johnny didn't hesitate. He instantly called for the attention of one of the many store employees roaming about behind the counter, leaving Nina shocked at how abruptly her request had been granted. The store clerk stopped, then turned to attend to Johnny's needs. She was a tall, pale-skinned woman, with short-cropped hair and hard brown eyes that gave measure to Johnny the very minute he'd called for her.

"Can I help you?" she asked, the politeness of her voice sharply contrasting the smugness of her gaze.

Johnny flashed his patented bright, white smile.

"How are you today?" he asked. "Would you mind wrapping that necklace up for me, please?"

The eyes of the store clerk stiffened, showing just as much disbelief as Nina was feeling inside.

"Sir," she said pointedly. "This is a Palomi Gibanno, limited edition. It costs an even eighty-thousand dollars. Are you sure…"

"About buying it? Yes," Johnny interrupted smartly while pulling out just one credit card from a large stack of credit cards that filled the inside of his wallet. "About the quality of your customer service, I'm not sure it's worth my patronage."

His smile disappeared in an instant and was replaced with one of absolute seriousness.

"Run my card, check my credit, and when you're done, make sure it's gift-wrapped neatly; it's the package and not the contents inside that makes a gift what it is. Now, hurry, Mami!" he snapped roughly while making a shooing gesture with his hand. "Hurry up and do your best to satisfy me. I'm sure that you NEED the commission, so hurry up before I change my mind."

Nina couldn't help but to be a bit impressed by the manner in which Johnny handled the clerk's snobbish attitude, and even smiled while watching the woman's face turn beet-red while accepting his credit card.

I'm gonna have it like that, Nina thought while forcing herself to pretend to enjoy Johnny's sudden and unwelcome embrace. *New York is gonna recognize just who the fuck I am.*

When Johnny said the trip to Maine would be a four-hour drive, he meant exactly that. The journey was long and uneventful; there was nothing but cars, buildings, and sometimes open and empty land for Nina to see as she fought not to fall asleep while on her way out of the state.

It was North's difficulty with trailing Johnny that had inspired her to remain awake. This might be the only chance for them to learn something that may prove useful in the long run. Through half-closed eyes, Nina watched as they entered into the parking lot of what appeared to be a group of warehouses, all of them combining into one, huge commercial area. Nina exited the car along with Johnny, and followed him inside and to an office at the rear of the building.

The inside of the warehouse was alive with energy, and buzzed noisily with all sorts of activity. Warehouse workers busied themselves in between the sky-high piles of cargo boxes that combined to resemble gigantic supermarket aisles, checking and inspecting the paperwork on both the merchandise, as well as whatever was scribbled on the clipboards they carried around. Forklifts were hard at work, either loading, or unloading huge packages and wooden crates to and from the open ends of tractor-trailers, which were backed up and parked at the mouths of the loading docks. Nina's eyes worked frantically to scan and record everything she was seeing.

This is definitely a place of importance, Nina thought to herself. *Maybe this is where the coke comes from...it has to be*

Her attention immediately switched focus from the forklifts, and suddenly onto a short, overweight Dominican man who was slowly approaching from the rear end of one of the tractor-trailers. Unlike everyone else in the warehouse, he was extremely well-dressed in the most expensive clothing, which not only told of him being in control of whatever was going on in the warehouse, but half-revealed to Nina that he may indeed be Johnny's supplier as well.

The closer he got to her and Johnny, the more she knew she was correct in her assumption. Aside from the man's extravagant style of dress, was a distinct air of royalty about him. He seemed to command respect from everyone in his presence, even from Nina. He smiled while approaching them, stopping for a brief moment or two to hand his clipboard to one of the warehouse workers before finally arriving.

Now standing face to face with this fat Dominican man, Nina was totally convinced that he was far higher up on the criminal food chain than Johnny. His hair was well-trimmed, combed back and streaked with gray, and his suntanned skin provided him with a rather grand and regal appearance. He and Johnny greeted each other warmly.

"Johnny!" the man finally said after breaking away from a lengthy embrace. "How've you been?"

"Good, Papo, good," Johnny replied while ushering Nina a bit closer to the fat, jolly old Dominican. "I want you to meet Nina. We've been seeing each other for a short while now. Que linda, verda?"

Seeing each other?! Nina raged angrily but silently. *For a short while?! This bastard's got a lot of fucking nerve showing me around like I'm his woman!*

"Hello, Papo," she said with a smile before leaning forward to kiss his cheek. "It's nice to meet you."

Papo flashed a pleasant smile. Everything about him seemed refined and at ease with life. He was definitely a wealthy man.

"Iy, Mami," he replied. "It is I who am pleased to meet you."

He examined Nina with a sharp appraising eye, which didn't quite fit with the warm, father-like demeanor he was so smoothly projecting. There seemed to be a dark, almost vicious undercurrent beneath his soft, loveable disposition, and it chilled Nina to the bone.

"I wish I could've met you sometime earlier in my life; you're gorgeous!"

Papo's look of sincerity turned into one of pure humor as he nudged Johnny's elbow with his own.

"But, hey," he joked. "Johnny's not a bad looker himself. You two look good together."

Nina forced her lips into a smile as Johnny squeezed her tightly around the waist while kissing the side of her face.

"Alright, alright!" Papo said. "Let us go inside."

The office was small and a bit cramped, just the right size for Nina to stand and stare out of the window and not appear to be listening in on Johnny and Papo's conversation. She focused her attention on the trucks that came and went out of the yard, wondering what they may have been carrying inside, while at the same time eavesdropping on their talk of various "shipments" and "locations", one of them being Elizabeth, New Jersey. It was indeed a location Nina felt inclined to remember.

After more than an hour of "business talk," Johnny and Papo began saying their good-byes.

"Nina," Papo said while grasping both of their hands in his, "I'll be having a get-together a few days from now down in Manhattan. I'd be delighted to see you there."

Playing the role of a subservient girlfriend, Nina turned to Johnny for confirmation.

"If Johnny doesn't mind," she said rather shyly.

Again, Johnny motioned behind Nina, placing his hands firmly upon her hips.

"Of course it's okay," he replied before planting a kiss on the side of Nina's face.

Papo smiled.

"Well then," he said jovially while showing them to the door. "It's settled. I'll see you two lovebirds in a few days."

With that, Nina and Johnny walked back to the car arm-in-arm, only as lovers would.

<hr/>

North wasn't the least bit thrilled to learn of Johnny introducing Nina to everyone as his new little girlfriend. The fact of Johnny now being so easy to follow made North even more disgruntled. With Nina now behind the wheel of the car and successfully following Johnny from New York to New Jersey, she seemed to be a good luck charm for both North, as well as for Johnny.

They both kept a safe distance away from Johnny as they followed him through the industrial area of Elizabeth, New Jersey. With the street nearly free of any traffic, Nina had to be extremely careful not to be noticed. She parked at the entrance of the warehouse parking lot and watched as Johnny drove toward a long line of buildings. She then hurriedly followed behind him, noticing that his black Mercedes Benz was parked near a group of tractor-trailers.

Through a pair of binoculars, she quickly recognized the fat, well-dressed Dominican man who Johnny was avidly speaking with.

"That's him, Shay!" she said excitedly. "That's Papo, the guy I was telling you about."

While peering at the fat man through his own pair of binoculars, North began to recall how Nina was guessing that Papo and Johnny were dealing heavy volumes of cocaine through their tractor-trailer business. Any past doubts about her story disappeared when spying a semi truck heading directly towards them.

It was now North's turn to become excited. He tossed his binoculars to the side and quickly slipped on a pair of black leather gloves. It was only when hearing the metallic click of a bullet being cocked into the firing chamber of a pistol that Nina's attention had abruptly shifted away from Papo and Johnny. She nearly lost her mind when seeing North armed with a chrome forty caliber automatic, looking as if he was preparing himself to do something reckless. He was now staring straight ahead at the oncoming tractor-trailer with eager and anticipating eyes, licking his lips while readying himself for the moment of truth.

"Shayome!" she snapped.

"Dig, Ma," North interrupted. "All you gotta do is wait until the truck gets close enough, then just pull right in front of it. I'll take it from there."

Nina couldn't believe what she was hearing, but then again, she actually could. North had always been a loose cannon, sometimes being all too consumed with the thrill of the moment to carefully weigh out all of his options.

"Use your head, Shayome," Nina remarked coolly. "Don't be silly. Now's not the time, Pa. We'll get our chance soon enough."

It was now North who couldn't believe what he was hearing.

"What?" he asked, not taking his eyes off the approaching tractor-trailer. "What the fuck is you talkin' about, Nina? You know it's mad drugs in that mafucka! What's up, Ma? What the fuck?"

Being all too familiar with North's temper, Nina knew how close he was to falling into his "I don't give a fuck" state of mind; she had to respond quickly and make the best sense in the world while doing so.

"Shayome, listen to me," Nina began. "There's no guarantee that they'll have coke in the truck. Right now, we're closer than we ever were to hittin' the jackpot. We're dealin' with some smart men, Shayome; men who are smart enough to set up all this warehouse shit as a front for the 'real deal'. We've worked too hard to take the chance of having everything go up in smoke over a simple hunch. You feel me, Shay?"

North didn't respond. He continued to stare hungrily at the truck, all the while tightening the grip he'd been holding on his pistol. Nina found herself becoming nervous.

"Shay!" she screamed. Do… you… hear me? Don't fuck this up, Shay! Do you hear me? Answer me!"

With the blink of an eye, North seemed to have been suddenly transported back to the here and now.

"I'm with you, Ma," he replied, sounding a bit resigned. "I'm with you, man. It's whatever."

Nina breathed a hidden sigh of relief as the tractor-trailer came and passed without any harassment. With the truck now a short distance away, Nina started the car and began to follow behind it.

"Now, let's find out just where this shipment is headed," she said out loud to no one but herself.

North remained silent, only bothering to purse his lips while beginning to roll himself another blunt.

<hr />

After a long, exhaustive drive all the way to Elizabeth, New Jersey from Maine, the tractor-trailer had finally started towards another group of warehouses similar to those in the New England territory.

Just what I thought! Nina said to herself while watching the truck driver exit the vehicle and began conferring with the warehouse foreman.

Nina glanced over at North, who was staring at the truck with sleepy, weed-reddened eyes, and was quite sure that he was still entertaining the thought of hijacking the tractor-trailer.

Be easy, Shay, Nina thought to herself. *The puzzle is almost put together. Now, my question is that if this is truly the cocaine shipment, then why is it going from Main to New Jersey without stopping in New York first? It just doesn't make sense!*

One way or another, she silently vowed. *I'm gonna get to the bottom of this shit. It's only a matter of time, baby; just a matter of time.*

Chapter Twelve

The entire day Nina spent in bed trying to recover from her exhaustive game of cat and mouse wasn't nearly enough to rejuvenate her liveliness. Her sleep was terribly plagued with anxiety and an overdose of night sweats, only for her to awaken and try the best she could to soothe North's appetite for action.

The car they were using to follow Johnny in and out of state with was no more than a neighborhood ride that was used mainly for liquor runs and things of that nature. Rah-Rah was reluctant to let North borrow his only means of transportation without being fully informed of why it was so badly needed in the first place, and he was truly unhappy to see the results of it being constantly driven from one state to another. Rah-Rah didn't complain though; he knew there had to be some sort of profound intention behind what North and Nina were doing in secret, but the cost of it all was soon beginning to overwhelm him. Not one member of Rah-Rah's crew had anymore coke to sell, and his only means of transportation was practically on its last legs. The direness of his situation was beginning to strain his and North's relationship, and it was shown on North's face, which often left Nina feeling a bit uneasy.

⚜️⚜️⚜️⚜️⚜️

Two days had passed since Nina and North had followed Johnny from Maine to New Jersey, yet she was still exhausted. Recollections of Johnny calling her earlier that morning to remind her of their plans to attend Papo's party later on that night, happened to be only a few minutes away from now.

Her more immediate concern, however, was of North's reaction when seeing Johnny parked outside of their project building and awaiting her arrival. North was under a great deal of stress; the very sight of Johnny may be more than enough for him to lose control and do something that he may very well regret later on in the future, and Nina wasn't about to take the chance. Fearing that North may lose his composure and quite possibly blow everything they've been working so hard to accomplish, she called and asked for him to meet her upstairs. North was there in a matter of minutes.

He was dressed in a pair of baggy denim jeans, a bubble-goose down jacket, and a fitted cap, and his eyes were red and as hard as the cold late November winds.

"Damn, Ma?" North said after taking a gulp from the fifth of Hennessy he was holding. "You look sexy as hell! I wish my nigga 'don could see you lookin' like this, but instead you all dressed up for this duck-ass nigga!"

Nina was dressed in a skin-tight, emerald green dress that flared out just above her ankles. The fake diamond earrings that dangled from her earlobes matched perfectly with the fake diamond necklace that rested just above the cleavage of her breasts, which bulged teasingly from the top of her dress. With her hair styled high in a butterfly wrap, Nina's beauty was just too much for North to indulge in. Surprised by the sense of attraction, he instinctively turned his gaze away from his childhood friend.

"Do your damn thing, Ma," he said while turning away and taking another sip of liquor. "Go 'head and get that nigga ready for me to kill his bitch ass."

Nina immediately read the source of North's sudden feeling of discomfort. The fact of him being thrown off by her beauty was enough to make her blush; she could feel her own face beginning to redden while watching North struggling to cope with the surprise of him being so attracted to her.

After a few awkward moments of silence, she approached North and grabbed him gently by the chin.

"Hey, Shayome, hey," she said while turning his face towards her own. She then looked him square in the eyes, seeing far past the "I don't give a fuck – I'm a thug nigga" look that everyone else in the projects feared so much.

"I know what you're going through, and I know what you're feeling inside, Shayome. Trust me. I'm going through the same thing too, but we gotta be strong."

The unexpected ring of the telephone suddenly broke the short silence that followed Nina's words. It was Johnny, telling her that he was outside and waiting for her to come down and meet him in front of the building. After a few minutes of conversation, Nina returned to inform North that she was due to leave.

"Go see what you could do, man," he said. "I want the number to that nigga's safe; I wanna know where all the fuckin' keys are stashed at; I wanna rob that bitch nigga for as much as possible."

Nina's face went grim, her eyes every bit as cold as North's while nodding in agreement.

"We will, Shay," she promised. "That's my fucking word."

<hr/>

Everyone standing outside the project building, including Rah-Rah, was completely stunned by Nina's beauty and elegant appearance as she exited the doors and made her way past them. Most of the hustlers proceeded with a series of "o-o-ohs" and "a-a-ahs", while others remained quiet and simply stared.

"O-o-oh, a-a-ah what, mafuckers?" Rah-Rah barked.

He separated himself from the crowd and was now staring everyone down with a threatening glare.

"What the fuck is wrong with y'all niggas, man?" he raged.
"Y'all better respect my mafuckin' peoples, man. Word is bond!"
"Don't worry about it, Rah-Rah," Nina replied. "It's all right. Thank you anyway."

Recognizing Johnny sitting in a black convertible Mercedes Benz, and dressed to a tee, Nina continued her stroll as sexily as she could, twisting every muscle in her hips and thighs as she went.

With his hair slicked backward, and a custom-fitted topcoat draped over his black, tailor-made suit, Johnny looked something like a member of the Italian Mafia. His eyes lit up when spotting Nina walking his way. She wrinkled her nose with distaste as she drew near. She could smell the cologne seeping out of the open window of his car well before her closing the distance between them.

"Iy, Mami," he remarked while showing her to the passenger side of his car. "I'd die a thousand times over just to see you looking this good again."

I only need you to die once, motherfucker, Nina replied only in her mind while making herself comfortable in the leather bucket seat of the Mercedes. *Just once, motherfucker, just once!*

The drive from Marcy Projects to Pier 57 in Manhattan was brief, but listening to Johnny's overdose of compliments on Nina's remarkable beauty made the ride seem more like an eternity. She was more than happy to find that they'd finally reached their destination. They were near Manhattan's waterfront, where close to a dozen or so boats lay docked at their own individual piers.

"Oh, my God!" Nina said excitedly, using her surprise as a means to interrupt Johnny's overflow of corny compliments. "Are we going aboard one of those boats?"

"Not just one of those boats, Mami," Johnny remarked with smiling eyes. "But we're going aboard the biggest one here."

Papo's one-hundred foot yacht was every bit as large and impressive on the inside as it was on the outside.

With the temperature being chilly, the passengers all chose to gather on the lower deck. There were close to thirty people aboard, all of them Hispanic and seemingly very important. All the men were exquisitely dressed. The very air about them was dark, dangerous, and very, very wealthy. They reeked of power. The women were just the same; they were all fitted with the most extravagant outfits, their necks, wrists, fingers and ears glittering with jewels. There was a level of class amongst the party that Nina was very much alien to, making her feel way out of her league.

She clung tightly to Johnny's arm as he made his way through the crowd, shaking hands and exchanging kisses on the cheek with any and everyone along the way. Despite fancy clothes, expensive jewelry, and the help of the greatest plastic surgeons, there wasn't a single woman on the boat who could hold a finger to Nina's beauty. She did the best she could to smile at the daggers behind the glares of the jealous women she'd met. They were very much intimidated by her presence, and she knew it.

Nina and Johnny made their way to the front of the lower deck, where Papo seemed extremely happy to see them. He was probably the only one aboard who hadn't bothered to wear a tie, but then again, as Nina figured, it was his boat and his party. Dressed in a plain, but tailor-made suit, with a crew neck T-shirt beneath, it was clear that he wasn't one to abide by the unwritten rule of dressing for the occasion.

"Johnny!" he announced rather joyously. "It's good to see you again!"

Papo gave Johnny's hand a vigorous shake before engulfing him in a warm bear hug of an embrace. Johnny couldn't help but to show off Nina to Papo once more, and introduce her to him as his girlfriend.

"Papo," Johnny began proudly. "I'm not sure if you remember…"

"Nina!" Papo interrupted. "How could I ever forget such a beautiful woman!"

He then snatched Nina by the hand and placed his lips upon her knuckles. Nina smiled.

"You're looking quite handsome yourself, Papo," she replied. "And I love your boat, too."

"Que linda, trust me; I'd trade this entire boat and everything in it for you at the drop of a hat!" Papo said brightly. "Johnny better take good care of you."

Johnny was now smiling brighter than ever before.

"Don't worry about that," he said while kissing Nina softly on the lips. "I got that part covered."

Johnny's advance was a rather bold and unexpected move, catching Nina completely by surprise. She met his lips with perfect timing, even toping it all off with an appreciative smile. She rebounded perfectly.

Damn, it's gonna be a long night, she thought to herself while fighting not to show just how disgusted she felt for kissing him. *Something has got to give, and it's gotta be soon – real soon.*

⚜⚜⚜⚜⚜⚜

Nina spent the next few hours mixing and mingling with the other guests on Papo's yacht party, drinking as much as she could to wash away the creepy feeling of kissing Johnny on the lips. She'd never been much of a drinker, and her below-average tolerance for alcohol, along with the fatigue from following Johnny from one state to another, was finally beginning to catch up with her; she was more than happy to learn that Johnny was preparing to leave.

Nina lay sleepily in the seat of Johnny's Mercedes, vaguely hearing him mention something about spending the night in a suite and leaving first thing in the morning. Despite her misgivings, Nina quickly complied.

She perked up immediately when noticing that they'd crossed the bridge from New York to New Jersey, and were now heading into Elizabeth, New Jersey. They were only forty-five or so minutes away from Papo's loading docks. Bells of alarm now instantly began to sound off inside Nina's head as Johnny pulled into an alley in between what seemed to be a hotel and another building.

If this nigga thinks he's gonna get some pussy, he's sadly mistaken, she thought groggily to herself.

Johnny laughed out loud when noticing Nina's worried expression, and then went on to explain how, in order to assure complete privacy, he paid the hotel's superintendent to provide him with a key for him to enter through a fire exit at the rear of the hotel. It was one of the many ways he was able to come and go as he pleased without being noticed. Nina now saw first-hand one of the many ways Johnny was so able to elude North's surveillance.

The lavishness of Johnny's suite was a great reward for the seventeen stories they walked up via the stairwell. With a living room, dining room, a kitchen, and a larger-than-life bathroom, the hotel suite was unbelievably larger than Nina's tiny apartment in Marcy Projects. The plush, beige colored carpet brought much relief to Nina's feet, which were now free of the torturous high-heeled shoes she'd been wearing all evening.

She flopped onto the king-sized bed and stared up at the huge plasma screen television, which hung suspended from the ceiling, as Johnny informed her that he was due for a shower.

Nina changed into the clothes Johnny had given her, and after hearing his cell phone ring, she then crept over to the bathroom to eavesdrop on his conversation. Thanks to the loud and aggressive manner in which he was speaking, she could make out a good portion of what he was saying, over the noise of the shower.

Putting one and one together, Nina quickly figured that the caller was his cousin, Angel, who had been desperately trying to get in touch with Johnny all night. Johnny was enraged at his cousin for constantly showing up at one of his "spots", and he promised him a "whole one" anytime after twelve o'clock tomorrow afternoon if he didn't bother him anymore. Nina's eyes went wide when hearing those three magic words.

A whole one! He must be talking about a kilo, she rationalized while listening as Johnny relayed instructions to his cousin on how to make his way to the hotel, and threatening him not to be late.

"Iy, Dios mios," she heard him cry out in exasperation.
With that, Nina crept back into the bed and made herself comfortable under the covers.

A whole one; Those particular words rang inside her head over and over again. *It means a kilo,* she thought to herself. *It just has to mean a kilo.*

A kilogram of cocaine was nowhere near the goal Nina was trying to achieve, but it would undoubtedly quench North's thirst to make a few dollars, at least for a little while.

Johnny walked out of the bathroom wearing nothing but a pair of boxer shorts. His hopes of having sex with Nina tonight were dashed to bits upon seeing her balled up beneath the blanket, appearing to be in the deepest of sleeps. It was a bitter disappointment.

Coño! He thought dejectedly to himself. *I'll just have to take my time with her. Fuck it, it's better this way.*

There was something striking about Nina that Johnny had recognized when first laying eyes on her. He couldn't quite explain or even attempt to define what it was, but it was definitely there. There was a strong and fierce aura about her that touched anyone and everyone that happened to be in her presence. She enraptured everyone; she enraptured Sadon, Johnny, and even Papo.

Yeah, Johnny silently decided while standing and staring at Nina. *She is definitely worth the wait.*

He lay down on the bed beside her, careful not to get underneath the covers and take the chance of sending the wrong message of him trying to take advantage of her or something. To Johnny, Nina was of a rare pedigree, and he was determined to have her, no matter how long it took. Time is money, and Johnny was quite sure that he had a fair amount of both. Nina was going to be his sooner or later.

Nina, however, had totally different plans.

※※※※※※※

Nina slowly awakened to the feel of the sun's warmth beaming brightly through the glass double doors of the suite's balcony. Through squinting eyes, she saw Johnny seated at the dining room table, drinking a cup of coffee and glancing at a newspaper. When noticing that Nina was now awake, he flashed a smile that was every bit as bright as the morning sun.

"Good morning, Mami!" he said cheerfully while still maintaining his loving grin. "I'm glad to see that you're up."

Nina had quickly gotten up and placed herself on the edge of the bed.

"Damn, Pa," she said sleepily. "What time is it?"

"It's about nine in the morning," he answered. "You went down kind of early last night. Are you okay?"

His look was one of genuine concern.

This nigga really has the nerve to act like he fucking cares about me! Ha! Nina thought silently.

"I'm okay," she said out loud. "But, yuck! I gotta brush my teeth or something; my mouth feels all nasty and sticky. You didn't try to take advantage of me last night, did you?" Nina asked with a teasing expression.

Johnny blushed.

"Don't ever think like that, Nina," he replied earnestly. "I'm not that type of person, and you're definitely worth a hell of a lot more than that. I'm in this thing for the long haul."

The last part of Johnny's reply chilled Nina straight to the bone. The smile she flashed seemed frozen on her face as she made her way to the bathroom. Her brain was working at a fast and furious pace as she washed her face and brushed her teeth.

Johnny's cousin, Angel, was due to arrive here at the suite no earlier than twelve noon, which left her with a little less than three hours to drive all the way back to her home in New York, and return to New Jersey in time to execute her plan.

Patience, Nina, patience, she fought to remind herself. *Everything's gonna go according to how it's planned. There's no need to get overanxious and fuck up now.*

She exited the bathroom with a bright and loving smile. Johnny only stared as she approached, his eyes showing a mixture of both surprise and anticipation as she straddled herself on top of him.

"Thank you for being such a gentleman, Johnny," she said. "I feel so bad about leaving you high and dry last night. Can I make it up to you, Papi?"

She was grinding her crotch against Johnny's now rock-hard penis while talking. Johnny was speechless.

"You've been so good to me, and now I wanna be good to you," she seductively whined while scooting backward and fishing Johnny's erection out of his pants.

It was as hard as concrete, leaving Nina fearful that he'd climax in a mere matter of minutes. Johnny closed his eyes and sighed as she continued to stroke him up and down.

"Can I make it up to you, Daddy?" she asked.

Daddy! Calling a man "Daddy" is usually one of the quickest and easiest routes to a man's ego, Nina figured to herself while toying with Johnny's raging hard-on.

"Si, baby, si," he panted. "Lets… Let's go and take this to the bed."

"No," Nina replied while easing him back onto the chair. "I have an errand to run for my aunt, but I'll come right back – that is if you want me to come back."

"Of course, Mami, of course," he replied softly. "Take the key to the fire exit. I'll be waiting for you to return, so please hurry back."

I bet you will, motherfucker, Nina thought hatefully while quickening the pace of her hand-job.

Her entire hand was now slick with Johnny's pre-cum; it was the perfect lubrication. She gripped the shaft of his penis tightly, working it from the middle of his member to the very top, twisting her fist every which way as she reached its swollen head. In a short matter of moments, Johnny began to climax. His body went rigid as his eyes opened wide. Nina now began to work her hand as fast as she could when feeling his penis swell while in her grasp. Semen spewed everywhere, almost splattering against Nina's cheeks as she tried her best to direct his eruption somewhere other than her own face.

"Oh, Nina! Oh!" was all that Johnny could manage to say.

Nina, feeling despicable and dirty all over, hopped off of Johnny and rushed into the bathroom to scrub herself clean of his filthy bodily fluids. Determined not to cry out from the humiliation of having to satisfy a man she truly despised, she promised that she wouldn't come away from all of this empty handed; Johnny was going to pay for this, and so much more.

She exited the bathroom with a smile on her face. Johnny sat slumped in the chair, obviously still drained from the hand-job he just received.

"Nina, wait!" he called out as she grabbed the key and started towards the door. "I'm not gonna let you catch a cab all the way home from here. That's trashy. Let me drive you. The faster you get home, the faster you'll be able to handle your business; and the faster you handle your business, the faster you'll get back here to take care of me."

I couldn't have said it better myself, Nina thought to herself while smiling at what Johnny had just now said.

"That's what's up, Papi," she replied with a forced grin. "I want to hurry up and get back here just as fast as you do. So, what are you waiting for? Let's go!"

Chapter Thirteen

Nina barged into her apartment, making a big enough commotion to startle North out of his sleep. With his eyesight now a bit more focused than before, he didn't like what he was seeing. Aside from Nina's different set of clothing, and her hair being styled into a sloppy ponytail, she appeared totally disoriented and beside herself.

"What... what's up, Nina?" he asked while watching as she fumbled and fought to close and lock the door behind her.

"Shayome, I need a gun!" she said hurriedly. "Do you have a gun? I need to borrow your gun.
"

A gun? North thought groggily to himself. *What the fuck would she need a gun...*

A dark an alarming scenario had suddenly begun to materialize in North's mind as he slowly began piecing one and one together. His blood was now racing throughout his body at a fiery pace. He immediately jumped to his feet with his hands balled tightly into fists that his knuckles seemed as if they'd rip through his skin.

"Yo, man! What the fuck happened, Nina?" he barked, barely able to control his own breath.

North's reaction was shocking to Nina; she was taken aback by the abrupt and sudden change in his demeanor. He stood less than a foot away from her with his hands balled into huge, menacing fists, and his chest was now heaving at a frantic, almost uncontrollable pace. His eyes were ablaze with an inexplicable amount of rage. It was a side of him that everyone in the projects, except for Nina, was all too familiar with.

Refusing to display just how surprised and afraid she'd become, Nina moved in to neutralize North's burning hot glare with a cool, authoritative stare of her own.

"Nothing happened, Shayome," she replied evenly. "Johnny didn't do anything to me."

"Fuck that, Nina!" North spat back. "If he ain't do shit, then why the fuck you need a burner and shit?"

"If you calm down and give me a chance to explain, then you'll know what's going on," she snapped. "Now, do you want a 'whole one' or not?"

North's expression of pure rage and anger was now a combination of both hope and wonder.

"A whole one?" he asked. "What the fuck you mean by that?"

"What do you think it means?" she asked while staring straight into his eyes.

"A kilo?" he asked.

A kilo! A fucking kilo! I knew it! Nina thought happily to herself while maintaining a mask of seriousness.

"Are we both on the same page now?" she asked plainly.

North was all too surprised and full of joy to recognize Nina's sarcasm.

"A key!" he remarked. "A whole mafuckin' bird? You mafuckin' right, we on the same page! That's what it is, but what's really good?"

Seeing that North's attitude had gone totally in reverse, and was at complete ease, Nina seized the moment to regain a grip on her airtight schedule.

"Listen," she began seriously. "I don't have much time; I gotta hurry up and take a shower and get dressed. When I'm done, I'll come back and explain everything to you."

"I heard," North replied, not really liking the sound of Nina coming home after spending the night with Johnny and stressing the need for a shower.

Okay then, Nina he said inside his head while watching her rush into the bathroom to get showered and dressed. *Lemme find out you bout to come through.*

※▲※▲※▲※▲※

By way of the Brooklyn Bridge into Manhattan, and through the Holland Tunnel, Nina figured that she could make it back to Johnny's hotel suite in close to thirty minutes, but traffic in New York City is fickle. At any given time, she could easily find herself delayed for at least an hour or so. With that in mind, she moved as quickly as possible. In a little more than fifteen minutes flat, she showered, combed her hair down to the sides of her face, slipped into a cute two-piece outfit, and filled a knapsack with a black sweatsuit, sneakers, a pair of sunglasses and a black knitted cap.

Now dressed and all set for the occasion, she started out to the living room where North sat patiently waiting. With exception to the gross act of stroking Johnny's putrid erection, she'd told North everything that had taken place since leaving her apartment the night before. She spoke of Papo's exclusive yacht party, and how she pretended to be asleep at Johnny's hotel suite. North's eyes lit up like the fireworks on the Fourth of July when Nina told him of the conversation she overheard.

"Yup," North agreed. "He was talkin' about a mafucking key. But, if you need a burner, I'll hit you with somethin' like a twenty-five…"

"A twenty-five?" Nina retorted, the frown on her face showing just how disgusted she was with North's suggestion. "No, Shayome, I need somethin' that'll lay a nigga down if shit doesn't go the right way. I don't think it will, but I still want to be prepared."

North took a moment to ponder Nina's perspective, and then reluctantly agreed.

"How 'bout this nine?" he asked while pulling the nine-millimeter handgun from between the cushions of the sofa. "A mafucker gotta respect this shit here."

North cocked a round into the firing chamber as if the metallic click of the pistol's mechanical workings would emphasize his point. Nina glanced down at the weapon, and then nodded in agreement.

"Yo, let me show you how to handle it," North began. "This is…"

"Yeah, yeah, yeah," Nina interrupted. "That's the safety."

North eyed her with surprise.

"Sadon already taught me how to handle a gun, North," she went on to explain. "We used to practice shooting them in the Park."

North smiled.

"You never cease to amaze a nigga," he said honestly.

"Hurry up and give me that pistol so I can amaze you some more," she replied with an overwhelming tone of impatience. "Come on, Shay; traffic in New York can be murder sometimes."

Murder!

Nina almost smiled at her own choice of words.

"Here you go," North said while handling her the pistol. "Lemme see your work, girl."

Nina smiled while accepting the handgun and placed it into her knapsack along with the rest of her things.

It was now ten o'clock in the morning, leaving Nina with only two hours to meet Johnny in New Jersey, rob him of his kilo, murder him, and then escape without anyone seeing her. She was far from an experienced killer, nor was she a believer of committing the "perfect crime", and was deathly afraid of something going terribly wrong. Nevertheless, she refused to allow herself to be swayed from the decision she'd made. On the way out of the door, she was determined to make Johnny pay dearly for his arrogance and his disrespect towards Sadon, and she would make sure he did so very, very soon.

Despite Nina's fears, traffic along the Brooklyn Bridge was clear, and the ride through the Holland Tunnel to New Jersey was even smoother; she'd made it back to the hotel in a little more than thirty minutes.

Johnny was overcome with joy to see that she had returned so soon.

"Hey, Nina!" he said cheerfully before glancing at his Rolex. "It's still early. What happened to the errand you were supposed to run?"

"Iy, my aunt!" she lied. "She's so freaking impatient. I mean, since she didn't get a hold of me last night, she bothered my uncle to chauffeur her around."

"Well, I've been doing a little bit of running around myself," Johnny said while beginning to unbutton his shirt. "I'm going to take a quick shower. Go ahead and make yourself comfortable."

Nina smiled and nodded as Johnny turned and started toward the bathroom. She remained sitting on the bed, listening intently to what he may be doing inside. Satisfied to hear the water running, she began her frantic search for the "whole one", which lasted no more than a few adrenaline filled minutes. Sitting on top of a six-foot tall stereo system was a large leather bag. After standing on the tips of her toes and grasping a corner of the bag with her fingertips, she managed to retrieve the bag and opened it to inspect its contents. The very sight of the solid brick of cocaine wrapped in plastic was enough to numb her all over. A million and one thoughts were now racing through her mind as she stood still, captivated by her discovery; she was paralyzed with indecision.

What the hell are you doing, girl? Nina heard herself say. *You're standing around like shit is sweet or something; you still have to take care of Johnny!*

Nina's entire body underwent a strange, yet all too familiar change. Her skin felt ice cold, but the blood coursing through her veins was red-hot, seemingly on fire. It was the same feeling she had felt just before killing her father. The sense of indecision and apprehension had suddenly disappeared, and was now replaced with complete numbness. Nothing existed but the will to follow through with her plan of betrayal.

With the speed of lightening, Nina closed the bag and carefully placed it exactly the way she had found it; then, she hurriedly retrieved the nine-millimeter handgun from inside her knapsack and placed it underneath the bed.

Now sitting on top of the mattress, Nina was contemplating the best way to do away with Johnny. Shooting him as he bathed beneath the shower was probably the fastest and easiest way to dispose of him, but then it would deprive Nina of her satisfaction of seeing the anguish in his eyes when learning of her betrayal, and she couldn't have that. She wanted to repay him for all the humiliation, all the degradation, and all the pain she was forced to endure over the past few months. Since the very first day Johnny had dared to fix his mouth to proposition her, Nina had waited for this day; it has truly been a long time coming.

With her nerves now steeled, and her mind set to get things over and done with, Nina made her way into the bathroom where Johnny was just stepping out of the shower. It was the first time that she'd ever seen him completely naked, and she was even more repulsed at the very sight of him. His chest and stomach were out of shape and covered with hair, and his entire upper body was fat and undesirable. His erection had immediately begun to rise when seeing Nina enter inside.

"Uh, uh, uh," Nina said with a seductive smile while removing the bath towel from Johnny's grasp and tossing it to the floor.

She then ran her fingers through his hair and used the other hand to manipulate his erection while kissing him full in the mouth.

This was the moment that Johnny had been so desperately waiting for. The passion he felt pent up inside his being seemed impossible for him to control. He grabbed a fistful of Nina's hair and yanked her head backwards to smother her neck with kisses, while at the same time ripping apart the top piece of her outfit. The very sight of her firm, shapely breasts hanging free of her brassiere only intensified his lust. He grabbed one of her breasts and began licking and sucking its honey-colored nipple.

"Es Perate, Papi chulo," she said while taking a step away from him. "I'm all yours, Papi; just take it easy. Let's slow it down a little."

She took another step backward, and while staring into Johnny's eyes, slowly began to unbutton her skirt and allowed it to fall to the floor. Johnny was speechless. He could only stare dumbly as Nina turned around to model the red thong, which seemed to be wedged deeply between her huge, almost muscular cheeks of her buttocks.

"Why don't we go on into the bedroom so we can have a little fun?" she asked sexily.

Nina's physique was absolutely perfect; there wasn't a single blemish on any part of her body.

"Vamos, Mami," Johnny found the strength to say. "Let's go."

He followed close behind Nina, utterly transfixed on the switch of her hips, thighs and buttocks as she led him to the bedroom. Nina turned around to find Johnny face-to-face with her and wasting no time in kissing and groping her.

"M-m-m-m, Johnny, wait!" she said while grabbing his wrists. "I wanna do this right. I wanna show you what I can do with a can of whipped cream. Please tell me you have some whipped cream, baby. Trust me – you won't be sorry at all."

Johnny was now at the very peak of impatience; he couldn't stand too much more of Nina prolonging the inevitable.

"In the kitchen, Mami," he replied almost dejectedly. "Pero, hurry up, chica! You're about to give me blue balls!"

Nina matched Johnny's smile with one of her own before starting toward the kitchen as he moved to make himself comfortable on the bed. She returned to find him stretched out with his hands resting behind his head, smiling as his penis was now standing fully erect. His eyes held a sickening measure of anticipation.

Yeah, right motherfucker, she thought while smilingly approaching the bed. *Like I'm really gonna give you the satisfaction of sliding inside of me!*

"That's right, Papi," Nina cooed as she lay beside him near the edge of the bed. "I'm gonna make you feel so-o-o good!"

She moved to the side of the bed and began to stroke Johnny's erection, kissing him down his fat, hairy stomach, while at the same time switching the can of whipped cream for the loaded nine-millimeter handgun she'd hidden beneath the bed.

Johnny's intense moment of pleasure had suddenly vanished with the feel of his penis now being twisted into a pulp. His automatic reaction to rise up and protect his private parts was thwarted by a brilliant flash of blue, and the crunching sound of the bridge of his nose caving inwards. He fell back against the bed, blood splattering his entire face. With wide, innocent eyes, his once-blurry vision slowly began to focus on the barrel of a gun now aimed directly at his head.

Iy, Dios mios! He though to himself with horror. *I can't believe this is happening to me!*

Johnny stared at Nina in disbelief, and he trembled when recognizing that she was actually smiling.

After feeling Johnny's penis shrivel up while in her grasp, Nina released her grip and began trying as best as she could to wipe her hand free of the filth she felt from touching him.

Johnny could only stare at her, the pain of seeing her being disgusted from touching him hurting worse than the dull, aching throb of his broken nose.

How could this be? Was one of the many questions now storming about in his mind as he fought desperately to make sense of what was now happening.

"Nina…"

"Shut the fuck up, nigga!" she barked at him while rising to her feet with the pistol still trained on his head.

She took a moment to stare at Johnny's mess of a face. Blood flowed freely from a gash that lay horizontally across his smashed and battered nose, trickling down and mixing with the stream of blood now coursing from both of his nostrils. He gazed at Nina with a look of complete bewilderment, it was reminiscent of the look her father once held on that fateful night.

In the back of Nina's mind, she was eleven years old all over again. She was standing in the very same position she'd stood in a little more than a decade ago. The gun felt the same; the hate felt the same; and the look Johnny held was the same combination of fear and uncertainty that her father had. However, the scenario was the same. Nina's smile broadened, contrasting the darkness that blazed from within her cold, unloving eyes.

"Say you're sorry," she demanded.

Johnny was perplexed.

"Sorry?" he asked. "Sorry for what, Nina? What the hell did I…"

"I'm sorry, Sadon," she interrupted. "I shouldn't have disrespected you. I should have never tried to fuck your fiancée."

Johnny's mouth fell open.

"What?" he asked. You mean…."

"You got three seconds to say it, you fucking dickhead!" Nina forcefully interrupted. "One…two…"

Johnny cringed at the sight of Nina handling the pistol in such a menacing fashion. Having no doubt that she was more than willing to squeeze the trigger if provoked, he repeated Nina's words.

"I'm sorry, Sadon", he said numbly. "I shouldn't have disrespected you. I should have never tried to fuck your financée."
Johnny's eyes began to bubble with moisture. Nina only smiled.

With one single shot, it was all over. The squeeze of the trigger, the jerk of the pistol as the muzzle exploded, the bullet hole appearing in between Johnny's eyes, and the back of his head exploding all over the bed's headboard happened all within a fraction of a second. Johnny lay slumped against his pillow; a single stream of blood poured from a hole in between his still open eyes. The neatness of the wound to his face sharply differed from the mess behind him.

Nina took a brief moment to observe Johnny's dead body, and then immediately sprang into action. She placed the handgun inside her knapsack, and then slipped on a pair of latex gloves. After carefully wiping away any fingerprints she felt she may have left around the suite, she tossed the entire leather bag with the cocaine still inside, into her knapsack, then quickly changed into her "tomboy" clothing.

Now dressed in a pair of sneakers, baggy jeans, a sweatsuit, and with her hair tied and tucked into a stocking cap beneath a wool knot skull cap, she very much resembled a young adolescent boy, instead of a beautiful young woman. The sunglasses she wore only perfected her disguise.

Nina took one last second to stare at Johnny's now lifeless body. She smiled when noticing the tears from his eyes were still fresh and moist on his cheeks. It was only for fear of forensics that Nina didn't spit on him.

"Fuck you, Johnny Vega!" she said out loud.

With that, she exited the hotel suite by the same covert means she used to enter.

Chapter Fourteen

There were close to a dozen or so hustlers in front of the project building in Marcy Projects, all of them huddling around North, who was in a crouching position, preparing to throw his dice against the concrete wall. Only a few were wise enough to bet with him; the rest, to their dismay, refused to see North's four straight wins as nothing more than a simple stroke of luck. The atmosphere was electric. North seemed to take forever with jiggling the dice around in his hand, and finally, he tossed them onto the ground. Rah-Rah, one of the few whose money was riding with North, called out the victory before it even showed up on the dice.

"Fo, five, six, nigga!" he exclaimed. "C-Low, mafuckas!"

North, too, showed his excitement.

"Yeah, niggas!" he shouted out while snatching his earnings from the hands of the now disgruntled gamblers. "You know what time it is! Lemme get that paper!"

North's pleasure of winning had disappeared in an instant upon hearing Nina call his name from afar. He turned to find her walking swiftly from the parking lot with a hand on one of the straps of her knapsack, which dangled from her shoulder. The smile she wore may have fooled everyone else standing and gambling in front of the building, but North had grown all to familiar with the cold glint he recognized behind the happiness in her eyes.

"Shayome," she said while making her way through the crowd. "Meet me upstairs. I need to talk to you."

North accepted a half-smoked blunt from one of his fellow hustlers, and took a few drags before passing it around.

"Rah-Rah, I gotta go take care of somethin'," he said while handing over the dice and the cash he'd just won. "Hold the bank for me 'til I get back."

North followed closely behind Nina; either one of them bothering to utter a word until making it safely inside her apartment. The anticipation was killing him.

"What happened, baby girl?" he asked after locking the door behind them.

"Hold up, baby," Nina said. "I picked up a bottle of Moet on the way home, so have a seat on the couch while I get a couple of glasses."

North stared at Nina with surprise.

"A bottle of Mo'?" he asked, while taking a seat beside the leather bag she had tossed onto the couch. "You drinkin' now, too? Let me find out!"

Nina let out a childish giggle.

"Look inside the bag, Pa," she replied while fiddling with the cork of the champagne bottle.

The cork burst out of the mouth of the bottle with a loud pop, the sound of it signifying the shock in North's eyes when pulling an entire kilo of cocaine from inside the leather bag. Spying North's surprise while filling each of their glasses with alcohol, Nina couldn't help but smile.

"Word is bond!" North said numbly. "You got that nigga for a whole fuckin' key! Word is bond, Nina, you done woke me the fuck up! That's what the fuck it is!"

By now, Nina had well gotten over the period of celebration with North. She was far more focused on the next few moments ahead, and was even more concerned with how he'd react to her next proposal. She filled North's glass with another dose of champagne, and then took a seat on the sofa beside him.

"So," North said after taking a sip from his glass. "How'd you get it off?"

"Never mind all of that right now," she replied. "We have a more important issue to discuss, baby."

North finished the rest of his drink in one gulp, then, turned his full attention on Nina.

"What's good?" he asked.

Nina sighed while taking his hands into her own. North watched with curiosity as she moved closer to eliminate the distance between them. Their faces were now only inches apart from each other. She only stared at North, blatantly appearing to be unable to express what was on her mind. North was becoming unsettled; impatience was clearly beginning to surface in his eyes.

"What's up, Nina?" he asked. "Tell a nigga what's good."

Without warning, without uttering a single word, she leaned forward and tried to kiss North on the lips. His reaction was quick and evasive. He dodged Nina's kiss, while using his hands to create distance between them.

"Hold up, Nina! Hold up!" he said while rising to his feet. "Yo! What the fuck are you doin', yo? What the fuck, is you drunk or somethin'?"

Nina got up and started toward North, who was standing with his back turned and staring out of the living room window.

"I don't wanna hear that shit, Nina," he said when sensing her draw near. "You in violation right now; word up. What I look like playin' my nigga 'Don, like that? You wild the fuck out for even tryin' some shit like that."

Nina turned North around and tried to stare him in the eyes. He was looking everywhere but in front of him, where Nina was standing.

"Shayome…"

"I ain't try'na hear it, Nina," he interrupted. "Sadon…"

"Sadon is dead, Shayome!" she snapped. "He's dead. Now look at me! Goddamn, Pa!"

North was now staring at Nina with widened eyes. He was too overwhelmed with shock of hearing her speak in such a harsh, almost uncaring fashion for him to become angry at what she had just said. She then caressed North's face softly with both of her hands.

"Listen to me, North," she began. "Sadon doesn't just live on through you, and Sadon doesn't just live on through me either; he lives on through the both of us. We're about to move on to bigger and better things, Shay, and we can't afford to take the chance of stepping outside our circle for anything: not love, not protection, not revenge, not anything."

Despite North's discomfort with the idea of sleeping with his beloved homeboy's fiancée, he indeed saw the profound intent behind what Nina was trying to say. He could only stare at her as she continued to speak.

"Do you think Sadon would want me to lay down with someone that's not as thorough as he was? And any nigga that's as thorough as you or Sadon ain't nothing but a potential threat to what we're trying to accomplish. Feel me? Sadon wouldn't want it any other way, Shayome, and we both know that's the truth."

North fully understood where Nina was coming from, and wholeheartedly agreed, but he was too overwhelmed to say anything. He could only stare dumbly at Nina as she took him into her arms. He reciprocated her embrace, and began running his fingers through her hair while gazing deep into her eyes. Nina reached up to kiss him once more, and this time he accepted her lips as well as her tongue. She pulled away from him to look deep into his eyes before speaking once more.

"Sadon wouldn't want me to be with anyone else, Shayome; you know this."

"I know, Nina," North replied. "I know."

He kissed Nina once more, this time with much more passion and feeling, before scooping her up into his arms and carrying her into the bedroom.

Till death do us part, North thought to himself while preparing to make love to his childhood friend.

Little did he know that Nina was thinking the exact same thing.

Nina and North spent the following hours sharing each other in every possible way they could imagine. Now, after everything was all said and done, North lay naked in bed, smoking a blunt and watching as Nina stood in front of the mirror combing her hair. He was still struggling to believe what had just transpired between the two of them.

"I wanna make sure I heard you right," he said, while getting off the bed and approaching her from behind. "You shot him? You killed that bitch nigga?"

"Yep," she said matter-of-factly, while accepting the blunt North passed to her. "Right between the eyes, the same way Sadon was killed."

The deadpan look in Nina's eyes was even more disturbing than the nonchalant manner in which she confessed to killing Johnny. To North, Nina was still a young, inexperienced girl just now getting involved with a life of crime. He couldn't help but to inquire about the details of everything that happened before and after the murder. Nina told of how she cleaned up any and everything that could possibly be traced back to her being there, and she explained that the tomboy clothes she wore were for the sole purpose of appearing totally different from the sexy young woman anyone may have seen enter the suite. The murder weapon was tied to a brick and thrown into the Hudson River long before she had even made it back to her home in Marcy Projects.

Satisfied that Nina had covered all the bases, North could only smile while accepting the blunt.

"I did what I had to do, and I did it right, Papi," she remarked before giving North a kiss on the lips. "You don't have anything to worry about."

"Oh, yo, don't get it fucked up, Ma," North replied." I salute my hat to you, word up. I salute you like a mafucka. I've been sleepin' on ya ass for the longest, but you definitely woke a nigga up. Word is bond! I'm just glad to see you on point, that's all."

"I know, Papi, I know," said Nina. "But now's the time for you to play your part."

North's demeanor immediately changed from cool and subtle to excited and combustible.

"Oh, now I can do what I do best," he said anxiously. "I'm 'bout to get shit poppin', believe that!"

North got dressed, then, left to return to the bedroom with the plastic wrapped kilo of cocaine.

"Shit," he began. "I'm 'bout to go holla at Rah-Rah and bubble weight all over this mafucka!"

North's attitude was just as Nina expected it would be.

"Hold up, Pa," she said. "Don't call Rah-Rah just yet; we have a couple of things to talk about first."

North placed his cell phone back into his pants pocket and turned to face Nina, who was now tying her hair into a ponytail.

"A'ight, Ma," he said while taking a seat on the bed. "What's good? Let a nigga know somethin'."

"All right, listen," Nina began. "First of all, I don't want you and Rah-Rah selling nothin'. Keep your hands as clean as you possibly can, baby. Put some thorough niggas together, and establish some type of chain of command. But I don't want you dealing with too many niggas, Shayome. Let Rah-Rah deal with them, but you make sure that you keep a tight-ass leash on Rah-Rah -- remember that YOU run shit. Do you know where I'm comin' from, Shay? Second, forget about sellin' weight; break it down and sell it in all twenties."

North looked at Nina as if she were crazy.

"All twenties?" he remarked. "Nina, that's…"

"Smart, Shayome. That's what it is," she replied sharply. "We only have one kilo, Papi. We need to milk this motherfucker for everything it's worth."

North was now seriously listening to what she was saying. Every word she'd said so far was making complete sense. Much to his surprise, she was proving herself to be a very shrewd business minded individual. Nina had obviously given this plan a great deal of consideration. He was thinking of how raw the cocaine was, and how easy it would be for him to stretch it from one kilo to one and a half. The results of bagging up the entire product in nothing but twenty dollar vials was nothing short of staggering; he and Nina would be on top of the game in relatively no time.

"What's good, Ma?" he asked, noticing the distant look in her eyes. She appeared to be seriously deep in thought. "It looks like you got some shit on your mind."

"Yeah," she replied, seeming suddenly to snap back to the here and now. "Listen; Johnny was big, Papi, but Papo's bigger. I gotta find a way to plug into him. This coke is raw as hell, and we need to make sure it stays that way."

"Hell, yeah!" North agreed.

"We gotta maintain this grade of coke," she continued. "And with that being said, we need to stay on top of Papo's truck shipments."

Again, North was thoroughly surprised at how sharp Nina's mind worked about the drug game. He was just now beginning to see what Sadon had fallen so deeply and madly in love with – a woman with the potential to inspire a man to achieve great things in the game.

***

After an entire day and night of making love, as well as making plans to take over the projects, North stepped outside onto the street, feeling more than ready to get things underway.

"Aye, aye!" he yelled over to two little kids who were racing their bicycles up and down the project's parking lot.

They immediately recognized North and began pedaling towards him.

"What up, Shay-North?" the dark skinned kid said with a smile.

"What's poppin', North?" said the other.

North squatted down between the two boys.

"What's good, my lil' niggas?" he began. "I got a deal for y'all, but first, I gotta know what time y'all bad-ass mafuckas is 'posed to be in the crib."

The dark-skinned kid looked upward at the sky while trying to figure out his curfew. The light-skinned, freckle-faced kid answered immediately.

"As soon as it gets dark," he replied. "Why, what's up? You need us to do somethin' for you again?"

"You know I do, lil' homie," North replied while pulling out a wad of money from inside of his pocket. "And, I'ma show y'all some real love, too."

He then gave them each a fifty-dollar bill. Both little boys stared wide-eyed at the money he'd just given them, and then quickly stuffed it into their little pockets.

"Now dig," North began. "I know y'all bad-ass niggas be playin' with matches and shit, so now y'all gon' get paid for it."
He gave them both a pack of firecrackers and some matches, and then continued.

"Check me out; me and a few of my big homies is gon' be taking care of some business in the laundry room in the building. I want one of y'all to post up on one end of the hallway, and the other to post up on the other end. I need both of y'all to look out for us. If y'all see anybody, and I mean ANYBODY come into that hallway, y'all light that whole pack of firecrackers and then haul ass, ya heard? Can y'all niggas handle that, or what? Tell a nigga what's good."

Both kids gave North a firm nod of surety.

"Most definitely!" they both said at the same time.

North smiled and gave them both a ghetto-style handshake before heading towards the laundry room of his project building.

Everything was set. Rah-Rah had personally picked five of his most trusted and well-respected soldiers to meet with North in the laundry room. North entered inside to find them each sitting on top of the washing machines, smoking blunts and listening to the radio. They all watched with curiosity as he began to pull out a number of glass plates from inside one of the book bags he was carrying.

"Lemme hit that weed, my nigga," he said to Rah-Rah. "And you," he said, pointing to one of the hustlers closest to the boom box. "Lower that music, we got a lot of work to do, homie."

"A lot of work to do?" everyone asked almost simultaneously.

They all waited for North to finish taking a toke of the blunt to hear what he was going to say next. He passed the blunt, then retrieved the cocaine from inside of the other book bag.

Everyone inside the laundry room, including Rah-Rah, gasped at the very sight of North's package.

"What the fuck is that, my nigga?" Rah-Rah asked, needing North to confirm what he, himself, was seeing with his own eyes. "I know that ain't no mafuckin' bird!"

"Yes, sir! Yes, sir!" North replied happily. "All twenties, too. We gon' break this shit all the way down and blow the fuck up!"

The room came alive with happiness. All five of Rah-Rah's soldiers had gotten to their feet and were now exchanging smiles, handshakes and pounds. Everyone was eager to get things started. Despite their blatant look of being overcome with joy, North could clearly see that they were all completely high, and he didn't like it.

"Yo, man!" he barked while handing everyone a glass dish. "Y'all niggas is all high and shit. I got some lil' homies watchin' out for us on both ends of the hallway, but y'all niggas stay on point, man. Word up!"

He then began passing each of them a bottle of bleach.

"And pour this bleach inside the machines, too. You gotta be ready to get rid of this shit in case them mafuckin' pigs try to run down on us. What the fuck is y'all doin'? C'mon, let's get it poppin'," North barked. "It's seven of us in this mafucka. It shouldn't take us forever to get this shit over with."

⚜⚜⚜⚜⚜

After blending the cocaine with synthetic additives, and then straining it into tiny pebbles, came the job of packaging the product. Each one of the hustlers now stood in front of a dish filled with cocaine, which sat on top of a short row of washing machines. They all knew how much time it would take to package all of this merchandise, and were well aware of how tiring the process was going to be, but in the end, as they also knew, it would definitely be well worth the effort. In the back of each drug dealers' mind was the anticipation of making it big.

Chapter Fifteen

It seemed like centuries since the criminal elements of Marcy Projects had seen the likes of the high quality cocaine that North and Rah-Rah was distributing. The fact of them selling nearly a kilo and a half in little more than a week was proof enough of how much the neighborhood addicts appreciated their merchandise.

While sitting up the street in Nina's Honda Civic with Rah-Rah, and watching the overwhelming traffic of coke fiends bustling to and from the workers in front of his project building, North almost began to regret that he had made the twenty-dollar vials so large. With his quality of cocaine being head and shoulders above any and all of the competition, the product would have sold like water regardless of its size. It was indeed something for him to remember in the very near future.

North and Rah-Rah sat inside Nina's car sharing a blunt, the both of them being thoroughly satisfied with how smoothly things were going.

"That's what the fuck I'm talkin' about!" Rah-Rah said excitedly while tapping the blunt's ash into one of the car's ashtrays. "Look at that shit, my nigga!" he said in reference to the steady flow of customers running back and forth from the drug dealers congregated in front of the building. "This shit is fuckin' beautiful, man! Word up!"

North only smiled at the sight of their success. The thought of what happened between Nina and him over these past few days hampered him from truly reveling in his accomplishment of bringing the 'hood together with such strength. With that in mind,

North got straight to the point after finishing the weed he'd been smoking with Rah-Rah.

"Aye, yo," he said while hoisting the huge, brown paper bag from off the floor and placing it on the seat between his legs. "You sure this is thirty-two?"

"Nigga, listen," Rah-Rah said while preparing to roll another blunt. "That's thirty-two G's in that mafuckin' bag. I counted every dollar of that shit my mafuckin' self like three times."

Again, North only smiled at Rah-Rah's show of enthusiasm.

"A'ight, a'ight," he replied. "Just make sure you don't forget to lock the doors when you finish in here. I'm 'bout to go make some shit happen, baby!"

With the brown paper bag tucked securely beneath his arm, North exited the car and made his way through the crowd in front of his building, and started inside.

<hr />

Nina was sitting at the living room table smoking a joint when North entered the apartment. Her hair was parted from the corner of her head and styled into a tight-fitting bun, revealing thoughtful eyes and an ever-worried expression. For the past several days, she'd been mulling over two issues that continuously nagged at the back of her mind, and prevented her from sharing North's joy over how well everything was going. For Nina, there would be no peace of mind until a certain amount of numbers and problems were resolved.

Papo was undoubtedly her greatest and most important concern. Despite his charming, father-like persona, he was, in fact, far from a fool and wouldn't be as easily wooed by Nina's beauty as Johnny had been. He was a very unique and versatile individual, whose charisma was more than a subtle technique used to disarm the guard of those he dealt with, and interpret their true intentions. As sharp and as attentive as Papo may be, he was still a man, and all men in Nina's mind had a soft spot for women. Be it as a lover, mother figure, daughter figure, or whatever, men always sought the company of a woman for one purpose or another. The trick was for Nina to figure out what angle to strike from without being exposed, and possibly being killed, for her attempted deception.

Rah-Rah was another one of Nina's more immediate concerns. He was nowhere near as dangerous as Papo, but still, he was someone for her to keep a watchful eye on. She'd been watching Rah-Rah from her living room window, taking notice of how he kept his hands in nearly everything that went on out there in the streets, with a little too much initiative. He was always in the midst of commotion, directing traffic, dictating orders to his workers, and carrying himself in an overly flamboyant manner in front of those outside his circle.

To North, a fellow drug dealer from Marcy Projects and one who is also prone to the child-like street thug attitude as well, Rah-Rah's antics were perfectly understood and accepted. Nina, however, saw something totally different. To her, Rah-Rah was letting his position go to his head, causing him to sometimes test the limits of his duties, which meant that he was a little too ambitious and could very well prove himself to be a problem in the future if he were to go unchecked. Nina found herself constantly having to warn North to keep and eye on his "second-in-command", but for whatever reason, North felt that there wasn't too much cause for him to be overly concerned.

Nina wasn't the least bit surprised, though. Contrary to popular opinion, she felt it was more so men, and not women, who were creatures of the heart, and were more easily duped by their so-called love for a woman, or the so-called loyalty of a fellow hustler. Fearing the strength of North's overwhelming love and trust for Rah-Rah, she resolved to keep an eye on him by herself, and hopefully nip any problems in the bud before they blossomed into something dangerous.

These were only two of the many other thoughts that plagued Nina's mind, which in turn, combined to give off a rather cold, unfeeling aura when kissing North's lips after he'd entered the apartment and took a seat at the dining room table.

"How much, Pa?" she asked.

"Thirty-two thousand," he replied while emptying the contents of the bag onto the table, which was now a mountainous pile of twenty, fifty and one-hundred dollar bills. "It would've been a little bit more, but niggas had to get paid too. And dig; we only got like a hundred clips left before we're all sold out. So, what's poppin'? How do you wanna do this?"

"Papo," she replied while beginning to separate and sort out the money North had poured onto the table. "You're sure this is thirty-two thousand dollars?"

"Rah-Rah counted that shit three times, Ma. But, hold up. What do you mean 'Papo'? Papo who? Johnny's Papo?" North seemed confused.

"Yes, baby. Johnny's Papo."

"Are you fucking serious, Ma? You just murdered that nigga's underdog."

"And? Papi, please! I don't want to talk about it. Let me handle this. You just need to trust me."

"Fuck it then! That's what it is. Do your thing, girl. I know you'll holla at me if you need me to put a nigga under the dirt," North smiled.

Nina returned his smile with one of her own, then she remembered hearing North say that Rah-Rah counted the money three times.

"Baby, did you count this money yourself?"
"Nah, Ma."

Nina didn't have to say anything else. The look that she gave North helped him realize that he was slipping.

She made it clear that she only slightly trusted Rah-Rah, and North completely understood. After all, she had no knowledge of all the crimes that he and Rah-Rah had committed together in the past. Over the past ten years of them knowing each other, North and Rah-Rah had been involved in more robberies, shootings and murders than anyone would ever believe. Even as a child, Rah-Rah had always possessed the characteristics of a "stand up guy." Not even Sadon knew of all the criminal activities North and Rah-Rah had indulged in over the years for he surely wouldn't have approved of North getting a much younger guy like Rah-Rah involved in what he pointedly referred to as "how real gangsters get down".

The possibility of Rah-Rah betraying him over drugs or money was the very least of North's worries, yet he understood Nina's doubts about Rah-Rah's loyalty and chose not to argue. His only concern was to count the cash as soon as he could, so Nina could be on her way to find out if she can score with the fat Dominican drug lord he knew only as "Papo".

⁂

It was a clear, but extremely cold November day as Nina sat parked in the near-empty parking lot at Pier 57. She remained still in the seat of her car, staring into the rearview mirror as she continuously practiced what she was planning to say to Papo. Deep down inside, however, she knew that it was of no use even to try conning him with some well-rehearsed and memorized tale of deceit. It was better to let things flow more naturally. Papo was a very sharp listener, and God forbid if he was to see through her. One stammer or inkling of untruth was all it would take.

Fuck it, she thought to herself, sickened by the thought of being afraid to face Papo. *Let's get this shit over and done with.*

After exiting the car, Nina threw the weighty book bag over one shoulder and started on her way down to the waterfront.

Being so close to the water made the temperature exceptionally cool, and despite being dressed in a black bomber jacket, black skintight jeans, and black heeled boots, she almost shivered each time the wind blew.

The absence of Papo's yacht only added to her urge of wanting to turn around and call it quits. She removed her black colored sunglasses and peered about the waters, hoping to find Papo's enormous boat somewhere along the Hudson River. It didn't take long for her to spot it; in fact, the yacht was heading directly into dock where she was now standing. The sound of the yacht blowing its horn while drawing near was deafening.

HONK! HONK! HONK!

"Iy, Dios mios!" she muttered out loud. "That shit is fucking loud as hell!"

Nina put on her shades and focused on the short, pudgy man who was dressed rather debonair in his navy blue, double breasted suit jacket, matching well with his fancy captain's cap, and a red scarf tucked beneath the collar of his crisp button-down shirt which stood out strikingly.

Oh, my God! She thought to herself while returning Papo's wave. *That's him! There he is!*

For women like us, Mami, strength and beauty are one and the same; make them respect you as much as they admire you.
Bearing her mother's words of advice close to heart, Nina smiled heartily at Papo as he instructed one of his deckhands to lay down a ramp for her to come aboard.

"Nina," he said while straightening his jacket, which was struggling not to burst open from his large, oversized belly. "How'd you figure to find me here?"

Papo's smile was one of genuine surprise; even his eyes twinkled as he questioned her. Nina refused to allow him the chance to ease beneath her guard. Keeping in mind that his warm, father-like demeanor was no more than a façade, Nina moved in to engage in her own game of deception.

"I actually had no idea that you'd be here," she replied with an awkward smile. "I was just trying my luck, and thank God, you're here."

"Iy, Mami," he said when seeing the mix of emotions now beginning to surface on Nina's face. "It's okay."

He caressed Nina's face then kissed both of her cheeks.

"I miss him too," Papo said ruefully.

Miss him too? Nina thought to herself. *He actually thinks that I'm mourning Johnny's death!* She couldn't have been happier to stumble upon the chink in Papo's armor so easily.

"I was waiting for him to call me Papo..." Nina began, careful not to overdo it with the dramatics. "He never called me. I had to hear about him being murdered from someone else in the streets, Papo."

Instead of playing the grieving, near hysterical woman of poor old Johnny, Nina opted to go with a more dignified expression of grief. She stared off into nothingness with sorrowful eyes, allowing her lips to tremble ever so slightly. It was a look that would easily have melted the coldest of hearts.

"Vamos, Mami," Papo replied. "Please, come inside."

Nina followed Papo through the glass doors of the yacht's upper cabin, and down a short aisle, which led into one of the many large and extravagant private lounges on the boat. The carpet was plush and charcoal gray in color, which went well with the expensive-looking black leather couches that were situated along the walls of the cabin. A huge bar was lined up against the wall opposite of the couches.

"Sienta te, Mami, please, have a seat," Papo said with an overtone of hospitality. "Can I fix you a drink or something?"

"No, Papo, gracias, though," she replied thoughtfully while sitting down on one of the leather couches. "Have you heard about who may have killed Johnny? It's not right, Papo. It's just not right!"

Nina began chewing her bottom lip as she turned her gaze toward one of the many black-tinted windows, hoping to give Papo the impression of her being terribly upset. It seemed to have worked like a charm.

Papo sighed, while fixing himself a drink with more juice than alcohol.

"Iy, Nina," he said rather regretfully. "Unfortunately, I don't have a single clue, Chica. It really is a mystery. I mean, Johnny didn't have any trouble with anyone, at least not to the extent to where someone would murder him."

Papo then took a seat on a black recliner chair, which was in the corner of the cabin and in between two leather couches. He propped his feet up and took a sip of his drink.

"It's truly a puzzle," he said with a hidden touch of bewilderment. "I have no idea."

He then took another sip of his drink before turning his gaze onto Nina.

"So, what do you know, Nina?" he asked. "Can you think of anyone who may have held some type of animosity toward Johnny?"

Papo's warm, sparkling eyes twinkled as he stared softly more so into Nina's eyes than her face. He seemed to be searching for something that Nina may be hiding, and it unsettled her.

"You can't imagine how bad I wish I could help, but I don't have the slightest idea, Papo," she lied convincingly. "I really don't. I mean, Johnny's death hit me on more than just a personal level, Papo. It's one of the reasons why I came looking for you in the first place. Johnny was the only person I did business with, and now that he's gone, I have no one else to turn to but you."

Papo's eyes went sharp, showing how heightened his attention had gotten when hearing Nina's words.

"What do you mean, Nina?" he asked. "What, are you saying that you need a few dollars or something?"

"No, no, no," Nina quickly replied, while at the same time shaking her head. "With all due respect, Papo, I have too much pride to beg anyone for a handout, especially you. I wouldn't even allow Johnny to shower me with gifts."

Nina then took the bag off of her shoulder and proceeded to open it.

"Johnny wasn't just my lover," she continued to lie. "He was my connect as well."

Papo remained silent, his eyes narrowing as he stared first at Nina and then to the bag she was holding, with an odd combination of both humor and caution.

"What is that you have there, Nina?" he asked in reference to the book bag she was now holding on her lap.

"Its thirty-thousand dollars in cash," she replied while dumping it all on top of the marble coffee table sitting in front of her. "Johnny usually…"

Nina's response was cut short by a simple wave of Papo's chubby finger.

"Did you come here looking to score some type of drug deal with me, Nina?" he asked with the eyes of a hawk. There was now a mixture of caution and uncertainty that heightened the feel of discomfort in the air.

"Papo," Nina tried to explain, "I just…"

"It's a question that you'll answer by either saying yes or no," Papo replied curtly with his eyes never leaving hers. "It's as simple as that."

"Yes," Nina replied, trying the best she could not to show how uneasy she was feeling.

Papo nodded while giving her a simple purse of his lips while lying back against the cushions of his recliner chair – still, there was a climate of apprehension that continued to loom between the two of them. Nina remained silent, unsure as to whether or not it was in her best interest to press the issue. The silence between them was finally broken by the sound of Papo dialing and speaking into his cell phone, ordering for someone to bring him a bathrobe.

A tall, slim Dominican man with plain facial features and haunting eyes entered almost immediately with a white cotton robe securely in, what appeared to Nina, as an ironclad grasp. Although he was obviously very much younger than Papo and very well-dressed, the blankness of his eyes, which matched his aura, told of him seeing, and perhaps even being responsible for imposing acts of brutality that were far too gruesome for Nina to even imagine. His hollow, almost lifeless eyes darted from Papo to Nina, and to the money spilled all over the coffee table, and then back to Papo before he spoke.

"Que pasa, Papo?" the man asked in a rough, gravelly voice.

Again, Papo raised his finger, this time to quiet the man from asking any further questions. The man stopped talking within an instant, and only continued to stare at Nina. She turned to find that Papo, too, was now staring at her as well.

"Mira, Nina, I'm going to have to ask you to stand up and remove your clothing," he said. "Everything—your bra, your underwear, socks and all."

Seeing that Papo's silent henchman had been summoned to bring a bathrobe along with him, Nina quickly figured against any thoughts of them mistreating her. Still, she felt uncomfortable about taking off all her clothes in front of their blank, expressionless eyes. While doing so, she felt like a bleeding sea lion in the midst of a pair of bloodthirsty sharks. Now totally naked, Nina stood before the two of them, anxiously awaiting their next set of instructions.

"Forgive me, Nina," said Papo. "But please do us the favor of turning around. I promise you that this will be over shortly."

Nina complied, making sure to raise her hands high in the air as she did so. Both Papo and his associate watched intently as Nina turned around, seemingly unimpressed with her flawless physique. The two men had undoubtedly seen and sampled better.

With a wave of Papo's hand, the tall, menacing man moved forward and handed Nina the bathrobe.

"Please allow me to apologize for the inconvenience. My friend, Carlito, is going to take your belongings to another room so we can talk. I just need to make sure that I'm speaking to you and only you. I hope you don't mind," Papo said as his silent partner began to gather all of her belongings.

"Oh, not at all," Nina honestly replied. "I understand the need to take precautions."

Papo nodded and smiled slightly.

"Please," he said with his hand outstretched to one of the leather couches. "Have a seat and explain your situation."

"I was buying coke from Johnny and finally worked my way up to two kilos before he was murdered. He was planning to sell me two for eighteen thousand a piece. Not only am I four thousand dollars short, but now he's gone. He's gone, and I'm on my own. I feel so embarrassed for coming to you like this, especially when I'm short, but I really need your help. Papo, please…"

"Sh-h-h, quyeta un momento, Nina," Papo interrupted. "Nina, this is a complete surprise, you know, the way you're coming to me. And Johnny…" Papo took a second to shake his head as if scolding a child. "Johnny knows, well *knew* better than to do business with you in this fashion."

Nina fought not to let the panic she felt beginning to well up from deep within her being able to find its way to the surface. She looked over at Papo, who, while taking another moment to stir the ice in his drink with one of his fingers, was now staring at Nina and trying to decide whether or not to turn her away.

"Papo, please," Nina started. "I've been working too hard to get where I am to just let things blow off into the wind. Soon, I'll be able to retire from this life with a little bit of satisfaction, just a little bit, Papo. I'm almost at the finish line. Please don't turn me away when I'm so close, Papo, please."

Papo stared Nina in the face, rubbing his stubby, clean-shaven chin while listening as she pleaded her case. Nina only stared back at Papo, appearing as honest and as sincere as she possibly could. After what seemed like an eternity to Nina, he finally opened his mouth to speak.

"You know what, Nina?" Papo remarked with a smile. "I can see why Johnny was so crazy about you. My God, you're a keeper! I'll tell you what. Today's your lucky day."

Papo rose from his seat and started around the bar, and then hoisted a duffle bag to the top of the counter. He then retrieved two kilos of cocaine from inside the bag.

"I'll give you two kilos for, hm-m-m, thirty-thousand," Papo said. "Si, fifteen-thousand dollars a piece for each kilo. You can keep the money you brought here with you and take the keys on consignment. You bring back the money, and I'll charge you fifteen thousand a key from here on out."

Nina couldn't believe what she was now hearing.

"You're talking about spotting me?" she asked, realizing how silly of a question she had asked only after hearing it.

"Si, Mami," Papo replied. "It is in honor of the man we both knew and loved. Consider it as my gift to you."

Papo's associate then reentered the lounge room with Nina's belongings and placed them on the couch beside her. Papo then joined his partner at the door.

"Now, I shall allow you to get dressed and prepare to go on about your business," he said smoothly. "I'll be waiting for you outside on the upper deck."

With that, Papo turned and left Nina alone to scrabble and get herself together.

Thirty-thousand dollars and two whole kilos of the best cocaine in Brooklyn! She thought wildly to herself while slipping into her clothes. *Oh, my God! Oh, my fucking God!*

⁂

Now fully dressed from head to toe, and with two kilos of raw cocaine and thirty-two thousand dollars in drug money stuffed inside her backpack, Nina was all set to head back to Marcy Projects. After kissing Papo on both of his cheeks and saying goodbye to his silent, brooding associate, who only nodded in return, she started her way down the yacht's ramp and towards her car. She could only hope that North was making as much success with following Papo's truck shipments from Maine to New Jersey as she had been with scoring the deal of a lifetime.

Nina drove slowly down the street, staring intently at the swarm of people now buzzing around the entrance to her project building as she made her way into the parking lot. It was terribly crowded, and everyone there seemed alive with excitement; they all seemed to be captivated by some sort of a grand spectacle. While observing all of the activity and realizing that everyone was indeed watching a fight, Nina couldn't help but to get angry with

North for allowing such a thing to take place directly in front of their place of business.

I can't believe this nigga! Nina thought angrily to herself as she exited the car and locked its door before starting out of the parking lot. *We're about to start playin' in the major leagues, and Shayome is still acting like a little fucking kid! I swear, he's gonna have to grow the fuck up.*

With a book bag full of money and two kilos of cocaine tossed over her shoulder, Nina walked briskly up the street. The closer she got to the crowd, the more disgusted she became with what was going on. There were well over a dozen spectators, all of them rowdy and wildly excited. They were all whooping and hollering, some cheering while pumping a fistful of money high in the air at the same time. Neither North nor Rah-Rah could be seen amongst the crowd. The bystanders were all packed tightly together as they rooted and cheered for what Nina now saw was a gruesome and brutal street fight.

"Hook that nigga!" someone shouted.

"Man, knock that nigga the fuck out!" screamed another.

Nina fought her way through the crowd to find a pair of men, both of them bruised and bloodied, circling one another with their hands raised in a boxing form. The entire atmosphere was electrical.

"What the fuck is you waitin' for, man!" someone shouted. "Go 'head and swing! Knock that nigga the fuck out!"

"Word up!" exclaimed another voice. "Knock that nigga the fuck out!"

The scene was alive and combustible. Nina too found herself somewhat hypnotized by the two bloodied fighters circling around one another.

Despite the cold pre-winter temperature, both fighters were shirtless. The short, somewhat stocky kid known by everyone as Paco, circled around cautiously with his hands balled and guarding a bruised and terribly battered face. His light-skinned face was now dark red, almost purplish, and one of his eyes was nearly swollen shut, while the other eye bore a long streaking bruise beneath it. Blood trickled freely from both his nose and his mouth.

Nina didn't recognize the man Paco was fighting with. She rationalized that he must have been a hustler from one of the many other buildings that combined to make up March Projects. He was a rather tall fellow with a trim, but muscular build, with long braided hair that was set backward in more than a dozen cornrows. With exception to his expression of being totally exhausted, the stranger's face wasn't the least bit bruised or swollen. His mouth, or maybe his jaw, seemed to be the most damaged, and helped to make him appear to be in worse shape than Paco. His mouth was hanging open and appeared awkwardly crooked, closed only when having to spit out the blood that poured profusely over his lips and onto his bare chest. It was a terrible sight to see.

It was only when hearing the sound of Rah-Rah's voice for the fight to continue that Nina snapped from out of her gaze and noticed that he had been standing beside her all along.

"Man, what the fuck!" he bellowed. "Is y'all niggas gon' rock or what?"

North was standing across the scene from Rah-Rah. He was also too consumed with the fight to notice that Nina was present.

He stared wildly at the street brawl, holding a fistful of dollar bills, and screaming and yelling just as loudly as Rah-Rah.

Paco ducked beneath his opponent's lurch and countered with a solid two-punch combination. His left hook landed on the man's jaw with a crisp popping sound, which was just as soon followed up by a right hook to the temple. The crowd gasped and cheered as the tall, braided man wobbled from the blows to his face and head, but regained his composure fast enough to land a stiff right jab and a bone-crunching left hook.

To see both North and Rah-Rah so oblivious to any and everything going on around them sent Nina through the roof with anger.

"Shay!" she exclaimed while walking directly between the two fighters. "Is this how y'all handle business?"

"Yo, man!" everyone cried out. "What the fuck is she doing?"

Nina turned around and stared at everyone with a threatening enough glare to silence any more ill remarks. She wanted to curse each and everyone out for being so stupid. She wanted to warn them of how reckless activities like the one they were all participating in was no more than an invitation for the presence of the police, even if only to be nosy. In the back of her mind's eye, Nina was schooling them all about how a true hustler is supposed to handle his business while hustling out in the streets, but the reality of it was very clear.

North was the only leader amongst the bunch, and it would be North whom Nina would reprimand for such foolishness because he was supposed to be the law. Rah-Rah was just an enforcer, and everyone else was to simply follow instructions.

Knowing how important it is for North to appear to be in control of everything at all times, Nina fought to keep her temper in check and not to say or do anything that may take the chance of undermining his authority.

She looked over at North, who was, in turn, staring back at her with a slight glint of comprehension. Then, as if reading Nina's mind, North began asserting his authority.

"A'ight, a'ight," he began. "Chill the fuck out, everybody; fall the fuck back."

Everyone, including Rah-Rah, began staring at North with disbelief.

"What the fuck you mean, fall back?" asked a bruised, battered and bloody Paco. "How you know I wasn't gon' knock that nigga out? I'm tryin' to get paid, man. What the fuck!"

Paco's remark immediately initiated protests from many other thugs who had laid odds on who would win the bare-knuckle brawl.

"Hell yeah!" said one hustler.

"Word is bond, that's some bullshit!" said another, "Niggas got dough on the line, man!"

The crowd was now becoming unsettled and growing noisier by the second.

North's first instinct was to bitch-slap anyone who went against his decision, but the sight of Nina standing at the door was enough to quell his urge to turn violent. To see her looking so nervous while in possession of some serious baggage made him a bit more anxious than usual to walk away from the possibility of trouble. North could see the unease in the faces of his loyal street soldiers, yet he could also recognize their willingness to enforce whatever command he issued. Seeing that his word was still received, and that he had urgent business with Nina that needed his immediate attention, he decided to give both Paco and his adversary a few dollars for the entertainment that they provided.

"You wanna get paid, nigga? Huh?" he hissed while pulling a wad of cash from inside his pants pocket and peeling a thousand dollars for the both of them. "Here. Y'all mafuckers deserve this shit. Word up, both of y'all niggas got chipped the fuck up."

Paco and his one-time enemy smiled at each other while stuffing the dollar bills deep into their pockets, and even took a moment to shake hands and embrace each other before parting ways.

"Well, ain't that a bitch!" said Rah-Rah with a grin.

Not everyone was amused with their show of good sportsmanship as Rah-Rah was.

"I'm sayin' though," said one of the disgruntled gamblers. "How the fuck is you gonna just tell them niggas to fall back like that? Shit, nigga, I put money on them mafuckers too."

"You don't get paid to make bets, nigga!" North barked while jumping into the hustler's face. "You get paid to sell coke! You done with that pack yet?"

The explosive look in North's eyes was a big enough warning for the hustler to back down.

"Nah, dawg," he replied without a sign of the gusto he'd shown just a few minutes ago. "You got that."

"There goes your money right there!" North said angrily while pointing at an addict now making her way towards them. "Go get your money, mafucka, and stop wastin' time over here bitchin' about some bullshit!"

After witnessing North's near-violent reaction to his own worker's complaint of losing money behind the cancellation of the street fight, there wasn't a single soul who'd dare say anything else. Everyone remained quiet as North and Rah-Rah scanned the crowd, waiting to see if anyone else had something negative to say. Satisfied with the silence, North started towards Nina, who was standing and waiting for him at the door of the project building.

"Yo, Rah-Rah," he said out loud. "We almost there, baby! Make sure you keep shit runnin' smooth out here, man."

"No doubt, my nigga," Rah-Rah replied. "I got this."
With that, North turned and followed Nina inside the building.

👑👑👑👑👑

The inside of Nina's apartment was disturbingly quiet; the noise of her bath water being prepared was the only sound to be heard. North sat on the living room couch thinking about how ashamed he was for Nina to catch him behaving so immaturely. The face that she'd given him the silent treatment while on their way up the stairs only added to his feelings of regret.

She ain't even tell me what happened today, North thought to himself while rolling a blunt. *Baby girl be trippin' sometimes.*

Just as North finished rolling his blunt, Nina entered the living room holding a knapsack. Despite the urge to appear nonchalant, North couldn't help but to glance down and notice that she wasn't wearing any panties beneath the T-shirt she wore, which barely covered her thick, shapely hips.

"So, what happened?" he asked while lighting the blunt.

"First things first," she replied while sitting down on the couch beside him. "How're things going with you and that shipment?"

North wrinkled his nose at the curt manner in which she was now dealing with him. Still, he didn't bother to make a fuss about it.

"Everything is good," he answered. "All I know for sure is that the coke comes from off the boat in Maine. Gimme a couple of days, and I'll know for sure if it's the same shipment that goes down to Jersey."

Satisfaction was now showing on Nina's face. There was no way she could possibly hide the relief of her hearing that North was proving successful with his stakeout.

"But, yeah, I'm handling mine," North said while passing Nina the blunt. "Tell me what happened with Papo.
"

Again, Nina couldn't help but to smile.

"I got two kilos, and I got the thirty-two thousand," she said before pulling out the two kilos of cocaine from inside the book bag.

North was speechless. His eyes darted back from the two kilos in Nina's hand, to the cash filled knapsack, and then to Nina who was now sitting cross-legged while smoking the blunt. The overwhelming look of satisfaction from a job well done was etched across her face.

"You got the cash and the coke?" he asked with surprise. It was a silly question, but at the same time, it was all North could fix his mouth to say. "How'd you pull it off?"

"He fronted me," Nina replied smilingly.

"He fronted you?"

"At fifteen-thousand apiece," she added while handling North the blunt.

"Two keys of the best coke in New York for fifteen G's apiece?" he remarked with sheer disbelief before taking an extra long drag on the blunt to calm his nerves. "Goddamn!"

Sensing that North's imagination was beginning to run wild, Nina moved quickly to bring him back to reality.

"Listen, Pa," she began. "Fuck Johnny – Papo's the real deal. We really gotta make a good impression on him to keep his business. I'm trying to double the profit off this, but at the same time, get his money back to him as soon as possible. Can you make that happen?"

It took North less than a second to answer Nina's question.

"Hell yeah!" he replied while finishing the rest of his blunt. "Man, listen. I could cop a bird from somewhere else and use that shit, plus a whole key of cut to smash on the two keys we got from Papo. We'll get close to five birds out of this shit."

Nina was listening closely to every word North was saying, all the while tallying up an estimated profit from the entire scheme.

"What's the least you think we'll make off all of this?" she asked.

North took a moment to ponder Nina's question.

"How much profit?" he asked out loud to no one in particular. "Ma-a-a-n... four keys... we'll break that shit down into all twenties like we did before, then..."

North was now becoming visibly excited.

"We gon' move fast and lock shit the fuck down," he replied. "Matter of fact, remember that bitch-ass nigga, Rock from out Fort Green? Yeah, I'm gonna lock his shit down too. Word up! Fuck it!"

"The profit, Shayome," Nina reiterated. "What kind of profit are we lookin' at?"

"I'm sayin'," North said while staring upwards at the ceiling. "I gotta pay niggas for movin' it, and I gotta put together a mean-ass team, so that would probably leave us with at least a hundred and fifty G's. But then again, we 'bout to take shit to a whole 'nother level, so we gon' need to spend a good – maybe thirty-thousand for guns, silencers, and shit like that."

Nina watched North with skeptical eyes as he seemed to be talking only to himself.

"Thirty-thousand dollars for guns?" she asked doubtfully. "I thought you already had guns, Pa."

"Man, listen," North replied. "Shit is serious out here. You could never have enough guns. If niggas ever act like they want it, I'ma give it to them, feel me?"

Recollections of Sadon lying dead on the sidewalk was more than enough for Nina to be swayed into agreeing with North to buy as many guns as he saw fit.

I feel sorry for anyone who tries to play Shayome, Nina thought to herself, while vocally granting North permission to buy as many guns as he wanted.

Feeling her blood beginning to run cold, Nina moved quickly to combat her moodiness. She straddled her body on top of North's and kissed him full on the lips. North, instinctively gripped her naked buttocks, with both of his hands.

"My shower's been running forever, Pa," she said with a smile while seductively looking into North's eyes. "How about getting your sexy ass in the water with me?"

North responded by grabbing Nina by the hair and kissing her full on the mouth.

"Mmf!" was all Nina could manage to utter while being flipped over and onto her back as they shared each other's tongues.

"Well," North said with a smile as he pulled his tongue from out of Nina's mouth. "What the fuck is we waitin' for?"

Chapter Sixteen

It was nine o'clock in the morning when Rah-Rah entered the diner, which was far too early in the day for North to be calling and all but demanding for him to show up to talk about something.

Man, this nigga gots me up all early and shit, he thought grumpily to himself while sidestepping one of the many early morning customers moving busily about the place. *This shit ain't what's happenin' man. Word up!*

Although dressed in a plain black sweatshirt and fitted cap, North was still easy to spot amongst the collage of everyday nine-to-five workers who were busy preparing themselves for another day of the workweek. Rah- Rah straightened the collar of his jacket and then started towards his old friend. North smiled while rising up out of his seat to greet him.

"What's good, my nigga?" he asked.

"Shit," Rah-Rah replied while sitting down in the booth. "You the one that's callin' niggas all early in the morning and shit. I'm the one tryin' to find out what's poppin'. Tell me somethin', my nigga, word up."

"Four keys, nigga," North replied flatly. "That's what's good."

Rah-Rah stared across the table at North as if not fully comprehending what he'd just heard.

"Four keys?" he asked, trying the best he could to be sure that he'd heard North correctly.

"Four keys, my nigga," North answered. "Four mothafuckin' birds. That's why ya ass is over here at nine in the morning. Feel me?"

Rah-Rah-s bright toothy grin far outshined North's reserved, almost sly expression.

Just then, a tall, thin white woman with pale skin and blood-red colored hair suddenly appeared at North and Rah-Rah-s booth. The cold, business-like attitude she gave off matched her straight, starch-stiffened waitress uniform.

"Can I help you, gentlemen?" she asked rather pointedly.

"Gimme some scrambled eggs and some home fries, and I want a large orange juice while I'm waitin' for y'all to cook it," Rah-Rah answered cheerfully.

He then peeled off a fifty-dollar bill and placed it on the table.

"And I'm payin' for whatever my nigga's gonna eat too."

The waitress appeared a bit uneasy with Rah-Rah's use of the word 'nigga', and it made him smile even more.
"I'm good," North said.

"It'll be about fifteen minutes," the waitress replied before turning and leaving them alone to continue their conversation.

"All right, listen," North began. "The stakes is high, my nigga. We about to be on a whole 'nother level, so that means the consequence for fuckin' up is gon' be on a whole 'nother level too, feel me?" Ain't no games gon' be played this time around; anybody can get it."

It wasn't hard for Rah-Rah to read in between the lines, and he smiled at North's indirect warning; there was no need for him to feel offended. Both North and Rah-Rah had seen friends betray each other over much less than four kilos of cocaine, and it was only right for North to let it be known that he was on point. Besides, they both shared the same goal, which was to get rich in the drug game. There was no way Rah-Rah could see the possibility of betraying the man who was helping him become a living legend in the projects.

The waitress delivered Rah-Rah's orange juice and then disappeared. Rah-Rah guzzled a good portion of his juice and then emptied a miniature bottle of whiskey into his glass. North eyed him disapprovingly.

"What?" Rah-Rah asked comically. "You got me up early in the morning. I gotta get right!"

"Anyway," North remarked, "Listen. We gotta put together a serious ass team, you know what I'm sayin'?"

Rah-Rah gave a nod of agreement while taking a sip of his drink.

"But I want you to keep your hands clean," North continued. "Don't sell a mafuckin' nickel bag. Let them niggas do the dirty work. Shit, that's what the fuck they're getting paid for anyway, feel me? I want you to take three of these keys and break them down into all twenties."

"All twenties?" Rah-Rah asked, his mind racing to calculate the possible profit that would come about from packaging three kilos of cocaine in such a fashion. "That's a lot of clips, son."

"Exactly," North replied. "We gon' need like sixteen niggas working two twelve hour shifts. I'm talkin' 'bout some sunup to sundown type of shit. We gon' have two pairs of niggas breakin' down a key apiece into all twenties, while another two pairs hit the block immediately with some product. Then, when them niggas get tired, we just replace 'em with another two pairs of fresh hands and fingers. From niggas paid to look out to niggas on the block hustling, we gotta make this shit airtight. I wanna lock Rock's shit down too."

"Fort Green?" Rah-Rah asked.

"Fort Green," North confirmed. "I want to flood that nigga's projects with an entire key of twenties; we gon' do our fuckin' numbers off this shit, for real!"

North took a moment to drop fifty cents into the slot of a tiny jukebox, which was fastened onto a wall by their booth, as the waitress delivered Rah-Rah-s breakfast. "For the Love of Money" by the O'Jays seemed a rather appropriate song.

"Check it out though," Rah-Rah said after the waitress left them by themselves. "You said four keys. What's up with the other one?"

"I was thinkin' about finding somebody to push it in weight," North answered.

"What about my cousin, Dee?" asked Rah-Rah. "He could bubble that shit off his cell phone. It'll work good for everybody."

"Whatever, my nigga," Said North. "Whatever you do, just make sure you do it right. We can't afford no fuck-ups. Make sure niggas bring back six off each G-pack too. Them niggas is gon' love you for that."

Rah-Rah's appetite was now overshadowed by his hunger to hit the streets and begin to make things happen. Sensing the anticipation in Rah-Rah's eyes, North cut straight to the conclusion of the matter by sliding an envelope filled with money across the table.

"The keys are in the bag underneath the table," he began. "And it's four G's in the envelope right here. I want you to rent an apartment somewhere out of the 'hood. We gonna use it as our lab. We could keep everything there just as long as you don't get on some greedy shit, like try to hustle out of there, then everything will be straight. Just make sure you be careful, my nigga. Start takin' cabs wherever you go. We gotta switch up on these niggas, feel me?"

Of course, Rah-Rah felt where North was coming from; after all, they had spent many nights in front of their project building dreaming of this very moment.

"Most definitely," he replied with a smile. "I'm ready to get shit poppin'. It's time to get rich, my nigga!"

North smiled while giving Rah-Rah a ghetto-style handshake.

"I'm about to spin off, my nigga," he said while rising to his feet. "Hit me on the cell when you get shit in order."

With that, North slipped on the jacket he kept lying across his lap and began making his way out of the diner. Like Rah-Rah, North too was anxious to get things underway. He was only one flip away from not just taking over his projects, but quite possibly Brooklyn, and it was all thanks to Nina.

If only Sadon could see her now, North thought silently to himself while getting inside his rental car.

If it wasn't for him having to follow Papo's truck from Maine down to New Jersey, North surely would have driven to the cemetery and paid a heartfelt visit to the gravesite of his fallen comrade.

"I miss you, my nigga," North said out loud. "This is all for you, word is bond, all for you."

Chapter Seventeen

With what seemed to be an endless supply of good quality cocaine, packaged in the form of some of the biggest twenty-dollar vials Marcy Project had seen in years, business couldn't have been going better for North and Nina. Money was coming in almost faster than they could count it. Both Nina and North spent their money slowly and carefully, upgrading their wardrobes only slightly, and not doing much more than keeping the bills paid. They were more so concentrating on saving and stacking their cash, than spending it.

Rah-Rah, on the other hand, was living life to the fullest. His clothing was top of the line, and his neck, wrists and fingers glimmered with jewels. All of Marcy Projects, including neighboring 'hoods from abroad, bowed down to Rah-Rah and his entourage, and both North and Nina stood on top of it all.

⚜⚜⚜⚜⚜⚜

Maria was only half-finished braiding Nina's hair when she stopped to answer the door. Rah-Rah burst through the door and engaged in his ritual of greeting and groping her at the same time.

"Damn, girl!" he said as if he were sliding his hands down her pants for the first time. "Your shit is kind of fat back there!"

"Yeah, that ass feels good, don't it?" Maria replied smartly while breaking away from his grasp. "I just hope you got enough money to keep touchin' it."

With a duffel bag in each hand, North made his way past his homeboy, who was now arguing with Maria, and placed them both down by Nina's feet while bending down to give her a soft kiss on the lips.

"How much?" Nina asked.

"Ninety-thousand," he replied while massaging Nina's shoulders. "Forty-five G's in each bag."

Maria had long known that North, Nina and Rah-Rah were all heavily into the drug game, but despite Rah-Rah's new and extravagant behavior, she had no idea they were touching it to that extent. Her eyes went wide with disbelief when hearing how much money North had just now handed over to Nina. The cool, almost nonchalant way that Nina had taken in the news of it was even more shocking.

"Ninety-thousand!" she remarked, while fighting with Rah-Rah's still groping hands. "I know you said you were doin' a'ight, but damn! Ninety-fuckin' G's! Shit, if it's like that, can I get a fuckin' thousand?"

North pulled a thick wad of cash from inside his pocket.

"Aye, yo," he said while beginning to peel off a number of bills. "You know you my homegirl, Maria, so you could get that. Take this right here. Just make sure you give my nigga some pussy. I'm tired of seein' his ass chasin' and shit."

"Oh, no," Maria said while sitting down on Rah-Rha's lap and fighting to control where his hands were going. "As rough as this nigga is, he's gonna have to pay me a thousand his mothafuckin' self!"

Maria looked over to find that Nina was in her own little world, totally oblivious to everything around her. Nina's breasts bulged from a black sports bra, which matched the black riding boots she wore. Her miniskirt rose high above her thighs as she sat cross-legged on a sofa chair with North lovingly massaging her shoulders. While smoking a joint, Nina was the perfect picture of Maria's admiration. She dismounted Rah-Rah's throbbing erection to go and brighten the living room lights. Maria couldn't help but to comment on how regal Nina was looking.

"Damn, girl, just look at you," said Maria. "You're all laid back, smokin' a joint and shit, lookin' all good with ninety-fuckin' G's at your feet. I wish I could be you right now, Nina. Word up! I just wish Sadon could see you like this."

Nina, too consumed with her plans for tonight to pay any attention to what was going on, was alone in her own little world. The sound of Sadon's name triggered a recollection of what Maria was saying.

"What?" she asked while staring at Maria with blank, unfeeling eyes. "Be me? You wish that you could be me?"

Nina took a moment to exhale a long stream of marijuana smoke before continuing.

"I lost both my mother and father to this game," she went on to say. "I lost Sadon to this shit too. My man WAS and IS a part of this game; in fact, he IS this fucking game. The game is all I have left, Maria, and I'm just making the most of it."

Nina's cool mask of nonchalance was now slowly beginning to fall apart. Tears were starting to bubble and trickle from her eyes.

"Don't get me wrong," she continued. "I love Shayome. He's the best thing that has ever happened to me since Sadon died.

He's the only thing I have left, but don't think for one minute that having all of this money makes life any easier for me."

"N-no, sweetie," Maria said, suddenly realizing just how fast the mood in the room had gone from light and pleasurable to heavy and emotional. "I didn't mean to make you feel all fucked up."

She then wrapped her arms around Rah-Rha's neck as Nina went on to take a drag on the joint she was smoking.

"Don't ever wish to be like somebody else just because of what they have – especially me," Nina said. "Even when you see me sittin' on millions, Maria, 'cause I WILL be sittin' on millions; either that or lying in the dirt next to Sadon."

Nina's body was now visibly being overtaken with emotion. Her hands were shaking, her breathing was becoming a bit more labored, and most of all, her Puerto Rican accent was showing itself more and more as she grew upset.

"Chill, Ma," North said as he leaned over to kiss Nina softly on the cheek. "Don't even start talkin' like that girl, 'cause you know we gon' get this paper. On everything I love, Ma, we gon' make shit happen, but it's getting' dark. You know you gotta get ready to meet this nigga..."

North then pulled one of his long-nose .44 caliber revolvers from the waistband of his jeans and offered it to Rah-Rah.

"Huh," he said. "Let's walk Nina to her car."

Rah-Rah declined to accept North's pistol and pulled two Glock nine-millimeter handguns from the waist of his jeans.

"Shee-it," he replied with a smile. "I got my own heat right here."

North acknowledged Rah-Rah's preparation with a simple nod of agreement while tucking the .44 back into the waistband of his jeans.

"C'mon, Rah," he said. "Let's walk my baby girl to the car."

⸙⸙⸙⸙⸙⸙⸙

Nina pulled into the parking lot of the pier where Papo's yacht was docked. Due to the huge amount of traffic caused by the presence of a celebrity who just happened to be throwing a yacht party of his own, Papo instead instructed Nina to meet him at nine o'clock in the evening. The volume of people should have lessened by then, and with a little help from the darkness of night. She wouldn't appear too suspicious to anyone, who may just happen to notice a tiny woman trudging a shit load of money inside two duffel bags. Nina's wristwatch read 8:49, which left her with a few minutes to sit and meditate upon the event that was soon to take place.

The sky was pitch black. The dark murky waters of the Hudson River sparkled and glistened from the illumination of Manhattan's brightly lit buildings.

One more time, Nina thought to herself while observing the dazzling waterfront view. *If things go the way they're supposed to, this should be the last time I ever have to see this fat-ass Dominican motherfucker.*

Satisfied that it was now time to meet with Papo, Nina exited her Honda Civic, lugging two duffel bags filled with the money along with her. Without North and Rah-Rah present to haul her weighty luggage, Nina was just now realizing how heavy the bags were. It was truly a test of her strength to even drag them across the pier and up to the ramp to Papo's yacht.

The cruise ship behind her was still bustling with activity. There was still a lengthy line of passengers spilling halfway down its ramp, waiting to enter inside. Thanks to the remarkably beautiful scenery provided by the illuminated seaport, no one paid much attention to the petite little Puerto Rican girl hunched over and struggling with ninety-thousand dollars worth of drug money.

After what seemed to be an incredible show of strength, Nina had finally made it to the top of the yacht's upper deck. Now free of what felt like a thousand-pound burden, she stood upright and took a moment to stretch her limbs. The cool, wintry breeze of the maritime air whipped about her face as she did so, seeping into her pores and slightly awakening her from the sluggish effects of the weed she'd been smoking earlier.

With a newfound sense of rejuvenation, Nina felt more than ready to go and see Papo. She cupped the side of her face while pressing it against the window of the main lounge room. Through squinted eyes, she could see him relaxed on one of his reclining leather chairs, talking on his cell phone.

Nina made her way around to the black-tinted glass door of the cabin's entrance and knocked before entering inside. Papo was all too absorbed in his conversation on the phone to notice that she had arrived.

"No, you listen!" he barked angrily. "I've been doing business with this family for a very long time – thirteen years to be exact. I've come through on schedule every week for the past thirteen years, so I take it as a direct insult for me to deal with a middleman in order to negotiate any type of arrangement, and over the phone at that? Mira, man, listen. That's not the way I do business. Do you understand me? Now, you remind Angel to keep in mind who I am, and that I expect for him to come and see me in person. Tambien? Very good."

It was only after the heated conversation came to an end that Papo noticed Nina standing in the doorway of his private lounge. Nina, however, was in her own little world, now every bit as oblivious to Papo's presence as he was to hers only a few moments ago. She stood in a daze, the words of Papo's argument turning over and over inside her head:

"I've been doing business with this family for a very long time, thirteen years to be exact...I've come through on schedule every week for the past thirteen years..."

Fragments of Papo's conversation bounced around inside Nina's skull, ricocheting here and there until they all gelled together to make sense:
"...Doing business with this family...come through on schedule...every week...thirteen years to be exact... business... Angel..."

Recalling the conversation she'd overheard at the suite when Johnny was arguing over the phone, Nina recognized one familiar name; Angel. Angel was Johnny's cousin and quite possibly played a significant role in the shipments from Main to Elizabeth, New Jersey. And then it suddenly came to her. Yes, he was the slim, pale-skinned Dominican she and North had seen at the warehouse in New Jersey more than once during their stakeouts.

The sound of Papo's voice had abruptly snapped Nina back to the here and now. She found him staring at her with a grave look of concern.

"Nina," he said once more. "Are you all right? You look like you've seen a ghost."

Despite the obvious look of concern, Papo's eyes were sharp and inquisitive. He seemed to be wondering if she'd overheard any parts of his conversation, and if so, what she may have been thinking. It was enough to shake Nina out of her dream-like state and get straight down to business.

"Oh, I'm sorry about that, Papo," she replied with an appeasing, yet sincere apologetic tone. "I was just thinking about the look on my brother's face when I told him that I was done."

"Are you serious? Ta bueno, Mami," Papo said with an admiring smile. "I must admit that I was rather surprised to learn that you have finished so quickly. You are truly a remarkable woman. I look forward to dealing with you from here on out."

"Oh, no, Papo," Nina responded. "After this last flip, I'm finished."

Papo looked at Nina with a puzzled expression.

"Finito?" he asked. "You mean done, as in calling it quits?"

"Si, Papo," she answered with an expression of both relief and regret. "Thanks to you, not only do I have the thirty grand for the two keys that you spotted me, but I also have sixty-thousand more for another four kilos. After that, it's finito."

Papo stared off into nothingness, seeming to ponder Nina's words while slowly rubbing his chain. His eyes now went from Nina to the two duffel bags she'd dragged inside the lounge.

"Ninety-thousand, Papo," she said, hoping to press him on. "I appreciate everything you've done for me, Papo. I really do."

Papo smiled.

"Impressive, Nina," he finally said. "Very impressive."

Then he rose from off his recliner and made his way around to the bar to fix himself a drink.

"You know, Johnny was bragging an awful lot about you long before he introduced us at my place of business," he began. "He'd always been a sucker for a pretty face, so I never paid much attention to him when he talked so much about you. But now, after all of this, I understand what Johnny saw in you from the very beginning. Nina, you are truly one of a kind."

Papo returned to his seat on the recliner chair and then took a small sip of his drink.

"For you to make something of yourself in this lifestyle, and then retire without actually going through something terrible truly warms my heart."

Papo then raised his glass to Nina before taking another sip.

"Mira, Mami," he said with a smile. "Here's to you. I salute you for being smart enough to know when to get out of this life. It is truly amazing to see someone get involved with this business, make a few dollars, and get out without paying some horrible dues. In honor of your tremendous feat, allow me to give you an extra kilo on top of the four that you're buying. Mira, there's no charge; it is a gift from me to you. Congratulations, Mami, it's been an honor."

Despite Papo's overflow of compliments on her success, Nina was enraged at his assumption of her never experiencing anything traumatic. He knew nothing of the guilt she carried over the deaths of both her father and mother, while at the same time being mistreated by every relative she came across because of it. He knew nothing of Nina seeing her fiancee's lifeless body; he knew nothing of the pain, grief and humiliation she suffered while romancing and playing up to the bastard that Nina was sure had smiled and even laughed at the news of her beloved Sadon's murder. Papo had no idea that it was she who not only killed Johnny, but smiled as she squeezed the trigger, and he had no idea that she was planning to relieve him of an entire truckload of pure, uncut cocaine.

No, Nina thought coldly to herself as Papo moved to get the five kilos of cocaine. *You don't know me at all, you fat Dominican bastard. You don't know a damned thing about me.*

After turning the five kilos Nina brought back from Papo into eight, and breaking six of them down into all twenty-dollar vials while selling the other two kilos in weight, Nina and North quickly began monopolizing the drug market at a record speed. No one in the criminal history of Marcy Projects, as well as, a great majority of those in Fort Green, sold anything but their cocaine.

For North, it was all a dream come true. With a squad full of nothing but the most thorough hustlers money could buy, and a huge supply of the best cocaine in the streets, his name was now ringing bells throughout every square inch of the projects and beyond. Topping it all off was the fact that he had the most beautiful woman in the world faithfully by his side. North couldn't be happier and much more content with his life than right now.

Nina, on the other hand, wasn't nearly as content as she showed. Her spirit seemed hardened. Her shrewdness and distrust of everyone except North had only increased with the money they made.

Nina was particularly wary of Rah-Rah, who, with is flashy and flamboyant ways, seemed to be slowly trying to get himself closer and closer to them on a more intimate basis. Rah-Rah was far too ambitious for Nina's liking. Him being like a brother to North called for enough caution as it was. For him to be involved with Nina's one and only friend was just a little too close for comfort.

✦✦✦✦✦✦✦

The sun was now beginning to set on Marcy Projects, bringing to life the unpredictable characters and life-threatening situations common to the streets of New York. This, along with the anticipation of what was sure to transpire a few hours from now, combined to chill Nina straight to the bone. For Nina, tonight was undoubtedly the moment of truth; tonight will be the night in which their destinies will ultimately be made clear.

Nina stood in front of the vanity mirror dressed in a black, hooded sweatshirt with the hood pulled over her head, checking to make sure the sides of her face were properly hidden from view. She had trafficked drugs back and forth a great deal of times. She'd even committed murder, but never before had she robbed anything or anyone at gunpoint, especially a huge tractor-trailer containing something very important to perhaps one of the biggest drug dealers in the New York underworld. Despite everything being planned down to the very last detail, she still felt uneasy.

North was all too familiar with the art of committing armed robbery, and was feeling totally at ease. He may have never pulled a heist on a grand scale such as this, but he was certain that it wouldn't be much different from any other robbery; after all, every victim pretty much reacts the same way when facing the barrel of a gun. A successful robbery for an experienced criminal like North was only a matter of timing, and with Nina masterminding it all, he had all the confidence in the world. It didn't matter much to him whether the tractor-trailer was transporting cocaine or not. After months of restraining from any forms of violence, and concentrating on staking out tractor-trailers and supervising drug sales, he was more than eager for some action.

North sat on the bed fitting a silencer onto his black .38 revolver. Like Nina, he was dressed in a black pair of jeans and a black, hooded sweatshirt. The quiet atmosphere between him and Nina only magnified the anticipation. Satisfied that the gun was now loaded and thoroughly prepared for tonight's event, he rose and approached Nina slowly from behind. With the .38 revolver left on top of the bed and the .25 automatic he'd loaded for Nina still in his hand, North wrapped one arm softly around Nina's neck while aiming the pistol at the mirror, which was directly in front of them. The sight of them together, dressed in all black and set to pull off the heist of a lifetime was enough to bring a smile to both of their faces.

"You ready to get this paper, baby?" North asked before gently kissing the side of Nina's face.

Nina was already warmed by North's mixture of fearlessness, eagerness, and above all, his strong and caring embrace. It was definitely perfect timing. With a renewed sense of confidence and appreciation for him being there, she reached and placed both of her hands on the arm North held lightly around her neck.

"No doubt!" she replied with a smile before turning and kissing him softly on the lips.

Their treasured moment of intimacy was interrupted by Rah-Rah's sudden emergence into the bedroom. The sight of both Nina and North dressed up in "stick-up" attire was a tremendous shock.

"Oh shit!" he exclaimed while shifting his gaze from the .25 automatic handgun in North's hand to the .38 revolver lying on the bed with the silencer attached to it. "What's poppin', son? I don't give a fuck dawg! Bring me in!"

Nina's urge to shoot Rah-Rah point blank in the face for his intrusion was offset by her anger at North for giving him a key to their apartment in the first place. Rah-Rah had suddenly stumbled upon something that he wasn't supposed to have any prior knowledge of, which was proof that she'd been right to argue against giving him a duplicate key.

After making sure the gun's safety mechanism was secure, North tucked the tiny handgun into the waistband of Nina's jeans, and then turned to face his friend.

"Listen to me, my nigga," he said. "Everything ain't for everybody. Me and Nina 'bout to handle some business real quick, but it's somethin' light, so you know, you could just fall back."

"Somethin' light?" Rah-Rah remarked while staring at North and Nina with complete disbelief. "Y'all dressed up in murder gear and shit with guns all over the place, and you gon' tell me it's somethin' light? Man, get the fuck outta here with that bullshit! What's really good, my nigga?"

"Just hold shit down 'til we get back," North said, this time with a bit more authority. "I'ma holla at you once everything is all said and done, a'ight?"

The cold, penetrating stare of Nina's gaze only verified the seriousness of North's words. Although not liking how he'd been kept in the dark about whatever North and Nina were up to, Rah-Rah complied without bothering to press for information.

"True, true, I feel you," he agreed with a simple purse of the lips. "Holla at me if you need me, my nigga. You heard?"

"I heard, I heard," North answered while tucking the .38 caliber revolver with its silencer attached, down into the waistband of his jeans. "Just make sure you hold shit down out here."

"No doubt, my nigga," Rah-Rah replied with an assuring smile. "No fuckin' doubt."

Nina didn't speak a word. She instead slipped on a pair of black cotton gloves, and then gave North a soft kiss on the lips.

"You ready, Papi?" she asked.

"I was born ready," North replied confidently. "Let's make it happen.

Chapter Eighteen

Neither North nor Nina bothered to utter a word as they drove across the state lines and into Maine; in fact, there wasn't anything left to say in the first place.

North lay reclined in the passenger seat, anxiously awaiting the time for him to put his gun to use. It had been a long, long time since he'd commanded his respect from a stranger by way of his pistol, and he was all too eager to get it started.

Nina too sat behind the steering wheel of her Honda Civic, totally absorbed in the anxiety of what was soon about to transpire. She'd gone over the plan a million times in her mind, each time checking for anything she may have missed or overlooked. To Nina's discomfort, everything seemed too perfect.

Nina and North turned onto the street that led down to Papo's warehouse to find the tractor trailer parked on the side of the road just as they predicted it would be. Nina stopped just a few yards behind the truck.

"Hurry up, Shay," she said when spotting the short, stubby truck driver waddling out of the door of the convenience store with an armful of snacks.

"I'm on it, Ma," said North with a slight pant. "I got this."

With that, North quickly made his exit from the car and hurried toward the driver before he made his way back to the truck. The sky was pitch black, and the road was barely lit. It wasn't until North had approached him with the gun already drawn that the driver noticed him approaching. He froze in his tracks and stared slack-jawed at North while feeling the end of the silencer poking deep into his jelly-like stomach. Seeing that the man was now totally in a world of fear, North spoke quickly and clearly to his soon-to-be hijacking and kidnapping victim.

"A bullet in the gut is the worst way to die, dawg, believe me," he said coolly but forcefully. "If you follow my instructions, you and your buddy will make it through the night. You got three seconds to open the door and get inside; one... two..."

Before North could make it to "three", the driver had already opened the door and scrambled inside the truck. The slim, hook-nosed passenger smiled at the sight of his friend scurrying up and into the seat.

"Damn, buddy," he joked. "What, you missed me or something?"

His sense of humor was cut drastically short when he saw North climb inside behind the fat man with his pistol showing.

"Hey! Hey, man!" he exclaimed with both of his hands raised. "We ain't..."

"Shut the fuck up!" North snapped while at the same time aiming his pistol at the terrified man who was now shrinking at the very sight of the lengthy barrel.

"Okay! Okay!" the man replied forcefully.

North then tossed the man a pair of handcuffs.

"You!" he barked. "Cuff yourself."

Seeing that his instructions had been followed without incident, North then turned his pistol back to the driver who had been sitting quietly in between the two of them.

"You. What's your name?"

"W-W-Walter," the man stammered with dread-filled eyes.

North remained harsh, but his voice became more relaxed and assuring.

This ain't nothin' personal, Walter," he began. "Today just ain't your day. If you do exactly what I tell you to do, everybody'll be happy, and you and your little buddy will be all right. Can I count on you, Walter?"

"S-sure," Walter frightfully replied.

"First things first," North then said. "Let's switch places."

The two men smoothly and easily traded places. Walter was now behind the steering wheel, and North was now in between Walter and his passenger.

"Now, let me see you make a peace sign," North demanded.

The man quickly obeyed.

"Now stick it out the window and wave it up and down."

<hr />

Nina was sitting patiently in her car, constantly glancing back and forth from the truck to her wristwatch over and over again. She had predicted that the hijacking should take no more than three minutes for North to take over and secure the truck before forcing the driver to comply. He was now thirty seconds overdue.

Goddamn, Shayome, she thought nervously to herself. *What the hell is taking you so long?*

It was then that Nina recognized North's signal. She couldn't help but to smile at the sight of the man now sticking his arm out the window of the truck and frantically waving a peace sign in the air. Relief now swam all throughout her body. Nina quickly drove up and around to the front of the truck, and after seeing it slowly beginning to start behind her, she began leading them southbound towards New Jersey.

✦✦✦✦✦✦✦✦

It was just after midnight, as Rah-Rah stood in front of his project building with a group of neighborhood dealers, all of them dutifully selling Nina and North's product. Dressed in the fanciest clothing and the flashiest jewelry, Rah-Rah stood out strikingly from the rest of the crowd. His neck, wrists, fingers and earlobes glistened and sparkled brightly beneath the parking lot street lamps.

Despite the abundance of weed and liquor they'd spent the entire night consuming, not a single member of Rah-Rah's crew failed to notice the black Navigator SUV. With huge tires and sparkling rims that, after driving through more than once, finally came to a stop a few feet away from where everyone was standing.

A small, dark-skinned man with braided hair and tough looking eyes leaned out of the truck's window and called out for Rah-Rah.

"Yo! Yo! Aye, yo, Rah-Rah!" he hollered. "Let me holla at you for a minute, yo!"

Rah-Rah, along with everyone in his entourage, started suspiciously at the man inside the huge, customized truck.

"Yo, who the fuck is that mafucka?" asked someone from Rah-Rah-s crew.

"I don't know," Rah-Rah answered while finishing off the rest of his blunt. "But we about to find out."

With that being said, he tossed what little was left of the blunt down on the concrete and started warily toward the man sitting in the late model Lincoln Navigator. With one hand gripping the door, Rah-Rah climbed on top of the truck's footrest and leaned into the window.

"Yo, you know me, dawg?" he asked.

"Nah," the man answered. "You don't know me either, but I'm here to holla at you about you and your peoples out here cuttin' everybody's throat and shit. You dig what I'm talkin' about?"

Rah-Rah wasn't the least bit surprised at the guest appearance made by rival hustlers who were either trying to get down with the program, or politely asking for him to slow down and take it easy. It was something that came along with success from the drug game, yet and still, Rah-Rah couldn't help but to feel some type of way.

Who the fuck this nigga think he is? Rah-Rah asked himself while staring the stranger up and down.

In the back of his intoxicated mind, he was unsure of why the man had come around, and above all, he didn't fully understand what the man was really trying to say. By now, however, it didn't matter. The stranger was laid back, staring at Rah-Rah with a most menacing glare, and that alone was enough to arouse his anger.

He kept a firm grip on the edge of the door panel so as not to fall while taking a moment to lean backward and suck his teeth.

"Listen, homie," Rah-Rah said smartly. "I ain't tryin' to hear none of that shit you talkin', feel me?"

"Word up?" the man asked, his gaze turning from cool to red-hot.

"Word the fuck up," Rah-Rah snapped back, meeting the man's threatening stare with one of his own. "That shit comes with the game, nigga. So, what's poppin'?"

The man only smiled while turning up the volume to his stereo system; The Notorious B.I.G.'s voice was now sounding at full blast: *"Somebody gots to die/If I go, you got to go/Somebody gots to die/let the gunshots blow..."*

The man's hand quickly and swiftly moved from the knob on the stereo to a crevice in between his car seats. In the blink of an eye, Rah-Rah found himself nearly face-to-face with the barrel of a .357 Smith and Wesson handgun.

"This right here comes with the game too, you bitch ass nigga!" the man shouted, punctuating his statement with six shots at pointblank range.

The first shot struck Rah-Rah high in the chest as he moved to avoid the barrage of bullets from the man's pistol. The second landed square in his chest, knocking him backward, and two more punched into Rah-Rah's midsection as he fell off the truck and onto the street.

Rah-Rah's crew was already keeping a watchful eye on their boss as he seemed to be engaged in a rather heated conversation with the man inside the truck. The shooting was quick and unexpected, catching everyone completely off guard. The gunshots were swift and in rapid succession, the four thunderous roars of the gun barrel simultaneously followed by one brilliant flash after another.

"Oh, shit!" everyone seemed to exclaim at the same time when seeing Rah-Rah absorb the full impact of the stranger's attempt on his life.

The man was even brazen enough to lean outside the window if his truck, aim his pistol and fire two more slugs into Rah-Rah's chest. It took only a short moment for everyone to snap out of the shock of seeing their leader being gunned down in such a cold-hearted and blatant fashion, but their reaction seemed too little, too late.

Everyone pulled out pistols from inside their pants, pockets and boots, and emphatically began squeezing their triggers while giving chase to the truck as it now began to speed off. The sparks from the bullets landing and ricocheting off the truck proved it to be bulletproof, as the driver made his escape.

"Goddamn, man! What the fuck!" the drug dealers cried out or mumbled in frustration on seeing the truck get away unscratched.

Their attention was now focused on Rah-Rah, who appeared in their eyes to have been nothing now but a memory.

※※※※※※

6:30 a.m.

After nearly seven hours of driving from Maine to New Jersey, North and his "traveling companions" had finally arrived at Nina's grandmother's home in Vineland, New Jersey. It was a small house with a larger-than-life three-car garage, which was situated on a twenty-acre plot of wild, unkempt land, and was the perfect place for Nina and North to stash and get rid of a huge tractor-trailer. The fact that Nina's grandmother was away on a church trip made their plans all the more sweeter.

Even if there weren't any drugs to be found inside the tractor-trailer, North would still be satisfied; his long-standing thirst for action had been thoroughly fulfilled.

Word is bond, Nina, he thought to himself with a smile while fidgeting with his pistol, which had been pointed at the driver the entire time they had been on the road. *I love the shit out of you for this, girl.*

The garage was every bit as large as Nina declared it would be. Unfortunately, it proved to be quite difficult for Walter to turn the truck around and back it inside without causing much damage. A great number of branches were snapped off of neighboring trees as they found themselves caught between the trailer and the entrance of the garage.

After nearly a half-hour of careful maneuvering, the tractor-trailer was parked and out of sight. North then tossed Walter a pair of handcuffs.

"Cuff yourself to the steering wheel, dawg," he ordered. "Just relax, it's almost over."

Satisfied to see that both Walter and his partner weren't going anywhere, North exited the truck to meet Nina, who was already at the rear of the trailer. He undid the hatch to the door and opened it with a mighty heave. There was a harsh, thunderous sound as the door rumbled upwards and slid against the ceiling of the trailer. North made his way inside, then grabbed Nina by the hand to pull her inside as well.

The trailer smelt of mildew and sawdust; it was a sickening stench. Scores and scores of cardboard boxes lay stacked together against the walls of the trailer, to the point where there was only a narrow path that was almost too small for North to walk through. He traveled up and down the passage thoroughly inspecting the boxes, which were all marked "Fragile" on the sides. To both Nina and North's surprise, each package was much lighter than they'd expected.

Please, God, Nina silently prayed. *Let this be the shipment Papo was talking about, please!*

She opened one of the boxes to find it filled mostly with Styrofoam. Beneath all its protective cushioning was a statue of a Spanish saint known as Lasado. Nina found herself slowly beginning to feel disheartened by her seemingly fruitless discovery.

Oh, God, no! She thought dejectedly.

She could feel her eyes begin to tear while checking another package. Meanwhile, North was rummaging through the packages with just as much intensity as Nina. He fondled, twisted and turned every statue, thinking that he may have to break one of them to see if there was anything hidden inside.

What the fuck! He thought to himself while pulling the bag all the way out of the figurine.

The package was hidden beneath several layers of plastic wrapping; only the label with "5-K" written on it gave hint to what may lie inside.

Oh Shit! North was now screaming to himself while tearing away at the plastic. *I know this ain't five keys!*

With an overwhelming sense of joy, North was now holding a huge quantity of plastic wrapped powder in both of his hands.

Five keys! Five Keys! His mind exclaimed. *This is five motherfuckin' keys!*

He looked over at Nina to find that she too was just now discovering the statues' hidden contents. Unlike North, who was fighting to show just how happy he was to learn that they'd just hit a once in a lifetime jackpot, Nina stood in front of the package with her hands clasped up to her mouth, mumbling, "I knew it!" over and over again.

North took Nina's face into his hand and began to kiss her full in the mouth. Nina was taken completely by surprise.

"M-m-ph," was all she could manage to say while accepting North's tongue.

"Look around us, baby," he said. "I'll bet there's coke in every last one of these boxes!"

North tightened his embrace around Nina and kissed her once more.

"I'm gon' have to start callin' ya ass the Queen of New York, Ma! Word is bond, you... You made it happen! You made all this shit happen!"

"Easy, Papi," Nina replied while at the same time releasing herself from North's loving caress. "Don't call me the Queen of New York yet. It ain't over 'til it's over. Come on, Shayome. We gotta hurry."

North ran through each and every box with the speed of Superman, ripping the Styrofoam away from each statue and removing the product inside before tossing it over to Nina, who, in turn, stacked it in a pile on the floor of the garage. After nearly an hour of intense hustling and bustling, the task was completed. The entire inside of the truck's cargo trailer was a total mess. Empty boxes and torn bits of plastic and Styrofoam was all that remained of the merchandise; the floor panels were littered with the remnants of the statues that were smashed and broken apart in the process.

With the coming and going of the early morning hours, the sky had gone from jet black to dark lavender, and was now slowly beginning to brighten with morning sun. Struck with a newfound sense of urgency, North got back into the front of the truck and uncuffed the driver.

"You've been a good dude so far, Walter," North said. "Just one more stop, and everybody'll be home free. Start the truck and follow that little Honda down the road."

Walter did as he was instructed. He followed Nina's car a little more than five miles down the road where the path was now beginning to grow dense with weeds, trees and a thick volley of underbrush. The volume of plant growth increased as they continued to drive further down the trail, and soon, when it became clear that they'd be unable to press on any further, Nina stopped and clicked on the car's hazard lights.

The driver and his companion instantly became afraid.

"Hey, hey man!" Walter said fearfully. "You said…"

Poof! Poof! Poof!

Blood sprayed and splattered against the window of the truck as all three of North's hollow point bullets ripped into Walter's head and face. North could have sworn that he'd heard Walter sigh one last breath of life as he slumped backward against the corner of the truck seat, dying with his eyes still open in surprise.

Walter's companion remained quiet, staring at North with horrified eyes. Not wanting to crawl over Walter's bloodied corpse to exit the truck. North opted to go the other way.

"You don't wanna end up like that over there, do you?" North asked referring to Walter.

Still too terrified to speak, the man could only shook his head "no".
"Alright," North remarked. "Then act right while I make my way across you and get out of here."

After crawling over the man, North remained on the stepladder. The sight of the silencer being aimed at the man's face was more than enough inspiration for him to utter what would soon be his last words.

"Wait a minute, man!" He cried out. "You said…"

Poof! Poof!

His head tilted upward from the first shot; the second knocked him backward. North reached into the truck and made sure the last bullet made it directly into the man's brain.

Poof!

With the one more squeeze of the trigger, it was all over.

North stared at the two bodies with a strange combination of both sympathy and guilt. He'd never killed a man that didn't deserve it, and although these two men hadn't done or said anything disrespectful to him, they were, however, in his way. As hard as he tried to see the two dead men as potential witnesses rather than unwitting victims of the drug game, it just didn't seem to work.

Damn, he thought sadly to himself. *I wish it ain't have to go down like this, but hey, man, fuck it!*

Nina sat inside her car, watching North through her rearview mirror as he handled his business with the truck driver and his companion. She wondered what was running through his mind as she watched him hop off the stepladder and take a moment to stare at the men he'd just killed, before slamming the door shut and starting towards the car.

What the hell is on his mind? Nina thought to herself. *I know Shayome's not gonna crack up on me now.*

North entered the car feeling as cold as the mid-January air.

"You alright, Shayome?" Nina asked with concern.

North took a moment to let loose a deep breath. "Yeah, I'm good," he finally answered. "You know what it is, Ma."

Nina's face went tight, her eyes growing sharp with apprehension.

"Shayome," she began. "Don't start…"

"Man, listen," North interrupted with a smile. "I told you, I'm good, girl. We done came up a thousand fuckin' keys, you know I'm good. Don't get it fucked up neither. Every queen needs a king. So let's get it poppin'!"

Recognizing, the all too familiar glint in North's eyes, made Nina almost sigh with relief. Happy to see the cold-blooded, murderous personality she had now fallen so deeply in love with, Nina could only smile while starting the car.

11:00 a.m.

Weary from a long night of robbery and murder, Nina and North pulled into the parking lot of Marcy Projects with every intention of getting a full day's rest. They walked with their arms closely around each other's waist, as all loving couples do, up to Rah-Rah, who was sitting by himself on a milk crate in front of the project building.

It was only getting up close to him that North realized just how wrong things felt in the neighborhood. Rah-Rah- stood up as North and Nina approached.

"What's good, my nigga?" North asked when noticing his bullet-riddled sweatshirt.

Nina released her grip on North as he moved in closer to further inspect Rah-Rah's beige, Gucci sweater.

"Damn, dawg!" he snapped. "Where the fuck everybody at? What the fuck done happened out here, nigga?"

Rah-Rah took one more sip of his bottle of Hennessy before setting it on the ground, and then used both of his hands to pull what remained of his sweater up to his chin. The bulletproof vest he was wearing beneath his clothing was still holding the six rounds from the barrel of the would be assassin's pistol.

"What the fuck!" North raged.

"Yeah!" Rah-Rah remarked while pulling down his sweater. "Bitch-ass nigga tried to take me off the planet and shit."

North stared at Rah-Rah's sweater with eyes that were reddened more so with anger than the lack of a full night's sleep.

"Who the fuck did this, son?" he asked.

"I don't even know, man." Rah-Rah answered while stooping down to retrieve his bottle of cognac from off the ground. "This nigga came through in a black, bulletproof Navigator talkin' about me and you is cuttin' his throat, then he just started dumpin' and shit."

"Just like that?" North asked.

"Just like that," Rah-Rah confirmed. "I think it's them niggas from Fort Green and shit."

North immediately agreed.

"Man, word is bond!" he exclaimed. "Go put on another vest, dawg. I'm 'bout to go break out the suitcase, my nigga. Fuck it! We just take these pussies to war!"

North was beside himself with anger, and Nina moved quickly to remedy the situation.

"Calm down, Papi," she said while wrapping herself around North and kissing him softly on the side of his mouth. Seeing that North's temper was now slowly beginning to subside, she now focused her attention on Rah-Rah, who was getting more and more drunk with each guzzle of cognac.

"Look, Rah-Rah," she began. "You said that you really don't know this guy, that nobody knew him, right?"

Not knowing where Nina was going with her line of questioning, Rah-Rah flashed a look of suspicion while nodding in agreement.

"Yeah," he answered. "So, what you tryin' to say?"

"Look," she began. "Unless you see him again or somethin' like that, then just fall back and charge it to the game. We can't stand a war right now. Fall back and let it ride. If you do me this one favor, Rah-Rah, I promise you that we'll be rich real soon."

Rah-Rah couldn't believe his ears; even North found a hard time accepting what Nina had just proposed.

"Fall back and let it ride?" Rah-Rah asked with a combination of anger and amazement. "Charge it to the game?"

He pulled up his sweater once more, showing Nina the six slugs embedded into his bulletproof vest.

"You want me to charge this right here to the game?" he said this time with more anger. "What the fuck is you talkin' 'bout, Nina? Do you really think I'm gon' let niggas live after tryin' to pull some shit like this?"

Choosing any course of action other than retaliation, for Rah-Rah, was unheard of. There was no way in his mind that he could ever see himself not avenging an attempt on his life. Nina, however, had other plans.

"I know how hard it is for you to let this go, Rah-Rah. Trust me. I know," Nina began. "If you do me this one favor, then I promise you that I'll give you a half a million dollars in cash for every one of those bullets in your vest."

Again, Rah-Rah couldn't believe his ears. He took a moment to count the slugs lodged into his vest as if he hadn't done it a million times already.

"One…two…three…four…five…six," he counted out loud. "That's six bullets, Nina."

"No!" she replied sharply. "That's three million dollars."

Three million dollars. The very thought of possessing such a large amount of money was nearly enough to short-circuit Rah-Rah's brain.

"Word is bond?" he asked, turning his question to North, who'd been silent during the entire conversation. "Holla at me, son. What's really good?"

"What?" Nina asked with an almost offended tone of voice. "Since when have I ever steered you wrong, Rah-Rah? Oh, now you need verification, huh?"

Nina's face was hard, her eyes as tough and as glinted as the shine of a chrome-colored pistol. North's face was just as serious, which proved to be all the verification Rah-Rah needed.

"Nah, nah, Nina," he replied while scratching through his now ragged box braids. "It's all good. But, what's the deal? Holla at me."

"You'll see in due time," Nina answered. "But what's left off that pack though?"

"About half a key," Rah-Rah replied, never quite liking it whenever Nina asserted authority in such an aggressive fashion.

"Check it out," she began. "It's all over and done with, we gonna shut shit down for a minute, so keep only eight of your thoroughest soldiers and just split the rest of the key between y'all. Get rid of everyone else, Rah; tell 'em it's a wrap -- that we're done. Then fall back."

Nina could tell from the look in Rah-Rah's eyes that he wasn't too fond of leaving the streets alone, especially after almost being killed by one of his many rivals.

"Remember what I said Rah-Rah," Nina said to reinforce the need for him to keep cool. "Five-hundred G's for each bullet. That's three-million dollars."

With that, she turned and gave North a pop kiss on the lips before telling him that she'd meet him upstairs, then left him alone with Rah-Rah, who was still a bit hypnotized by Nina's multimillion dollar proposal. North tapped him on the shoulder while at the same time freeing him of his grip on the bottle of Hennessy.

"What's poppin', my nigga?" North asked as he took a sip of the cognac. "You alright?"

"Yeah," Rah-Rah said, snapping out of his daze. "Yo, what type of shit your girl on? She's over here acting like she's the Queen of New York and shit. Yo, man. What the fuck did y'all do last night? Y'all talkin' like shit is sweet."

North fought not to smile while replaying some of Rah-Rah's words in his head.

She's over here actin' like she's the Queen of New York.

Keeping in mind that he referred to her as being, the Queen of New York, just a few hours ago, absolutely convinced North that it was indeed a fitting title for his lady.

"Dawg, all you need to know is that you about to get a half a mill for each bullet," said North to a still dazed Rah-Rah. "You rich, my nigga! But, yo. Nina's right. Fuck dude. Let's just concentrate on that half a key. Still bring like eight niggas together, but fuck all that splittin' shit up with them. We gon' need some more silencers and shit like that. You with me, dawg?"

"Hell, yeah!" Rah-Rah answered. "Shit, I can handle that. I've been dying to get shit poppin, my nigga. Word up!"

Chapter Nineteen

After almost three months of staying away from the streets, both Nina and North agreed that it was finally time to begin their mission to sell one-thousand kilos of cocaine as fast as they possibly could. They picked the Hyatt Hotel, in New Brunswick, New Jersey to set up shop, where they rented a luxurious suite on the sixteenth floor to be their temporary place of residence.

Nina orchestrated how business was to be conducted: two additional rooms would be rented under an alias; one of which would be located down the hall and used to monitor the main suite where she and North planned to meet their customers. The other room, whose sole purpose was to be used as none other than a place to package and house the product, was located on the tenth floor.

The order of operation was somewhat complex, yet remarkably simple:

The living room in the suite where North and Nina lived and conducted business would be fitted with surveillance cameras, and would enable their armed street soldiers down the hall to keep a close eye on all transactions. Inside this room were four members of Rah-Rah's personal team, all of them armed to the teeth with state-of-the-art handguns with silencers to match.

The room on the tenth floor was set to hold no less than one hundred kilos at a time, and was guarded by two armed street soldiers at all times.

Lastly, there were two more members of Rah-Rah's crew who remained posted at different parts of the hotel's lobby and sports bar. Their jobs were to simply keep an eye out for any suspicious activity.

Everyone was to maintain contact with each other by radio, and as time would go by, nobody would be able to feel as if they weren't eating.

In a mere matter of months, Nina and North had sold a little more than nine-hundred kilos. Although they agreed to break their product down to halves and quarter keys to appease their customers, it didn't matter; with kilos of pure, uncut cocaine selling at fifteen-thousand dollars apiece, business couldn't have gotten any better than it already was.

٭٭٭٭٭٭٭

The suite on the sixteenth floor was extravagant. While relaxed on the huge, cushiony sofa, North still couldn't help but to marvel at how luxurious the room was. While sipping a glass of Remy Martin, he sat with his legs crossed at the ankles, watching a Black Panther documentary on a huge screen television set, which was fitted inside a larger than life entertainment center. The beige colored carpet was plush and matched well with the walls, whose colors were brightened by the sunlight beaming brightly through the glass doors of the outer balcony.

North's interest in the struggles of Huey P. Newton and Bobby Seal was interrupted by a knock at the door of his room. He took a moment to finish his drink, and then rose to his feet before Nina yelled out for him to answer the door.

"That's him, Pa," North heard Nina say from inside the bathroom.

North tightened the ends of the quilted bathrobe he was wearing before opening the double doors to his room.

"Jamil!" he said with a smile. "What's good, my nigga?"

The two shook hands and half-embraced one another.

"Yo, man," Jamil replied while taking a step back to give North a glimpse of his pinstriped designer suit. "Same ol' shit; you know how it is."

"What the fuck you got on, my nigga, Armani?" North asked. "I see you got on some real classy shit."

Jamil took a moment to break away from his stone-faced, no nonsense expression to flash a bright, gold toothed smile.

"Don't get it fucked up, though," he said while beginning to unbutton his jacket to display the bulletproof vest and two holstered pistols. "A nigga always gon' keep it gangsta – even down to the socks!" Meaning to punctuate his statement, Jamil raised the legs of his pants to reveal a handgun holstered on both of his ankles. He then made a slow three-sixty spin before stopping to strike a pose. "Do you feel me, my nigga?" he asked.

It was Nina and not North, who answered Jamil's question.

"Boy, you know you look good!" she replied while entering the living room wearing a bathrobe that was identical to the one North had on. It was the sight of the briefcase, and not Nina's presence that snapped Jamil out of his playfulness. He quickly re-buttoned his suit jacket before leaning in to kiss Nina softly on the cheek.

Killing people had long been a lucrative business, and for Jamil, someone who'd always had a special gift for committing murder, he found himself doing Sadon the favor of killing Rock a little more than a year ago. In fact, Jamil was now a professional killer. The tailor-made and top of the line wardrobe he wore was only a small display of the wealth he'd accumulated from the dozen or so murders he'd been paid to commit.

Jamil's precise and efficient work had practically made him a household name amongst big time drug dealers, ranging from Florida all the way to New York, and that, among other things, is what made him such a valuable commodity to North and Nina's endeavors. He was connected to a great variety of major drug dealers who'd kill to score a deal involving kilos of prime cocaine for fifteen-thousand dollars apiece.

The problem was, however, that Jamil wasn't the least bit interested in the business of drug dealing; in fact, he more or less despised it. Citing the open door for betrayal on either end of the game, not to mention the innocent victims, Jamil opted to keep his hands clean of that particular line of work. Besides, murder for hire was faster money. He was more effective with it, and above all, he thoroughly enjoyed it. Jamil's love for Sadon was the only reason why he'd even bothered to give Nina and North's plan a chance. With the going rate of a Kilo being twenty-five thousand dollars, it would be no problem at all for him to help move the product.

Knowing how passionate Jamil was about his decision not to involve himself with drug dealing, both Nina and North agreed that it was only right that they'd accommodate their fickle friend and break a cardinal rule by having the merchandise waiting for him when he arrived. It was more or less a compromise of principles on both Jamil and Nina's behalf.

North clicked on a Tupac CD by remote control as Nina popped open a bottle of Crystal and filled three champagne glasses, after placing a briefcase on top of the dining room table. Jamil pulled out a blunt from his inside pocket that he had already rolled, and set fire to the end of it.

"I guess you got somethin' for me," he remarked indifferently.

She clicked open the briefcase to show Jamil the five kilos of cocaine neatly wrapped in plastic.

"Just for the sake of formalities," Jamil said after exhaling a stream of smoke, "Let's run this down the line one more time. I'm gon' make sure my man down in V.A. gets this little package, and then get him to spread the word. That's it, right? Oh, yeah, and nobody from New York."

"That's the plan, my nigga," North replied.

"No problem," Jamil said with an expression that could easily pass for either a smirk or a strained grin.

Nina closed the briefcase and smiled.

"Thank you so much, Jamil," she said while giving him a tight, heartfelt hug. "We owe you one, for real."

Jamil passed North the blunt and downed his glass of champagne.

"You don't owe me shit," he replied. "I loved Sadon too."

Hearing what Jamil had just said moved North to grab Nina and hold her tight. Nina felt her own eyes begin to well up and leak with moisture. No one bothered to say a word and fell silent. The sounds of Tupac sorrowfully rapping about one of his dead homeboys was the only thing to be heard in the entire room. Never one for sentimental moments, Jamil was the first to break the mood.

"Well, listen, man," he said while snatching the briefcase from the dining room table. "Call me if you need me, and I don't mean for no drug shit neither."

Nina and North matched Jamil's close-mouthed grin with a solemn smile of their own.

"Thank you so much," Nina said earnestly. "We'll be in touch."

Forever the gangster type, Jamil answered with a simple nod of his head and purse of the lips. With that, he turned and started out of the hotel suite.

⚜⚜⚜⚜

Jamil made good on his promise, and soon thereafter, Nina's plan was meeting great success. There were big-time drug dealers coming from as far as Texas and Minnesota to take full advantage of Nina and North's too-good-to-be-true deal of a kilo of cocaine for fifteen-thousand dollars. Some were regular customers, buying sometimes ten to fifteen kilos, while there were some who'd sometimes by a hundred kilos all at once.

Vincent Caltorre and his short, pudgy partner, Anthony, were perhaps two of North's favorite customers. They were both members of a South Jersey Mafia outfit, who, despite their boss order not to bother with narcotics, were sneaking behind his back and buying three to four kilos a week. They were a well-dressed and charming duo that got along easily with both Rah-Rah and North.

After a month or so, Rah-Rah and North were getting along with the Italian mob members to the point where their business acquaintance now seemed more of a genuine friendship. Vincent and Anthony would often bring along homemade Italian food and play video games, while promising to show North and Rah-Rah the time of their lives if, by chance, they ever bothered to travel further down south of Jersey.

Although Nina enjoyed their company just as much as North and Rah-Rah, she was all too familiar with the need to keep business separate from pleasure. The fact that these boundaries were now becoming blurred while at the same time dealing with Mafiosos was a disturbing concept, and she didn't like it one bit.

▞▞▞▞▞▞▞

After a feverishly busy day, as all Fridays usually were, North, Rah-Rah and Nina were now enjoying a clam and peaceful evening. With the five grams of exotic weed almost gone, they all sat watching a kung-fu movie on the huge screen television set. North sat in the middle of the couch wearing nothing but a pair of boxer shorts, as Nina, dressed in nothing but a knee-length T-shirt, lay curled up in fetal position with her head resting on his lap. Rah-Rah sat on the far end of the couch dressed in a tank top, denim shorts and a pair of suede Timberland boots.

The sound of an electronic voice interrupted everyone's enjoyment of the blunt they'd been smoking together. Nina stirred as North reached down by his side to grab the walkie-talkie.

"What's good?" he asked.

"Mario and Luigi," the voice replied laughingly.

North smiled.

"All right, cool," he finally replied.

A few minutes had passed before there was a knock at the door. Nina arose and allowed North to get up and answer the door. Rah-Rah immediately began rolling another blunt. Both Vincent and Anthony entered the suite carrying a duffel bag in their hands. Nina remained on the couch with her legs curled beneath her, watching as Anthony glanced around while his partner shook hands with North. She then watched as Vincent too began looking around as Anthony greeted North in the same fashion.

Fucking guineas, Nina thought suspiciously to herself. *Those motherfuckers are always scheming.*

She answered their greetings with a simple nod and then returned her attention back to the kung-fu movie.

"Oh, shit!" Anthony exclaimed while taking a seat on the sofa next to Nina. "What the fuck is this? *The Five Deadly Venoms*? I love this fucking movie!"

"Christ," Vincent remarked. "Anthony's such a fuckin' kid."

He then placed both his and Anthony's duffel bags on top of the living room table.

"Here's a hundred and fifty G's," Vincent said with his patented smile. "We're gonna need ten kilos this time around."

"Oh, shit!" Rah-Rah said after lighting his blunt. "It's about fuckin' time!"

Vincent only smiled at Rah-Rah's remark.

"Word up," North added. "I love to see niggas come up in the game. That's what the fuck I'm talkin' about!"

Vincent then unzipped both of the bags, showing stacks and stacks of one-hundred dollar bills wrapped in rubberbands.

"Let's get it poppin'!" he said, playfully imitating North and Rah-Rah's slang.

"No doubt, no doubt," North replied as he switched frequencies on his walkie-talkie and began placing the order.

"Yo, Flex," he said. "Yo, you hear me?"

"What's good?" the voice asked.

"Bring me ten," North said.

"Christ, my feet are killin' me!" Vincent complained. "Let's take a seat in the living room until it comes. Besides, I got some killer weed you need to try."

North only smiled while leading the way to the couch.

***

The weed was every bit as potent as Vincent promised it would be. His and Anthony's usually chatty behavior, however, had proven to be a serious speed bump on North, Nina and Rah-Rah's road to getting high. Rah-Rah had just finished rolling another blunt when the runner arrived with a gym bag containing the ten kilos of cocaine North had ordered close to ten minutes ago. He placed it on the table and left without bothering to utter a single word.

Upon the runner's departure, both Vincent and Anthony immediately sprang into action. It was a sudden series of movements that caught everyone by surprise. Nina flinched and instinctively grabbed for North, as the two Italians jumped off the couch. Anthony pulled two nine-millimeter handguns with silencers attached, from inside his leather jacket, and kept North, Nina and Rah-Rah at bay as Vincent, with his .45 Magnum drawn, started over to the table.

North stared comically at the two would-be robbers now aiming their pistols at him. Rah-Rah only giggled as he continued to smoke his blunt.

"You can't be serious," North said humorously. "Y'all mafuckas jokin', right?"

The most light-hearted of the duo, Anthony, couldn't help but to break into a smile.

"Listen, North," he said. "Don't take this personal, man. I really like you guys, but don't make me hurt you. Where's the rest of the money?"

"Rest of the money?" North remarked almost confusingly while accepting the blunt from Rah-Rah. "The rest of what money?"

"Don't play no fucking games with us, North!" Vincent barked from across the room. "We've spent more than a hundred grand with you ourselves. I want that money and everybody else's. I know you keep it somewhere around here, and I want it now!"

Unbeknownst to Vincent and Anthony, a team of killers would soon be on their way to put an end to this situation. Rah-Rah and North were staring at the two men who were as good as dead, and they found it hilarious. Nina, on the other hand, wasn't the least bit amused. Rah-Rah's team was only a few doors down the hall, and it seemed to Nina that they were moving entirely too slow. Things were becoming incredibly antsy.

Suddenly, at that very moment, both Rah and North burst out with laughter.

"Yo-o-o!" North cried. "Y'all white boys is crazy as hell!"

Vincent and Anthony looked at each other with bewilderment, and then turned their attention back to North and Rah-Rah.

Vincent had had enough. He was only a heartbeat away from killing everyone inside the room.

"I'm gonna ask you black motherfuckers one more time; where's the fucking…"

Vincent's final demand for the money was interrupted by a flurry of movement that burst through the double doors of the suite at lightening speed.

Poof!

The entire front of Vincent's forehead exploded from the nine-millimeter bullet that ripped into the back of his skull.

Anthony turned around just in time to meet a brilliant flash of light from the muzzle of a silencer.

Poof!

Blood and bone matter exploded from the back of his head as he twisted halfway around and collapsed onto the ground with the two nine-millimeter handguns still in his grasp.

Glad to see the thousands of dollars spent on silencers and target practice for his crew had paid off, Rah-Rah only smiled while finishing the rest of his blunt.

"Shit! Shit!" Nina exclaimed. "Somebody hurry up and close the door!"

North drew himself a cigarette before rising from the couch. His eyes were bloodshot red, more so from anger than the weed he'd been smoking.

"What the fuck took y'all niggas so long to get here?" he barked.

North was only a second away from going ballistic, and everyone knew it. Slim, one of the two men who had just burst inside the suite and helped kill the treacherous Italians, was suddenly wishing that he had left to close the door, instead of his partner. At least then he'd be a safe distance away from North's potentially unforgiving temper.

"Man, you and Rah-Rah was laughing so hard that we ain't know if y'all niggas was for real or not."

"Word up," said his partner. "Y'all was laughin' like shit was a joke."

North's heated line of questioning was interrupted by Nina's frantic pacing back and forth.

"Alright, alright, listen. We have to be cool, y'all. Now ain't the time to go crazy," she said before pointing at Slim and his partner. "Get rid of those bodies, NOW!"

She then turned to Rah-Rah.

"Rah-Rah, we have to get these cameras out of here – down in the other room too," she said. "We gotta shut this operation down and strip it clean."

The flurry of activity had come to an immediate halt when hearing Nina's final command.

"Shayome, Papi, get rid of the rest of the coke," she said.

"And when I say 'get rid of it', Shayome, I mean get rid of it. Don't give it to nobody! Throw all of that shit away."

Everyone, including North, stopped to look at Nina as if she'd gone insane.

"Get rid of it? You mean like throw it all in the garbage or somethin'?" he asked.

"Nina, Ma, that's eighty-two keys of coke that you talkin' about. We might as well give it to Rah-Rah."

Placing eighty-two kilos of high-quality cocaine in Rah-Rah's hands, especially after they've just been tainted with the death of what they had previously described themselves as "made men", was the last thing Nina wanted to do. When it came to murder or the disappearance of one of their own, the Mafia proved to be every bit as persistent and as vindictive as the Feds, and Rah-Rah selling a kilo to the wrong person could put both organizations hot on their tails. Rah-Rah was just as fool-hearted as he was courageous and ambitious. And that, along with the reality of him or any other man for that matter, cooperating with the enemy to ensure his own survival, was a very likely possibility. It was a risk that Nina was definitely not willing to take.

"Rah-Rah, listen," she said when noticing the whirlwind of emotions now swirling about his eyes. "I got genuine love for you, you know that. I'm just saying that we need to cover our tracks. We've all made a lot of money, but now it's over. It's time to walk away from this before it catches up to us."

Then she turned to North.

"Papi, you know I'm doing the right thing," she began.

"We've made more than ten-million dollars. We…"

"Word is bond, North? That's how y'all doin' it?" Rah-Rah asked with his gun now pressed against North's temple. "How the fuck y'all gon' play me like that?"

"After all the shit we done been through, and you gon' go out on some sucka shit like this!" North said with his anger steadily building. "We supposed to be family! Nigga, we made you rich!"

Rah-Rah's eyes glistened with just as much range as North's. He licked his lips while adjusting the grip on the pistol, which was now aimed directly at North's forehead.

"Man, I ain't trying to hear that family shit, nigga!" he snapped angrily. "Your bitch is over there talking some bullshit, and you riding with her. Man, I ain't go through all of this bullshit just for her to close shit down just cause she scared. Man, fuck that! Fuck her and fuck you too, nigga!"

North's heart sank when finally hearing how Rah-Rah truly felt. Nina had warned him long ago to keep Rah-Rah on a short leash; she warned him that he'd never, ever be satisfied. To Rah-Rah, it wasn't just about the money; it was the power as well. His resentment for always being second-in-command had finally come to the surface.

Seeing Nina sneak and grab a pistol from one of the Italians lying dead on the floor left North struck with a strange sense of déjà vu. It seemed just a day or so ago, and not four years ago, that he was just facing J.T. in front of their project building in Marcy, watching as Sadon crept from behind with a brick in his hand.

"Rah-Rah," North said softly. "Listen dawg, you rich, You ain't gotta…"

"Yeah, whatever," Rah-Rah interrupted. "Get on that radio and call down to Flex. Tell him to bring the rest of that coke, and the money too."

"Rah-Rah, man…" North tried again.

"I ain't gon' tell you again, nigga," he said while cocking back the hammer of his pistol. "I'm gon' give you one last chance. Get on that fuckin' walkie-talkie and…
"
Poof! Poof!

The first shot to the side of Rah-Rah's head turned him halfway around. The second slug snapped his head backward as he began to collapse.

Poof!

Another slug ripped through his now lifeless body as it toppled down onto the carpet. He now lay dead with his eyes open, a great portion of his head and face bloodied and torn apart from the strength of Anthony's hollow-point slugs.

Nina stood above Rah-Rah's body with the pistol still trained at his face.

"You motherfucker!" she screamed.

Poof!

"You no good snake motherfucker!"

Poof! Poof! Poof!

"I hate you! I fucking hate you!"

Poof! Poof! Poof!

"Die, you snake motherfucker, die!"

Nina's eyes streamed with tears as she continued squeezing the trigger.

Click-click-click!

Seeing that the pistol was empty of all its rounds, Nina tossed it to the floor and began stomping her bare heels into what little was left of Rah-Rah's face.

North could only stare in shock as Nina went crazy on the lifeless corpse.

Oh, Shit! He thought to himself. *She's blackin' the fuck out! Baby girl is straight up losin' it!*

After a moment or two of allowing Nina to finish venting her frustrations, North wrapped his arms around her and then scooped her high into the air.

"It's alright, mommy," he whispered. "It's okay. Everything is cool. It's all over with."

Still unsure as to how Nina would react after letting her loose, North set her down on the ground, but maintained his grip on her body, which was still trembling with emotion.

"It's over, Ma," he whispered into her ear once more. "You okay?"

With her eyes still fixed on Rah-Rah's body, she slowly nodded 'yes'. Upon being released, she immediately turned and wrapped North tightly in her arms.

"I wasn't gonna lose you to that no good, snake motherfucker," she said. "You're all I have left. I won't let you go like that, Papi. Never!"

With that, Nina broke down and began to cry on North's bare chest. Of all the death and betrayal that had taken place, Nina's affection for North was clearly the most memorable event.

North struggled not to get teary-eyed while holding her tightly in his arms.

"Well, what the fuck is y'all niggas waitin' for?" he barked at Slim and his partner, who stood enrapt by what Nina had just said and done. "We ain't got all night! Start cleanin' up these mafuckin' bodies!"

Chapter Twenty

Although it had been close to four months since Nina and North had last seen Marcy Projects, it felt more like almost a million years as they parked in the parking lot. For North, it was almost as if he was coming home from Nap Nap State Penitentiary all over again. If it weren't for the circumstances, he surely would have spent a little more time in the 'hood where he first began his career as a nickel and dime drug dealer. There were so many memories, some of them good, some of them bad; all of them combining to revitalize his love for Marcy Projects, and inklings of regret for having to leave in such a hurry were now beginning to surface.

Not much had changed since leaving Marcy Projects. There were a few new faces mixed in amongst the crowd of drug dealers gathered in front of the building, but North's name and reputation had yet to be forgotten. The crowd departed like the Red Sea as he and Nina made their way to the front entrance. It was as if they were royalty. These were the moments that, as an up and coming hustler, North dreamed of experiencing. It made him wish all the more that he was returning home for good instead of stopping through to help Nina retrieve a few of her things.

The rent had been paid six months in advance, which left Maria with a little more than two months of "playing house" before having to rejoin the real world of doing whatever she had done to make a living before. Since becoming seriously involved with Rah-Rah, Maria had long ago quit working in order to fully enjoy the lavish lifestyle he was providing her. Nina had often warned her not to be so dependent on a man, but she would hear none of it. With Rah-Rah now dead and gone, Nina hoped that Maria was smart enough to have stashed away a nice amount of cash for a rainy day, but it was highly unlikely. Much to Nina's disapproval, Maria was always the spend-happy type.

The fight to try and figure out how to talk to Maria about the need to move on no longer existed as Nina entered her apartment.

"Oh, my God!" she screamed out loud at the sight of Maria's murdered body. "No-o-o-! Oh, my god, no!"

Maria lay sprawled on the couch with a telephone cord wrapped tightly around her neck and two bullet holes in her forehead. She had died with her eyes open, and the expression on her face was a mixture of both fear and struggle. Nina rushed to her side and began fumbling with the cord around her neck.

North remained a short distance away, observing the gruesome murder scene with a careful eye. There was no doubt in his mind that Maria had suffered terribly on her way out. The blood from the back of her head, which was splattered all over the end of the living room couch, was still fresh. It had yet to soak into the couch's fabric and begin to harden into the sickening crust that North was sure he'd been responsible for leaving on crime scenes countless times in the past. It was enough to start a small panic inside his being.

"The blood's still fresh," he said. "This shit just happened. Come on, Ma. We gotta get out of here before the cops come."

Nina was still apologizing to Maria's dead body while struggling to loosen the telephone cord from around her best friend's neck. She only heard the latter half of North's statement.

"What?" she asked. "What do you mean we gotta get out of here before the cops come? We can't just up and leave like that. We have to call the cops ourselves and tell them what we found."

North stared at Nina as if she'd lost her mind.

"What?" he remarked. "Call the cops? Nina, are you fuckin' crazy! We…"

"We can't just leave like that," Nina interrupted. "The apartment is in my name, which means they'll come looking for me, Shayome. Alibis aren't hard to come by when you can afford good lawyers and witnesses to match. There's no need for us to make things more complicated than they already are."

Although seeing where Nina was coming from, still North didn't bother to respond. He was all too preoccupied with trying to make sense of everything that had just happened. Just as he'd silently come to his own conclusion, Nina spoke to verify what he was already thinking.

"Papo!" she muttered out loud while dialing 9-1-1 on her cell phone. "Papo's behind this. He somehow found out that I was behind his truck being hijacked, among other things, and sent his goons here to get me. Maria was just at the wrong place at the wrong time."

The thought of her best friend being killed for something she had no part of made Nina weak with guilt.

"Damn, Maria!" she cried out while gripping the edge of the dining room table for support. "I'm so sorry!"

After being consoled by North's loving embrace and encouragement to be strong, Nina regained her composure and had once again tried dialing for the police. North too began dialing a number on his cell phone. He wasn't about to give Papo another chance to have them murdered, and decided to beat the vengeful Dominican drug dealer at his own game of revenge.

※※※※※

Little to Nina's knowledge, she was only half-right. It took Papo almost no time at all to do some investigating of his own to find that Nina was far from the honorable, standup Latin princess he thought she was. In fact, Nina was a traitor to her own kind for conspiring with the blacks to damage his business.

She'd killed Johnny and two of his couriers, one of which was a distant relative of Papo's, while at the same time, robbing him of a thousand kilos. The most unforgiving sin of all was that Papo himself had been deceived. One thousand kilos of raw cocaine was now being distributed all across the country at the expense of him being blind to her treachery. Papo was made a fool of in the eyes of his peers, and he was determined to make her pay. Not only was he bent on making Nina pay, but everyone around her would pay as well. Papo meant to make her a clear example of what happens to anyone who betrays his trust.

※※※※※

Jamil had been long expecting North's phone call. After all, it was he that had been paid by Papo to kill Maria – well not just Maria, but North, Nina, Rah-Rah, and anyone else they may have cared for. At five-hundred thousand dollars a head, it would have been one hell of a contract. However, Jamil had no plans on killing North and Nina. The two lovebirds had genuine love for Sadon, and it was undoubtedly vice-versa, yet someone had to pay for him being murdered. An eye for an eye, a tooth for a tooth, and a life for a life, was Jamil's lifelong motto. And, with that in his mind, someone definitely had to pay for his best and only friend's death.

Jamil was never fond of New Yorkers, and the thought of Sadon losing his life in the Big Apple left a bitter taste in his mouth. Not only had Sadon been killed in North's neck of the woods, but his killers hadn't been found and properly dealt with, and for that, Jamil couldn't help but to feel disgusted. Sadon was never an easy person to get along with, which meant that Nina and North had to be exceptionally thorough for them to bond the way they did. Out of respect for Sadon, and how Sadon truly felt for Nina, Jamil would never turn against them and would instead kill those closest to them. Maria and Rah-Rah would undoubtedly have to do.

⚜⚜⚜⚜⚜

It was a cold, winter evening. The sun had long ago set on the snow-covered forest where Jamil now stood watching the activity of Papo's warehouse in Maine. Today, he was in exceptionally good spirits. It was the first time ever that his black and white camouflage army suit would prove useful on an assignment. Blending in perfectly with the scenery, Jamil stared at Papo through a pair of binoculars.

The warehouse, for some strange reason, was incredibly busier now more than any day of the past week that Jamil had been staking it out. He'd been watching for hours as Papo stormed around the loading area, checking the cargo and screaming at his employees for one reason or another. They all swarmed around Papo, hustling this way and that while at the same time, inadvertently forming a human shield around the fat, Dominican kingpin.

While standing half-hidden behind a huge leafless tree, and keeping an eye on Papo's movements, Jamil began to wonder with amusement at how silly Nina was to think that she could possibly rob Papo of a thousand kilos without having to kill him. Papo was perhaps one of the biggest drug dealers that Jamil had ever worked for, and for Jamil, that said a lot.

What the hell was she thinkin', lettin' this fat motherfucker live like that? he thought to himself. *Shit, she was just beggin' to get her top popped.*

Just then, Jamil's silent conversation with himself was interrupted by a sudden shift in the tide of human bodies that once surrounded and protected Papo from a .22 caliber bullet. He was now standing by himself, yelling orders to a driver of one of the many tractor-trailers lined up against the edge of the loading dock. Jamil quickly pocketed his binoculars, and took aim with a sniper's rifle.

It's about time! he thought eagerly to himself while taking the time to get a clear shot of his soon-to-be murder victim.

A sharp, irritating feeling had suddenly appeared out of nowhere as Jamil took a moment to smile.

"Shit!" he cursed out loud when he ran the tip of his tongue against his bottom lip to find it chapped and split open. The feel of his lips damaged by the unforgiving winter winds was a painful reminder of how much Jamil didn't care to be so far away from the warm, comforting feel of the Florida sun. Blaming Papo for this sudden discomfort, Jamil was now determined to make sure that he suffered terribly before meeting his death.

⁂

After being duped then robbed by a woman who was clearly twenty years younger than he was, Papo was determined now more than ever to never again suffer such damage to his pride and his business. Checkpoints were now set up all throughout his routes, with armed guards scattered about and in between to monitor the safety of his couriers. Everything was arranged on an airtight timeline, and Papo was blowing a gasket about everyone being only minutes behind schedule. He cursed, threatened to kill, and had even physically assaulted anyone he felt was moving too slow.

After pacing back and forth at a furious pace, Papo now stood at the ledge of the loading dock yelling at his employees. He directed traffic with one hand while the other gripped a clipboard; the impatience on his face could be seen a million miles away.

"Come on, man; what the fuck!" he barked at one of his workers. "Hey, you! You wanna end up in a ditch tonight? Move your fucking ass, man!"

That's right, motherfucker, Jamil thought to himself while squinting into the scope of his rifle. *Stand right there. Don't fuckin' move.*

"Iy, Dios mios!" Papo cried out loud. "Why can't you motherfuckers…"

Papo's complaints were cut short by a bullet to the back of his neck, his throat exploding into a giant mess all over one of the warehouse workers he was standing face-to-face with while verbally abusing him. Papo's mouth fell open; his eyes went frightfully wide as he was trying to decide whether to clutch the back of his neck where the bullet entered, or grab at his throat which was now a gaping hole spewing a stream of blood with each beat of his racing heart. He did neither, and instead collapsed onto the ground in a fit of convulsions. After a few minutes of gasping and choking miserably on his own blood, he stopped moving all together.

The loading dock of the warehouse, which was at first buzzing with activity, had ceased all movement at the sight of Papo's bloody and lifeless body, and then all pandemonium broke loose.

Jamil watched through the scope of his rifle as everyone in the warehouse ran aimlessly around in an uncontrolled panic.

Adios, you fat mafucka!" he said out loud while disassembling his rifle and placing the pieces into an all white knapsack. After checking the two Glock .40 caliber pistols, which were both fitted into shoulder holsters beneath his army jacket, Jamil then began making his exit. He didn't scramble to get away from the scene like most amateur killers; he instead walked calmly through the thick, wooded area to the side of the road where his 1100 Series Ninja motorcycle was parked.

Not forgetting about his badly chapped and split bottom lip, Jamil chose not to smile at the notion of another job being well done, and chose only to purse his lips in acknowledgement of his success.

Carol City, here I come! Jamil thought to himself while mounting his bike and starting its engine.

This time, he couldn't help but to smile, and was instantly punished for doing so.

"Goddamn it!" he cursed out loud. "I hate this fuckin' weather!"

Jamil then reached down into a compartment of his motorcycle to retrieve a stick of medicated lip balm. After taking a moment to thoroughly remedy his wound, he then lit himself a joint and treated himself to a deep toke before tearing off down the deserted Maine highway with nothing but Florida on his mind.

Epilogue

It was an exceptionally clear and warm day for the end of February. The sun shone brightly through clear, blue skies. The mountains of snow below were slowly beginning to wither and disappear beneath the rare, almost sixty-degree temperature. A huge, customized Hummer all-terrain vehicle, with huge sparkling rims pulled up to the gates of the cemetery (the length of the truck was entirely too wide for it to fit through the gates of the New York burial ground).

Nina, who was seated comfortably in the passenger seat of the truck, reached forward to turn the volume down on the stereo system.

"What, are we gonna go visit Sadon, Pa?" she asked with wide, surprised eyes.

"Yeah," North said, while parking the Hummer along the side of the cemetery. "It's only right. Besides, I got a surprise for you. Come on, let's go."

With a blunt in one hand and a full bottle of Crystal in the other, North stood and waited as Nina made her way around the front of the truck. She was dressed in a waist-length mink coat and a black, designer dress, with high-heeled alligator skin shoes to match. North was dressed in a black sweatshirt, black denim jeans, and a black fitted cap, which was tilted to the side, and his leather jacket and suede Timberland boots matching the midnight green color of the Hummer.

Careful not to splash any muddy water on her thousand-dollar dress, Nina hiked up her dress while starting down the cemetery road with North. North, however, couldn't have cared

The Queen Of New York   Visa Rollack

less. He walked freely down the winding dirt road with Nina, while smoking his blunt, unbothered by the slushy and dirty water that coated and sank into the material of his boots.

They cut across the lawn and started through a maze of grave plots and tombstones, until they reached Sadon's final resting place.

Nina's eyes went wide with wonder at the sight now before her. She opened her mouth to speak, but was too surprised to say a word. She could only make herself comfortable in the loving embrace North had just placed around her body, while staring at Sadon's newly customized tombstone. The tiny square brick of granite had now been replaced with a huge, eight-foot slab of marble, with a large, roaring lion that was sitting on its hind legs with its paws outstretched in the air.

"Sadon 'The Don' Mitchell" was carved above his date of birth and death. "SEE YOU WHEN I GET THERE, MY NIGGA. LOVE ALWAYS, NORTH AND NINA" was etched at the bottom. It was the largest, most extravagant gravestone in the entire cemetery. Its glossy texture sparkled every bit as brightly as the jewels on both Nina and North's necks, fingers, wrists and ears.

"Oh, oh, Papi!" Nina gasped while clutching North's jacket with tears now spilling from her eyes. "It's beautiful! I love you so much more for doing this; I swear to God, I do!"

North kissed the tip of Nina's forehead while freeing her from his embrace. He then popped open the bottle of Crystal and began pouring its contents all over the lion perched on top of Sadon's tombstone.

Go 'head and drink, my nigga. We don' made it, baby, he said to himself while watching what little of the snow melted beneath the streams of champagne.

North then stepped back and took a hold of Nina.

"Listen to me," he said staring directly into her eyes.

He then grabbed her by the hands and licked his lips before speaking again.

"We made it, Ma, and there's only one thing left to do."

North pulled a huge diamond ring from his pocket. Each facet and cut of the massive jewel changed colors and glistened beneath the sunlight; its shine was almost blinding.

"Sadon would've wanted it to end this way," he said while sliding the ring on Nina's wedding finger. "Spend the rest of your life with me, Ma; marry me, Nina."

Nina only stared up at North, the tears from her eyes now spilling down harder than ever.

"Oh, of course, Papi!" she found the voice to say. "Oh, I love you so much!"

Beneath the bright, blue, sunny February sky, both Nina and North walked hand-in-hand back to their customized SUV, proving that some stories do indeed have happy endings.

Street Knowledge!
"So Real You Think You've Lived It!"

Street Knowledge Publishing
Order Form

Street Knowledge Publishing
P.O. Box 345, Wilmington, Delaware 19801
Email: jj@streetknowledgepublishing.com
Website: www.streetknowledgepublishing.com

For Inmates Orders and Manuscript Submissions
P.O. Box 310367
Jamaica, NY 11431

Bloody Money
ISBN # 0-9746199-0-6   **$15.00**
Shipping/ Handling Via
U.S. Priority Mail   **$3.85**
Total   **$18.85**

Me & My Girls
ISBN # 0-9746199-1-4   **$15.00**
Shipping/ Handling Via
U.S. Priority Mail   **$3.85**
Total   **$18.85**

Bloody Money 2
ISBN # 0-9746199-2-2   **$15.00**
Shipping/ Handling Via
U.S. Priority Mail   **$3.85**
Total   **$18.85**

Dopesick
ISBN # 0-9746199-4-9   **$15.00**
Shipping/ Handling Via
U.S. Priority Mail   **$3.85**
Total   **$18.85**

Money-Grip
ISBN # 0-9746199-3-0   **$15.00**
Shipping/ Handling Via
U.S. Priority Mail   **$3.85**
Total   **$18.85**

The Queen of New York
ISBN # 0-9746199-7-3   **$15.00**
Shipping/ Handling Via
U.S. Priority Mail   **$3.85**
Total   **$18.85**

Purchaser Information

Name: _____

Address: _____

City: _____ State: ___ Zip Code: _____

Bloody Money ___

Me & My Girls ___

Bloody Money 2 ___

Dopesick ___

Money Grip ___

The Queen of New York ___

Quantity Of Books? _____

Make checks/money orders payable to:
Street Knowledge Publishing

Upcoming Novels From Street Knowledge Publishing

Coming Fall of 2006

Don't Mix The Bitter With The Sweet
By: Gregory Garrett

No Love-No Pain
By: Sicily

The Hunger
By: Norman R. Colson

Coming 2007

Bitch Reloaded
By: DeJa King

Dopesick 2
By: Sicily

Playin' For Keeps
By: Gregory Garrett

Stackin' Paper
By: JoeJoe and DeJa King

Shakers
By: Gregory D. Dixon

Dipped Up
By: Visa Rollack

No Other Love
By: "Divine G"

M.U.C.C.
By: Ronald Jackson

Lust, Love, & Lies
By: Eric Fleming

Dirty Livin'
By: Fernando Seirra

Sin 4 Life
By: Parish M. Sherman

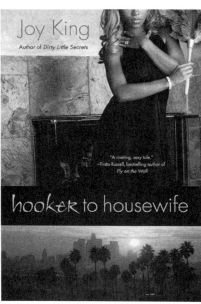

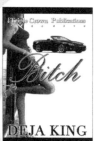
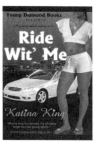